DON DESPERADO

**Center Point
Large Print**

L. L. FOREMAN

DON DESPERADO

CENTER POINT PUBLISHING
THORNDIKE, MAINE

This Center Point Large Print edition
is published in the year 2003 by arrangement with
Golden West Literary Agency.

The text of this Large Print edition is unabridged. In other
aspects, this book may vary from the original edition. Printed in
Thailand. Set in 16-point Times New Roman type by
Bill Coskrey and Gary Socquet.

ISBN 1-58547-365-0

Library of Congress Cataloging-in-Publication Data

Foreman, L. L. (Leonard London), 1901-
    Don Desperado / L.L. Foreman.--Center Point large print ed.
        p. cm.
    ISBN 1-58547-365-0 (lib. bdg. : alk. paper)
        1. New Mexico--Fiction. 2. Large type books. I. Title.

PS3511.O427D66 2003
813'.54--dc21

2003055163

Dedicated to Theodora

CONTENTS

1. GENTLEMEN OF FORTUNE

I N THE ROCKY MOUNTAIN HOUSE of Old St. Louis a shaggy white hunter roared out a deep and guttural Cheyenne chant. Others joined in, and some went to stamping the dances they had picked up far away in the Indian camps. The fair belles of the house, accustomed to such wild caprices, prudently withdrew. When mountain men gave themselves over to merry abandon, any startling thing could happen. There were buckskin leggins here trimmed with Comanche hair, and a blond curl or two always looked fine against the coarse straight black.

With the coming of spring the yearly horde had invaded Old St. Louis of Missouri—fur trade center, gateway to the Great Plains, jump-off for the westbound emigrants, and chief outfitting emporium for the mammoth trading caravans that annually rolled out onto the long overland trail to the Royal City of the Holy Faith, Santa Fe, capital of the Mexican Province of New Mexico.

Crowds swarmed in the muddy streets. Keelboatmen from the river thrust through idling groups of Delaware hunters, laughing French-Canadian *voyageurs* carelessly jostled rich merchants in ruffled shirts and tall beaver hats, and emigrant farmers stood aloof with their large families, indrawn and distrustful of everybody. Dark Spaniards in high sombreros, with remote but restless eyes, brushed elbows with their trade rivals, the Santa Fe traders—those keen-faced

9

Americanos in black broadcloth frocked coats that showed the creases of long months of disuse beyond the frontier.

Bronzed trappers, mountain men in flapping buckskins, strode their peculiarly soft-footed ways, their speech an outlandish jargon of English, French, Spanish and half a dozen Indian tongues. Mule-skinners, soldiers, packers, Missouri teamsters . . . and here and there a greenhorn, self-conscious in new fringed buckskins, knife and pistol in belt, as like as not under the appraising scrutiny of some hawk-eyed gambler looking for ripe pickings. . . .

Captain Con, sitting in the Rocky Mountain House, said to his three companions, "Well, gentlemen, tomorrow we start up the river for Independence and the caravan rendezvous. The landing stage was a madhouse this morning, everybody wanting passage and deck space. I had to fight to get our wagon aboard."

His voice, deep and flexible, gave the impression of being held in leash. As to that, his whole air hinted of restraint imposed upon a capacity for slashing speed and ruthless directness of action. In the course of his life, though still a young man, Captain Michael Connegan had handsomely succeeded in ridding himself of the nuisances of gentility, while yet not sacrificing the outward marks of a gentleman. However, none but the very rash threw it up to him. Nor was his title of captain often challenged. He had won that rank while fighting for the new Texas Republic. A dozen riverboats and a thousand gambling tables, from the Rio

Grande to the Mississippi, knew and remembered him as Captain Con. His friends usually called him Con, while his enemies used names more spectacular when recalling him to mind. He had the easy gift of swiftly taking a prominent place and keeping it, and the memory of him always lingered long after he had gone.

He raised his glass. "To a good trail—Santa Fe—and success to us!"

His three companions drank with him to that. Rael Elliot, gentleman impoverished but untarnished, sipped with slow moderation. Old Nick Gentry, grizzled buffalo hunter, opened a gap in his bush of whiskers and finished his drink at a gulp. Young Abel Fonley, greenhorn from Memphis, trying heroically to emulate Old Nick, choked on the potent Monongahela and spilled it down the quilled front of his new white buckskins.

Old Nick wiped a splash from his eye and opined the mishap might augur bad luck if not remedied promptly with a fresh round, while courteous Rael chose not to notice, in deference to young Abel's red embarrassment. But Captain Con was locating the cause of a slackening in the noisy chanting and stamping. The unpredictable mountain men were eying with vast approval a girl who appeared at the open doorway to the street. Vivid sojourns in the Mexican settlements had given them a strong liking for *la femenil español.*

"It's the girl from Santa Fe," muttered young Abel. "Don Chavez's niece. What's she doing alone in the streets?"

11

The roaring streets of the town were no place for a lady without escort, least of all for the niece of Don José Chavez y Salomain, *primer vocal* of far-off Santa Fe.

This year the great General Don Manuel Rajimo, Mexican military governor of New Mexico, was graciously visiting St. Louis in response to warm invitations sent him by leading Missouri merchants and all others with heavy interest in the Santa Fe trade. Don Chavez, head of Santa Fe's civil government, with his niece and many servants had accompanied the great Rajimo's glittering entourage.

All St. Louis was playing lavish host to the doughty general and the blue-blooded Don Chavez, and everybody had high hopes of at last cementing an unwritten agreement of goodwill that would remove future friction. The Missouri traders prayed particularly that this auspicious visit might result happily in increasing their profits and decreasing the huge taxes and special import duties that they usually were forced to pay at the Santa Fe end of the long and dangerous trail. With New Mexico under the Mexican flag, and all its laws subject to the whim and iron rule of General Rajimo, the Missouri traders had long ago found complaints useless. Santa Fe's civil government met and conferred, gravely presided over by Don José Chavez, but always the final decision belonged to Rajimo, who was said to have a short and shocking way of removing interference from his path.

The girl came another step into the smoke-hazed Rocky Mountain House, and if she was aware of the attention on her she gave little sign of it. She was interestedly examining a section of the world that was new to her, and being no more self-conscious about it than if she were a young queen paying an unannounced visit to her palace kitchen.

She wore a lace *rebozo* loosely around her shoulders, and Con gave her credit for not stifling herself in the styles of the North. Even the mountain men knew she was a lady; had she been less, her welcome into the place would have been more definite and direct. As it was, they paid her bold compliments with their eyes.

Rael Elliot murmured something, and Con was surprised to find him regarding the girl with an almost holy light in his eyes. It was strange to catch Rael looking like that at any girl. Con cocked a black and quizzical eyebrow.

"Why not step over, Rael, and . . ." He had no need to finish. Rael was rising, his entranced gaze still on the girl.

"H'm . . ." Con rose with him. "I think I'll take my own advice."

They reached her together and stood before her, bowing. When she could no longer ignore them she allowed her glance to travel up to their tall bared heads, one black, one fair. As if against her better judgment, she smiled, the slow curving of her lips exposing a white flash of small teeth, and Con then discovered that her dark eyes could be faintly mocking as well as soft and cool. There were other elements he sensed in her, too, without being able to fathom them on such short notice. His interest leaped.

"You will forgive, I trust, our lack of suitable introduction . . ." Rael was saying in his gravely formal fashion, his quiet voice sounding a little breathless.

"Peregrina!" A woman's voice, outraged, issued from a closed carriage that drew up smartly in the street. Two men, stiff and resplendent in full dress uniforms, stepped from the carriage. One, with a light skin and aquiline features, Con recognized as Don Chavez. The other, he judged, was no less than the great Rajimo—big, swarthy as an Indian, with a massive face and somber black eyes. Haughty, indifferent to the stares of passers, they silently waited for the girl to enter the carriage.

She, her back to them, paid no immediate attention. Her smile deepened. Her eyes lightly touched Rael's then Con's, and Con fancied he detected in them a tiny regret. She had not yet seen the two stiffly waiting men behind her. "Thank you for your kindness, but I must go. The *doña*—my chaperon—she has found me and is very angry, I fear." She moved to leave them.

Through the reek of liquor and tobacco her perfume reached their nostrils, pleasant and intimate. "I trust," drawled Con in his best manner, "we may meet again, *Señorita* Chavez—in Santa Fe, perhaps?"

"You are traders?" she asked, pausing, while the shocked voice of the scolding *doña* rose higher.

"No, but . . . I mean, yes," stammered Rael, never a ready liar even under the best conditions. "That is . . ."

"Permit me," Con cut in smoothly. "My name is Connegan—Captain Michael Connegan. My friend . . ."

"Connegan?" The dark eyes rose swiftly. The two silent men by the carriage betrayed a sudden alert attention. Con found three pairs of eyes scanning him with startled intentness. "Did you say—Connegan? Ah, yes—yes, of course . . . And now you must excuse me, *señores*."

The girl turned quickly, and for the first time saw her uncle and the general. She gave a start, hesitated, and without a word to them entered the carriage. They stepped in after, still in silence, and the carriage drew away down the crowded, narrow street.

Con stood gazing after it. He slowly drew out and lighted a long Havana, his eyes narrowed in speculation. Beside him, Rael whispered almost shakenly, "She's beautiful! More than beautiful! She has a—an inner quality of—of . . ."

"She's certainly got you dancing on one foot, I'll say that," remarked Con dryly. "Let's get on down to the landing stage. I feel the need of a walk."

He followed with his narrowed stare the route of the carriage, thinking of the way those three had reacted so strangely to the sound of his name. "I'll· have to step light," he thought. "Devil an' all . . . only five days here in St. Louis, and already trouble winks at me! I wonder how much they know? That girl . . . Peregrina. H'm. Pretty name, that. I want to see more of her. A lot more. Rael's right, she's beautiful . . . a beautiful minx!"

The landing stage was jammed with men, boxes, crates, bales, and here and there a wagon that had not yet found its way aboard. The steamboat, already loaded to the guards, was still taking on more cargo. Her upper deck bloomed painted wagons, bright red and blue Conestogas and Pittsburghs, massive and sway-backed, lashed wheel to wheel and heavily laden with goods for the Santa Fe trade.

Old Nick, with nothing worth stealing but his battered Hawkins rifle, his long skinning knife, and a fire-spotted buffalo robe for bedding, nevertheless was as chary of crowds as a New England emigrant. But he exchanged a grunt with a passing Shawnee hunter. He got along with most Indians and had married into several tribes.

"I hear Burgwin is like to be 'lected Caravan Captain when we organize at Council Grove," he mentioned to Con, and added that he didn't care for the man. Too biggity. But Burgwin was taking eighteen giant wagons this year, making him the chief proprietor in the caravan, so the other traders would probably elect him leader.

Con's eyes stilled. "Burgwin?"

"M-mm . . . Dall Burgwin. Ever meet him?"

Con nodded. Yes, he had met Dall Burgwin once, at a card table. "It was a couple years ago, on a Miss'ippi packet. I skun him. Then, of course, there's this matter of my brother Lorin. I want to keep out of Burgwin's way."

Old Nick hunched his shoulders. "Reason I spoke, I jest saw him. Here he comes."

Dall Burgwin had a reputation for violence and hard business capacity. A humorless, frowning man, the blood was red in his face as he came up to Con. He stuck out a thick forefinger and spoke his mind, while his wagon men formed a hard-eyed and ominously silent squad behind him.

"Connegan, I've heard you figure to go out with the wagon train. I'm here to change your plans!"

Con quirked one eyebrow. "Your confidence, suh, does you credit," he commented mildly. Back of him, Old Nick stood solid and stocky in his blackened elk-skins, squint-eyed. Abel Fonley, slender and consciously heroic in his fine new buckskins, his brown eyes big with tension, gripped the hilt of his belted knife. He had bought himself a stiff-brimmed *cibolero* hat somewhere, with a flat crown and a dangling chin-string, and wore it at an angle. Rael Elliot, never quite sure of himself when in sharp-edged company, looked on, worried.

2. GOLD GONE ASTRAY

RAEL ELLIOT had never before known any man who could be so maddeningly cool and insolent as Captain Con. The man had a gift for saying a simple thing, even a polite thing, and making of it a deadly insult. And always he wore that enraging air of quiet triumph, as if he had just come from a pleasant victory or was on his way to one. He would wear that jaunty manner, Rael thought, even when he crashed down to defeat.

Rael wished he could be like that, hard and tough-fibered, invulnerable to inner doubts and self-distrust, taking hold of things with both hands and careless of hurt. He was wishing that, when Burgwin flung up an arm and took to loud oratory. Attention had already been caught, and at the first bellowed words the crowd dropped all other matters on hand to listen, for Burgwin's importance demanded it.

"Hear me, everybody!" Burgwin ranged his commanding stare over the faces, and brought it back to Con, who waited with a look of faint interest as he drew on his cigar. "You all know about Lorin Connegan—that trickster who frauded me last year, when I was laid up with a broken leg and couldn't go out with the caravan. Us traders have got a short cure for that kind, when we catch!"

He pointed at Con. "This is his brother—and of the same stripe! Captain Con, they call him—gambler, sharpster, gunman! Some of you may've heard of him. Well, this—this blackguardly rascal of a Texan figures to join our caravan, like his thieving brother did . . . as an honorable trader!"

There were men in the crowd who straightened up with a certain agreeable surprise at learning that they belonged in the category of honorable traders. Some of them had been gun runners and worse in their shady days, and had climbed various tortuous paths to the dignity of a frock coat and tall beaver hat. But they bent stern stares on Con when he gave his silent laugh.

Burgwin swept on. He had the crowd with him. "This year," he stated, "the commerce of the Santa Fe trail becomes a respectable business, no matter what it may've been in the past. His Excellency, General

Rajimo, has as good as told me pers'nally that—uh—customs house conditions'll be easier for us at Santa Fe from now on. The general, as maybe some of you know, has even invested in some goods which I'm packing through for him in my wagons. There's no longer any room in this business for rascals and . . ."

"May I have the privilege of making a statement in behalf of Captain Connegan?"

It was Rael Elliot who spoke.

After Burgwin's forceful shouting it came as a contrast to hear Rael's modestly temperate tones. Yet there was an edge to Rael's voice, too.

Con turned and looked at him, and he thought in surprise, "Why, devil an' all, he's really riled. I'd never have thought he'd . . ."

A jet of impatience and pride rose in him. He had never allowed anybody to take up for him, as long as he was in any sort of shape to take up for himself. It came to him now as a wonder, as it had in the past, that so often there seemed to be somebody at hand ready and willing to fight on his side. And often it was somebody he least expected, somebody to whom violence was not a frolic as it was to him. It irritated him, gave him a vague sense of guilt.

"I'll make my own talk, Rael," he said shortly, and then was sorry, for Rael flushed painfully and bit his lip.

Con, his mood gone hard, turned to Burgwin. "My brother Lorin didn't want to borrow that cash from you, at your cutthroat terms. He wrote and told me. But you saw he had a good thing. He had the chance to buy up a good stock of silks at low cost, and he could clean up a fortune if he could swing the deal and get the goods to the Santa Fe market. But you black-balled him from borrowing cash here in St. Louis. He wrote to friends, and to me, trying to raise the cash. I sent him what I had. Elliot, here, sent him some from New Orleans. And Fonley, from Memphis . . ."

"Crooked his friends, too, huh?" Burgwin cut in.

Con shook his head. "Lorin wasn't built that way. Old Nick, here, lent him a little, all he had. But Lorin needed thousands. So finally he had to take your terms and borrow from you. The point is, Lorin was square. He'd have come back and paid off all his debts . . ."

"Then why didn't he?" Burgwin shouted angrily.

Con shrugged. "*Quien sabe?* We know he sold his silks in Santa Fe. The other traders all know that. Then, well—he just vanished." He snapped his fingers. "Vanished from Santa Fe, and ninety thousand dollars in gold vanished with him! That's all anybody knows, or claims to know. It's a mystery, and I'm going with that caravan to Santa Fe and find out for myself what happened to him."

Burgwin made an explosive sound. "It's no mystery! When last seen, your precious brother was riding south in a big hurry, the night before the caravan was due to start back north! A dozen or more men saw him, not counting a lot of Mex sheepherders who he passed next day while galloping hell-bent south to Chihuahua! I'm telling you, we'll not let another crooked Connegan into the caravan—nor any friend of a Connegan!"

Old Nick spoke up in his rusty growl. "Say that last easy, Burgwin! I never yet been banned from any wagon train—but I seen the day you couldn't spread your dirty blanket in an Injun camp!"

Burgwin started to speak again, but young Abel Fonley, unable longer to contain himself, sprang to the defense with a stuttering rush. "Listen, you! Wh-when Con heard about his brother, he hunted up the rest of us and got us together . . . and he had a stake and he sank it all in a wagon outfit and goods . . . and he made us partners in it, so we'd make back what we lent Lorin in case when we get to Santa Fe we can't find Lorin or that gold, and—and . . . Well, that's the kind of man this Captain Con is, that you're saying is such a low varmint! Why, damn your eyes, he's . . ."

It was unfortunate that he got choked up too full for mere words to relieve, at that point, and lost control of his voice so that it pinched off into a thin treble.

Burgwin snorted his contempt. "Either you're fools or crooks along with him!" he bellowed. "You're banned, Connegan, y'hear? You ran your tracks over me once, you cursed riverboat gambler, but not this time!"

He hooked an arm in command to his waiting wagon crew. "Run 'em off the stage . . . kick 'em through the town and leave your marks on 'em!"

Old Nick whipped out his skinning knife, a long and ugly thing of hammered steel with a bound rawhide hilt. Rael snatched up a broken board. Abel Fonley drew his shining new belt knife and took stance like a fair young god at bay.

"Take it easy, boys!" Con sent his warning as much for his own small party as for Burgwin's wagoneers. He had dipped his hands under his coat tails and now he held a pair of saw-handled Allen pistols, cocked and upraised, ready to chop down.

"Gentlemen . . ." The term was very elastic, and given in frank mockery. "Gentlemen, at four times this range I could pick the buttons off your shirts. Don't make me prove it. Burgwin, you called up a fight. Strip off that coat and I'll accommodate you with enough fight to last you to Santa Fe!"

He handed his pistols to Old Nick, and took off his own coat and broad-brimmed hat. His eyes shone like those of the wagon men, with the same love of battle, and without his elegant coat he stood as lean and tough as they, and as combative.

The wagon men regarded him almost fondly, as they would have scanned a particularly well-spurred fighting cock entering the pit. They critically appraised the length of his arms and legs, the breadth of his shoulders, and saw nothing to condemn. They judged men as they judged animals, by size and line and hardness of muscle. When they weren't fighting fractious horses, ornery mules and skittish oxen, wagon men of the trail fought men of other outfits for diversion. And if all else failed they fought among themselves. Irish, Swedish, German, men of the old barbaric bloods. Lean American plainsmen, rangy Kentucks, long-legged mountaineers . . . hard drinking, hard-living wanderers, restless, haunted with strong desires and eruptive moods. All sharp-edged men. They looked expectantly to Burgwin.

The trader flung his coat to one man, his beaver to another, and came at Con in a straight charge. His wagon men roared, while the crowd gathered thick around, then all settled down to watching with expert eyes as the first solid blows landed with the pounding impact of buffalo bulls meeting in combat.

And Rael Elliot, watching with the crowd, sucked in his breath as Con took a smash to the jaw, and he wondered that Con could still wear that jaunty air of triumph. He was what he was, and probably all that his enemies called him, but in this moment Rael felt more admiration for him than he had ever felt for himself. With all his faults, this Captain Con was a man, and to outweigh his vices he had the virtues of splendid courage, a strong and tough mind, and a queer kind of honesty and immaculate cleanliness of body. A self-sufficient man. A dangerous man. Arrestingly handsome in the virile way of a handsome animal, sleek of line, unconsciously graceful, and with a latent power for violence that struck at the senses.

With Con's hat in his hands and not knowing he was mangling it, Rael thought over and over, "If I could be like that—fight like that! God, if I could . . ."

LATER, walking through the shabby lanes of Vide Poche, that careless and improvident Frenchtown of Old St. Louis, Con licked his gashed knuckles and admitted that he hadn't helped matters.

"Burgwin's got more reason than ever now to get his knife in me. It doesn't do a man like that any good to take a beating with his crew looking on. And he took one—I swear he took one! I thought he'd never give up."

It had been a good fight, Old Nick allowed, and he added he'd never seen as good a beat since one Blas Leroux got caught stealing skins from a Shawnee cache. Rael spoke of their wagon outfit aboard the steamboat, and asked Con his plans.

"Why, we're setting out for Santa Fe tomorrow, aren't we?" Con returned. "Anyway, that's still my intention."

Young Abel fiercely seconded him. His brown eyes said Con was invincible. He was steering very close to hero worship. "I'm with you, Con. What's to stop us heading west without the wagon train?"

Con kept his face straight and said nothing. He liked the boy, for all his notions and fofuraw, and carefully refrained from ridiculing him. The lad was high tempered, enamored of the dashing, the histrionic, the wild tang of adventure. But he could be hurt too easily, could suffer too deeply, ever to become the kind of hard-bitten adventurer that he wanted to be.

Old Nick, with blunter sensibilities, asked Abel what he thought that Santa Fe trail was like, and then proceeded to tell him. "Thousan' miles o' grass, rain, mud, flood, deserts, mountings, drouth, fire, thirst an' starvation. Comanches skulkin' along, hopin' to ketch stragglers. Bogs to drag through, needin' five-six teams to each wagon. An' quicksands, an' drysands, an' storms an' buff'lo stompedes . . . wagh, I talk too much!"

24

"Well, it was a fine large idea, Nick, anyway, you got to admit," put in Con, and punched the red-faced Abel in the ribs. "And I wouldn't want a better man with me, come I had to try it. Rael, we better get along to the hotel. We've left your sister too long alone. She taking the boat back to New Orleans in the morning?"

Rael nodded. "She wanted to wait and see us off, but I wouldn't hear of it." His young sister, Phileda, had come up from New Orleans with him. She'd go on with them over the trail to Santa Fe, she said wistfully, if they'd only let her. Rael couldn't understand that. Phileda had always been such a quiet, home-loving girl.

Old Nick shot a look at Con. "You got some notion how to beat Burgwin's ban?"

"Well, there's that farewell traders' dance at the Planters' House tonight," Con answered. "Everybody'll be there, the Spanish party and the cream of the town. I'll be there, too. If I can strike up a quick friendship with somebody of that Spanish party, now . . ." He spread his bruised hands. "The Spanish are a courteous people. With only a hint, they come right out and invite you to visit their home. Nice custom, that. Even Burgwin'd hardly dare ban a man who has been personally invited to the Santa Fe home of some Don or other."

"But you've never met any of them," argued Rael, whose own processes of making friendships were slow and diffident.

Con sent him a grave glance. "I've met one," he murmured. "The more than beautiful Peregrina—

25

remember?"

Rael was shocked and showed it. "Would you really attempt to use her as a—well—a means to an end? I mean, just for . . . for profit?"

"I would, Rael—I certainly would," Con confessed humbly. "For profit and—Lord give me luck—for pleasure!"

3. WHO DANCES MUST PAY

P HILEDA ELLIOT had never before been more than a leisurely hour's ride from her New Orleans home, and this flamboyant St. Louis in the springtime should have thrilled her. Rael thought it did, and was amazed at the change that had lately come over her.

She went about nowadays in a dreamy radiance. She was a quiet and gentle girl with soft brown hair and soft brown eyes, just entering early womanhood. Her features, not as finely cut as Rael's, were regular and smooth, more rounded than his. In Rael the thin old blood of lineage was barely diluted by the strong strain that Phileda had fully inherited. Their mother had been a New Orleans French lady of family. Their father had been one of Jackson's colonels, able to trace his family back no further than to his grandfather, who had come from nowhere in the dark and kept his mouth shut.

She stood now at the window of her hotel room, watching the bustling street below. When she sighted her four men at last, the strain left her eyes and color rushed to her face. She put her small hands to her cheeks, panicked by their flaming warmth, fighting to quell the swelling fullness in her. But her shining eyes remained on the coming four—on one of them, the tallest, who walked with long strides, rangy and a shade rakish, an indefinable air about him of jaunty triumph.

But when they knocked and entered she was sitting with one of Rael's plain white shirts in her lap, repairing a worn spot with neat small stitches. She forced herself to look up slowly, calmly. Smiling, she made her eyes go first to her brother. "Rael, I just don't know what you'll do about your clothes after I'm . . ."

She saw Con's face then, and his bloodied hands. The shirt fell unheeded. "Oh, Con—you're hurt!" It was in the nature of a cry, as if his hurt were hers. She raised her hands to touch his smeared face, her modesty forgotten, and Rael stared queerly at her, while Abel winced as if hit hard in a place already sore and tender.

Con warded off her hands, laughing. "It's nothing, little sister," he assured her carelessly. "My oath, how you mother us. I don't know how we're going to get along without you. Excuse me while I wash, h'm? Got to make myself decent for the Planters' House ball tonight. Wish I could take you, but maybe Abel will if you coax him real sweet."

It was while he was bathing that a stray thought caught up with him. He stood for a moment, frowning.

Damn it, it couldn't be. She was just a child. Little sister. It was just that she had come to regard him as another big brother, like Rael, and she was such an affectionate little thing. Sure, that was it. Dammit, that was what it had to be.

He caught sight of himself in the panel mirror, his dripping body sleek and lean-limbed, the healthy skin clean and white where the sun did not touch. He muttered aloud, "You damned scoundrel, if you've done that to the child you ought to be shot!"

He thought of Peregrina next, and dwelt on her, and grinned at his reflection. . . .

They had done a proud job of this farewell dance, and the ballroom of the Planters' House was gay with light and noise. The windows were open to the mild spring air that blew in lazy gusts from the river, and candle flames fluttered in great hanging chandeliers, drawing shifting glints from gold braided uniforms, thin tall glasses and sheening hair.

The breathless reel and the following waltz ended. A chatter of voices took the place of music, feminine murmurs mingling pleasantly with masculine tones. Con deftly piloted Peregrina toward a small outside gallery that he had marked for his own, where the moon could be seen. His success so far, he considered, had been remarkably easy. The lady was quite receptive, wonderfully kind, and he was certain she had cheated somebody by giving him this dance. That dour young Spaniard in gold epaulettes, probably, standing over there by the potted rubber plants. Con felt the dark, brooding eyes following him, and other

Spanish eyes, too, including those of General Rajimo. He had to stifle a piratical enjoyment of the knowledge. These devilish proud Spaniards must become his friends, not his enemies. He must use tact.

He seated the girl with grave courtesy. They had the small gallery to themselves, the lighted windows behind them and the moonlight on their faces. He opened his campaign with care. "I look forward to visiting your Santa Fe, *Señorita.*"

She inclined her head. "You must call on us, Captain. We should take it as less than friendly if you fail to do so—my uncle and I."

Minx, he thought. To the devil with her stiff-necked uncle. He gazed fully at her while she sat slowly swaying her painted Chinese fan. She had fine-textured skin, smooth and creamy, and her features could have been carved by the delicate hand of a careful sculptor. But her mouth was warm, and the slow flash of her marvelous eyes . . .

He wondered what thoughts such a girl might have in her secret hours alone. They wouldn't be pale, surely. Not with eyes like those and a mouth so warm with life. Her dignity was flawless, but he suspected her of wearing it as she wore her clothes—with dainty perfection and a flair for graceful effect, and possibly some moments of impatient rebellion. He wished he might know her in those secret hours when she abandoned it and emerged as herself, vibrant and glowingly alive. The man who won her had better not be weak, or she'd rip him with scorn. Her chin bespoke a strong will.

He found that his hands were clenched, and was amazed at himself. Of all the women he had ever known, none had taken such a swift and vital grip of his senses. He lighted a cigar to break the spell, forgetting to ask her permission, but even as he held the match to it his eyes went back to her over the flame. With almost a shock he found he was meeting her direct gaze. And there was knowledge in her eyes, and he could read it there. She knew his thoughts, knew his speculations. She was flushing a little, but not, he fancied, in anger at him. No, her eyes were . . .

Why, devil an' all, her eyes were challenging him!

Her small round shoulders, bare and white above the rose-tint flounces of her low and close-fitting basque, moved in a slight shiver. The gold pendant brooch of her basque, a tiny Cupid figurine, swung and curtsied with an impudence of its own, as if in full accord with the coquetry of the moment.

Con rose swiftly. "You are cold—allow me."

He took her flowered silk shawl and spread it around her shoulders. His strong brown hands moved lightly at the task, sure and competent, until the scent of her hair, with its single small rose tucked behind a pink ear, filled his nostrils. His hand stilled. She tilted back her head and gazed up at him, and he bent and kissed her.

Down in the shadow of the street, Phileda Elliot, in blue taffeta and eagerly bound for the ball on the arm of Abel Fonley, looked up at the secluded little gallery and stopped dead. She uttered no sound, but her fresh young face went slack, all the eagerness drained from it. Beside her, Abel followed her gaze, and was afraid to look back into her face for fear of what he would find there. It seemed a long time before he heard her halting whisper.

"The—the music is—lovely. Isn't it, Abel? Shall we—go on in?"

"Yes." He nodded much too emphatically, his own voice tight and strained. "Sure, Phileda—let's go on in."

He was thinking fiercely, passionately, "I hate him! I'd kill him—if—if—he weren't Con . . ."

H OW DARE YOU!" said Peregrina.

Hearing that, Con's first reaction was of honest bewilderment. To kiss a girl on a balcony was harmless enough, as meaningless as the usual aftermath of feminine reproach, but this was different, and the girl was different. Why, dammit, his kiss had been solemn, gentle, not a trifling diversion. In another minute he would have been telling her he loved her, and that was one lie he had never seriously told any girl. Surely he hadn't wrongly read an invitation? Her warm lips had been receptive and willing.

"Peregrina, I—I . . ."

He was stammering like a backwoods swain.

Peregrina slid from under his arms and stood erect, her back to the gallery's iron grille. Something caught on Con's cuff from her dress, and fell to the floor. She darted her hands to the low neck of her basque, in urgent dismay.

Con stooped and searched, glad of something to do while he gathered himself together. It was the little

Cupid brooch, and it had broken from its pin. He straightened up with it in his hand, for once in his life feeling foolishly inadequate and blundering.

"I'm sorry," he said muffledly. "I apologize."

"For what do you apologize?" rapped a loud and brittle voice, and General Rajimo stepped out onto the gallery, looking bigger and more commanding than ever, with his arrogant black eyes and straight mouth. His loud demand brought his staff officers hurrying from the ballroom floor.

Con dropped the little gold trinket into his coat pocket, and kept his hand there while he briefly searched the group for prospects of sudden action. These Spanish military men were such fire-eaters. "It's a very small matter, General," he answered easily, while his mind raced seeking a way to ward off disaster.

General Rajimo turned his stare on the girl. "Has this man insulted you?" He did not lower his tone, and some of his glittering staff officers appeared embarrassed.

It came to Con that there was some element here that was not genuine. The same instinct had warned him many times before, at gambling tables. He searched for definite signs. The general's wrath did not ring true. A man of his steel-hard type would be icily controlled in his anger, not loud and blustering like this.

He swung his head and sharply scanned Peregrina, caught a look in her eyes, and then he knew. Her dismay was guilty, as guilty as that of another girl who once had tried to decoy him into a robbery trap and then backed out at the last minute. And shame struggled in her eyes, too, when he tried to hold her gaze.

Other men were gathering, merchants and traders, all anxious and worried. Burgwin came pushing through, hissing questions. The ladies in the ballroom were politely trying not to notice that there was any disturbance.

Con's impressionable years lay behind him, and he was not easily agitated by the sudden smashing of an illusion, but this thing left him sick and aghast. He had been decoyed by this girl into a damaging and dangerous situation. The game had been rigged for him, and he had walked into it like a green cully. His rage came flooding up, and the impulse leaped in him to tear away that dainty dignity of hers, to punish and shame her, turn the shoddy trick back against her with interest.

He met the general's stare. "I was amusing myself," he drawled, and made of each word an insult. "It resulted in a slight accident to her dress. Quite unfortunate, but of no great importance. Am I expected to apologize to you also, General?"

He sent Peregrina a studiedly disparaging glance. "I must admit," he added deliberately, "that I consider two separate apologies an unreasonably high price to pay for such paltry amusement!"

After he said it, there followed an instant in which he regretted it, though his rage remained. He had once seen a sheltered girl of breeding grossly insulted on a riverboat. His memory of that girl's face, with its blushing shock and stigma of shame, remained clearer

33

than his recollection of shooting the man who had done it. Peregrina had that same look. Her hot color flamed and spread, and she shrank back, her lips parted in a faint gasp. The savagely wicked thrust had cut through her defenses and raked her with its barbed edge. Yet she recovered quickly, and stood erect again, eyes blazing. Con's regret passed. He could not stand her hurt, but he could relish her fury.

General Rajimo gave out a strangled sound, and now there was nothing false in his anger. He groped behind him and spoke in Spanish, in what was a chill whisper compared to his former loud rasping. "Don José—your pistol, please!"

The thin white face of Don José Chavez intruded past the general, high-bridged nose thrust out like the edge of an axe. "Pardon, Don Manuel, but I have my own use for it!" Don José answered rapidly, and fumbled under his gold-braided tunic.

Con said swiftly, "Take care of yourself—I'm armed!"

The furious, haughty eyes stayed fixed upon him. A short silver-mounted pistol emerged from under the tunic, and Don José cocked it with a steady hand. With no time left for further warning, Con drew from his pocket and fired. The solid roar of the percussion cartridge brought a second report from Don José's weapon, but it was the impact of Con's bullet striking the Spaniard's arm that jerked the fine-set trigger.

Don José stood very straight, no flinch disturbing his narrow patrician face, while his emptied pistol clattered to the floor. He turned a little gray, but that was all.

"It would have been better, Don Manuel," he observed distinctly, "had I given you the pistol to use on this *Americano*. It seems that I am no match for these *raffines*."

Two of the officers caught him as he swayed a little, and sheer horror gripped the numbed crowd. A few small screams sounded from among the women in the ballroom.

The St. Louis traders and merchants stood frozen. They had performed miracles of diplomacy in trying to please the Spaniards, had made even the least of the officers feel like a visiting rajah, and served them the best with lavish disregard of cost. No spotless Spanish boot had so much as been splashed by the common mud of the streets. And now, before their eyes, on the last night before departure, here came disaster. There stood Don Chavez y Salomain—*primer vocal* of Santa Fe, no less—sick and bloodied, shot by a scapegrace Texan.

Nor did they miss Don Chavez's comment. He had used the term *raffines* as a synonym for *Americanos*. *Raffines:* ruffians, desperadoes . . .

Burgwin pointed a blunt-nosed derringer at Con's head. "Drop that pistol and put up your hands!"

4. QUICKER THAN HANGING

THE CELL WAS SMALL and none too clean. The door was of latticed strap iron, and through it Con could see only part of Rael's face.

35

Rael was distressed. "But, Con, it's fantastic!" he protested. "You're in no position whatever to challenge General Rajimo to a duel! After all, he's the injured party in this affair—he and Don Chavez. You passed the gravest of all insults by your—er—by certain references aimed at a lady of their party. If satisfaction is to be demanded, the challenge should come from the general. Besides, you're a prisoner in jail, don't you realize that? The whole town is against you, and they're saying . . ."

Con brushed that aside. "Never mind all that. I know I'm in a bad tight. It's not exactly a challenge that I want you to take to the general. I'm offering him satisfaction on the—h'm—field of honor."

Rael's emotions and loyalty, Con realized, were in a tangle and badly strained. The whole affair, particularly what he had heard of Con's treatment of Peregrina, had deeply shocked him. It was like him to withhold reproaches, but Con knew he stood condemned in Rael's discriminating eyes.

Rael said haltingly, "Con, I know you're a crack shot with a pistol. In fact, you're a bit famous as a . . ."

"Notorious is the word generally used," Con put in dryly. He regarded curiously what he could see of Rael's face outside the cell door. "Rael, I begin to suspect the reason you don't favor this proposed duel is not so much on my account, but because you figure I'll probably drop the general! Isn't that it?"

Rael met his inquiring gaze squarely. "Frankly, yes. I'm sorry, Con, but I can't help believing that the Spaniards were in the right. If you had insulted my sister like that, I would have done what Don Chavez tried to do. Also, *Señorita* Chavez is betrothed to General Rajimo, so . . ."

"The devil you say!"

"Yes, I learned of that this morning, from one of the Spanish officers," Rael affirmed, looking at nothing. "A family arrangement, I gather. Her parents are dead, so Don José is not only her uncle, but her guardian, just as I am Phileda's guardian. I can understand his feelings very well. And General Rajimo, of course, was perfectly justified in defending his betrothed from . . ."

Con interrupted with the guess that Burgwin and the other leading merchants were falling over themselves trying to smooth down the Spanish spleen. "A duel might hit them just right, if they could be sure the general would down me—and they'll make sure!"

"Then why do you want the duel?" asked Rael.

Con coughed uncomfortably. "I think I ought to try and square what I've done, Rael," he answered solemnly.

For some time there was silence and he felt guilty, but overshadowing his guilt was the fear that he was laying it on too thick even for Rael. Then Rael's voice came through the barred door, muffled with emotion.

"Con, I never quite know whether to admire or damn you! You can be—forgive me for saying it— such a blackguard that I condemn myself for sticking to you. And then I've seen you do such fine and decent things that I'm proud to call myself your friend. All right, Con—I'll do what I can, if it's what you want."

After Rael had gone, Con stared unseeingly at the barred door and empty passage beyond. Rael would put it through if anybody could. Right now, Rael with his ingrained courtesy and obvious good breeding was more valuable than Old Nick and his Hawkins rifle. The *code duello* required that all parties concerned be of approximately equal social rank. In the event of doubt cast upon a challenger's status, his second must vouch for him as a gentleman. There would be no question of Rael's being accepted as a gentleman. He could never be mistaken for anything else, by anybody.

As for what he could make of the duel, Con let that question ride for the time being. It would be enough to get out of this filthy jail, and that could be managed by Burgwin and the leading citizens.

But Rael's parting words . . .

Con scowled at the door. "Devil an' all," he muttered, and shoved his hands deep into his pockets. "Why does he have to say things like that, anyway?"

His right hand came in contact with a small hard object, and he drew it out. It was Peregrina's pendant brooch—Cupid *volant* on tiny wire-gold wings, all chubby grace and impudence. A pretty thing. He regarded it broodingly.

Burgwin, when he came, said bluntly, "I don't trust you a damn bit, Connegan. None of us do."

Con shrugged. Burgwin and Rael, in the shadowy passage outside the door, could see his face by the light of the small cell window and he had to guard his expression. "I'm asking for no trust or favors," he returned with fitting simple dignity. "On the contrary, I'm offering my life. Rajimo is said to be an excellent shot and experienced duelist."

"So are you," countered the trader, "and you're a snap shooter. You don't have to take aim. Rajimo does. He's a sight shooter. I wouldn't trust you to let him have the first fire. You'd get off the first shot—and we'd have Rajimo dead on our hands instead of you!"

"Captain Connegan has appointed me to act as his second in this affair," said Rael. "If we give our word of honor . . ."

Burgwin snorted. "I wouldn't take his word that rain makes the grass grow. There's only one way I'd trust him—and that's if he stood to his mark with an empty gun!"

"An empty gun?" echoed Rael. "Good heavens, we ask for at least the semblance of a duel, not an execution!"

Burgwin whirled on him. "Then let him hang! Rajimo is bitter mad, lays the blame on all of us, and all the old bad feeling has come back. He swears he'll close the Santa Fe markets to us if Connegan isn't hanged. A duel would be even better, I grant that—but only if it ended one way. Connegan can face him with an empty gun, or hang!"

Rael's face was white. "I'll never consent to taking part in such a dastardly affair!" he vowed.

"Connegan's gun could be loaded with powder and prime, but no ball," Burgwin went on relentlessly. "Then he could bang away and no harm done. They'd think he missed."

"But Rajimo wouldn't miss," commented Con.

"No," agreed Burgwin. "But it'd anyway be quicker than hanging. Take your pick, Texan!"

"I'll take it," nodded Con. "Rael, I'm asking you as a friend to sink your scruples this time and be my second. There's nobody else I can call on, and nobody else I'd rather have by me on that—ahem—field of honor."

When they had gone, his mind went back to that rigged trap on the Planters' House balcony. There was a strong and pressing motive behind it and behind Rajimo's eagerness to have him hanged. Peregrina had probably been acting as decoy under orders of somebody. Rajimo, likely. Not Don José. Not that Spanish blue-blood, full of rigid ethics and honor. No, Rajimo was the man with the motive. And the thing had gone farther than had been planned, certainly farther than Peregrina had expected it to go, for her dismay at the end had been genuine. The kiss, perhaps, had been the first step beyond bounds. Peregrina hadn't been prepared for that to come quite so quickly, and it had taken her off guard. What was more—and Con experienced a leap of mingled feelings at the recollection—for the first instant or two, before gathering her forces to repel him, she had not drawn away.

Yes, he could place his finger on that point and say to himself, "Right there was where the rig ran away with them." He had been expected and encouraged to make some sort of advance, but a genteel advance that could be checked, calling from him an apology.

40

Whereupon General Rajimo could raise much ado about it, and use it as an excuse for forbidding him to enter Santa Fe. Con recalled the strange reaction that the sound of his name had brought about, outside the Rocky Mountain House. His name had been familiar to them. They wanted no man of his name to come prowling around Santa Fe, seeking the answer to a year-old mystery.

There lay the answer: Those three—General Rajimo, Don José Chavez, and his niece Peregrina— shared secret knowledge concerning the disappearance of Lorin Connegan and ninety thousand dollars in Mexican gold. Two of them, at least, were ready to guard that secret with any means at hand.

THE PUNCTILIOUS FORMALITY of the *code duello* ruled the meeting, and Con rather admired the polite perfection of it all. These *grande caballeros* knew how to dress up such doings to a fine gloss. They brought to the occasion a meticulous exactitude of form and ceremony that somewhat overawed the less tutored Americans.

The field was a little depression of open ground thickly shut in by trees, a mile down river from the town. The spectators were now making their way up to the bare crest of a knoll overlooking it. Most of those present had ridden down from the town on horseback, though a few had come in carriages and open hacks. Horses and rigs were crowded under the trees. All in all, with the solemnity and the absence of any women, the atmosphere approached that of a semi-secret political meeting, marred only by the display of pistols and the ominous presence of the surgeons. The little group of official witnesses withdrew to the correct distance. The two surgeons stood by with spirits of hartshorn and black instrument cases laid open in readiness.

General Rajimo's second, an officer in full dress, wheeled smartly from his principal and saluted Rael. "If your friend is ready, *Señor* . . ."

Con stood to his mark, and examined the pistol they had given him. A fine weapon, one of a pair, and its mate was in Rajimo's hand. Mahogany stock, carved handle, silver breechplate and long octagon barrel. A very fine weapon, though he preferred the newer breechloaders. This was a muzzle loader using a copper percussion cap. He would have admired it more sincerely had it been fully loaded. The powder had been measured and wadded down into the .50-caliber barrel, the percussion cap fitted, but no leaden ball had been rammed in.

General Rajimo, cold as ice, held his pistol raised, waiting the word. Con touched the gold Cupid brooch in his pocket and wondered what thoughts Peregrina might be entertaining just now, back in town. He drew out the little figurine and flipped it in his hand.

"Good luck, Con!"

The boyish hail, sincere but as unhappy as Rael's eyes, came from young Abel, up on the knoll with the spectators. Old Nick beside him raised an open hand high to Con in the simple Indian gesture of goodwill. Con crushed the delicate wire-gold wings of the Cupid in his fingers and sent back the same mute signal. When he brought his hand down it was empty, and his pricked fingers bled from the breaking of the tiny wings.

"Gentlemen, are you ready?"

"Ready!"

"Ready!"

Rael, with suffering on his fine-carved face, lowered his head, hands clenched.

The final word came like a crisp expletive.

"Fire!"

Con saw Rajimo's pistol level out, one chill black eye taking close sight along the barrel. He brought down his own weapon, touched the trigger at once, and the kick of the quick explosion packed the butt solidly against his palm.

General Don Manuel Rajimo rose onto his toes, his body twisted half around, and teetered. He had not yet fired, but as he swayed his pistol went off and the ball cut leaves from the trees. In the stunned silence after the echoes, his sighing gasp could be heard plainly. He let fall his smoking pistol and fumblingly touched his left shoulder.

Consternation broke out first among those closest to him. His second ran to him. The surgeons snatched up their cases and followed, with the witnesses racing after them. The Spanish officers, grimly silent, came stalking down from the knoll, but the citizens remained transfixed and incredulous. Burgwin had passed confident word around that there was nothing to worry about in this duel, and given his oath on it.

Con stepped swiftly over to Rael. "Let's get out of here!" he muttered, but Rael could only stare at him.

The Spanish officers formed a somber cordon around their *comandante,* now lying on the grass with the surgeons hastily cutting away his stained white shirt. A stormy rumble sounded on the knoll, and the Missouri traders led the rush.

Con gripped Rael's arm. "Watch yourself—they're coming like Sam Houston!"

Five saddled horses left the trees ahead of the oncoming mob. Old Nick, astride of one and leading another, crowded both animals to a tight turn that cut up clods of turf, and brought them broadside to Con and Rael. He said nothing, being a man of few words in emergency, but merely stuck a thumb at the spare horse.

Con shoved Rael forward. "Take it. All right, Abel—don't pull up!"

He caught the short mane of Abel's led horse, then the cantle, running, and swung up into the saddle. Another rider flashed by, a slim lad he didn't know, wearing a big hat that looked familiar. Somebody fired a shot and Con's horse reared, pawing, spooked by the commotion. It took time to fight it down and get it straightened out after the others. Another shot thudded, and he glanced back. Burgwin was leading the charge into the clearing, a plume of smoke drifting from his derringer. Con wished he had another load in his dueling pistol. He waved the empty pistol, grinned to see them scatter, then was busy bowing his respects to the low-hanging branches as his horse took to dodging trees.

HE CAUGHT UP WITH THE OTHERS on the muddy banks of the Mississippi, and the first thing his eyes lit on was the slim young rider in the big hat, now talking with Rael. They had halted and were waiting for him. Old Nick was using the time to tighten girth, while Abel adjusted his stirrups. They had borrowed the first horses at hand when they came down from the knoll.

"Good Lord, Rael—!" Con got down from his saddle, and Rael almost flinched at his explosive anger. "Haven't you better sense than let her in for a thing like this?"

"I didn't know," Rael answered quietly. "I've just been talking to her."

Phileda Elliot, under the big hat, was pale. Con recognized the hat now as one of his own, and the clothes as Abel's. "Then it's your doing!" He turned on Abel and Old Nick. "You brought her—let her come to that duel, knowing damned well it was bound to wind up in a riot!"

Old Nick peered up from buckling his girth. "Ever try stoppin' ary female from doin' what she's set her mind on?" he queried shortly, and led his horse down to water.

Abel said, half defiantly, "She wanted to come, so I lent her some clothes. Don't blame her, Con."

Phileda looked straightly at Con. "They couldn't stop me. None of you can stop me from—from doing what I want to do. I'm not a child any more."

"No," said Con, staring down at her, and seeing

more in her face than he cared to see. "No, I can see that. Rael, this is your problem. You all better scatter for home. I've got considerable travel coming up, myself."

Old Nick came back with his horse. "I got no home."

"Nor me," said Abel. "I sold my father's grain store and loaned the money to . . ." He broke off.

Con began rubbing down his sweating horse and critically examining the others. "Not bad animals, these, not bad at all," he commented. "Expensive saddles, too. I guess they'll call this horse stealing." He went on rubbing, and spoke to them over his shoulder.

"You all went broke on Lorin. Even you, Rael. You and Phileda borrowed on your New Orleans property. Yes, Lorin broke you—but it was left for me to come along later and make horse thieves and outlaws of you. Dammit, I don't see why you stood by me like this, I swear I don't."

They had no answers to that, but Rael said modestly, "Con, I think what we're trying to say is, we've no reasons for not wishing to stay together. None of us can go back to St. Louis and board a boat out now, not even Phileda. We sort of look on you as our leader. Don't turn us down, Con."

"What about Phileda?"

"She refuses to go back, and I don't know that I'd care for her to go back alone into St. Louis, in any case, after what's happened."

Con left off rubbing down his horse. "Do you know what it means to stick with me? You do, Nick, but not the others. After what's happened, I'll be the most wanted man in Missouri, and the most hunted. They'll want to give my head to Rajimo. They'll send the best men they can get after me, put a price on me, post me in every town and settlement from the Great Lakes down to the Texas line."

"We got a head start on 'em," mentioned Old Nick.

"And I've got to hold it," nodded Con. "It's a long old way to the free and independent Republic of Texas, but there's where I've got to jump—and jump in a hurry if I aim to save my neck! They'll make an international affair of this. Government men will be on my trail, as well as the best gun shooters and bounty bloodhounds money can tempt. They put a price of ten thousand dollars on the head of Charlie Legrets a few years ago and ran him to ground in short order—and all he did was shoot a Spanish *alcalde* in a card game."

Phileda spoke for the rest. "We'll try to keep up with you, Con. And I wish you'd forget I'm a girl—till we get to Texas."

"You're not going to Texas," said Con. "We'll push on down the Miss' to Cape Girardeau, sell these horses and saddles to a man I know there . . ."

"Sell them?" Rael exclaimed. "But they're not ours!"

"—and catch the *Tiago* going down river," Con went on. "We've got to have money to pay our way. The *Tiago* makes pretty fast time. Abel, you drop off at Memphis and get friends to hide you for a while. Rael, you and Phileda do the same when we make

New Orleans. Nick, if you hanker to come to Texas with me you're welcome. I'm known in New Orleans and the hunters'll be hard on my heels. We'll take the first boat for Galveston."

He thought he had it all fixed up, until Rael said he didn't care to expose any New Orleans friends to possible trouble by hiding him. And then Phileda declared she wouldn't live on the charity of friends there. Abel came out flatly and announced he wasn't going back broke to Memphis, but he meant more than that, for he kept his eyes on Phileda. Wherever she went, there he would follow.

Their quiet stubbornness frustrated Con. He drew a long breath and let it out slowly, checking himself from saying things he might feel bad about later. They were like children, with only vague conceptions of the cutting edges of life. He felt like a father, unable to desert his too loyal family.

Abel took it upon himself to change the subject. "You—uh—must have hit Rajimo pretty hard, Con, the way he shook. I thought first you got him in the heart."

"I still can't understand it," mused Rael aloud. "There was no ball in your pistol, on my honor, and yet . . ."

"It was his heart I tried for," Con said briefly, and turned back to his horse. "But what can you expect from a pistol, when you use a cussed little Cupid for a bullet!"

48

5. BEWARE THE HUNTERS

G ALVESTON HELD a certain sentimental attraction for Con. He looked on it as a tough old enemy whom he had whipped and made his ally. It had been the first seaport town that he had ever seen when he wandered in one day, a thin and tattered youngster of fourteen from the far back-country, with no assets but his wits and a driving hunger. Among his liabilities was a stern set of ethics implanted into him by a scrupulous father, and a code of polite conduct imposed upon him by a gentle mother who had decorously ridden sidesaddle even in hostile Indian country.

He had soon learned that bustling Galveston had too much on its mind to give much attention to an orphaned refugee kid from the Comanche country. Commercially, it counted itself the most important place in up-and-coming Texas. Its harbor saw more shipping than all the rest of the ports between the Rio Grande and the Sabine. Texas cotton, cattle, horses, all poured out through Galveston to the Gulf. It was a rich town of men who made money and spent it, of high prices and waste, and some poverty on the fringes.

The day came when the always hungry kid took a good long look at it, the way his father had looked at lonely land that he had taken on the San Saba, with cool appraisal and a hardening purpose. His father, when about to tackle a job, whether the taking and holding of land, the breaking of a killer horse, or the chasing of Indian thieves, had been wont to bite his thumb for good luck and mutter, "Up an' at it, Michael—I'll do it or kiss the devil's foot!"

So the hungry kid bit his thumb real hard. "Up an' at it, Michael . . ."

When he left Galveston he had money in his pockets, and had acquired a clearly defined philosophy. His hands, large and supple, were clever with cards. Galveston had capitulated to him, taught him his cards and philosophy, and been tardily generous.

But now he hated the place.

He stood at the grimy window overlooking the busy waterfront, his moody eyes on the ships. For two weeks he and the others had been cooped up in this dingy back-street lodging house. His tongue had grown sharp, and the others had learned to leave him alone much of the time. Inactivity always corroded his good humor. They spent the days outside in the fenced backyard, Rael reading to Phileda, Old Nick and Abel playing seven-up.

He cursed himself for having allowed himself to be saddled with them, while the knowledge mocked him that he lacked the hardihood to abandon them now. They were such damned innocents, except Old Nick. Left alone, with dwindling funds in a strange land, the Lord only knew what might become of them. He didn't even dare take chances on his own account, with them so dependent on him.

And always the thought of Santa Fe tantalized him. Santa Fe, and the only known road to it running by way of St. Louis and the Missouri traders' trail. There in Santa Fe was hidden somewhere the secret of Lorin and ninety thousand dollars in Mexican gold. And Peregrina—she would be well on her way back there by now, with her grandee uncle and General Rajimo—curse his dark hide and soul!—and all their glittering entourage. Well, Rajimo wouldn't be riding easy, with that little gold Cupid imbedded in his shoulder.

"He's due for a shock, if they ever dig that out of him and he sees what I shot him with!" Con mused, and let his mind run aside to Peregrina. He hadn't yet decided whether that beautiful girl was better or worse than he knew, but she was a part of Santa Fe's entice-ment. He was filled with a wild impatience to get away from here, where dull gray monotony painted all days alike, and where he had to hide like a furtive thief.

The hunters had arrived. He had learned of that from Rondo Kissane, friend of old times, when he ran into him on the street one day. They had come to run him down, and take him or his scalp back to St. Louis.

Rondo Kissane, a swaggery old ruffian in plug hat and tailed coat, had stepped out of the best hotel, caught him by an arm without a word, and taken him up to his room. There he mixed two sherry cobblers, built on a generous foundation of Jamaica rum, and regarded Con from under bushed brows.

"Eh? Is there any reason why three strangers should be lookin' for ye, Con, and one of 'em named Tripp and he a bad customer from his looks?"

"Tripp, eh?" Con tried the sherry cobbler and found it familiarly good. "Eph Tripp. Yellow-haired fellow with eyes like robin's eggs? Uh-huh, that's Tripp. Missouri killer. Yes, Rondo, there's reason. How've the games been?"

"Eh? Fair—just fair." Rondo Kissane nodded at three strapped bags on the bed. "Too many kickbacks, though. This town's gone hostile to us professionals. I'm packed to leave on a jaunt."

"Where this time?"

"Santa Fe. I'm joining the Expedition at Austin."

Con put down his glass. "Did you say Santa Fe?"

"Eh? I did. Why not? Think of it—three hundred men breaking trail through unknown wilderness where nowt but Injuns have ever trod. The ranks'll be full o' moneyed men with sporting blood, out for the lark. The gallant lads'll be wanting their games and fun at night as they sit round the campfires. I'm packing my tools, o' course—cards, dice, a faro layout, even a small wheel. But don't tell me ye haven't heard about our glorious Expedition!"

"I've heard rumors, that's all," Con admitted. "For years Texas has been talking of opening up her own trail to Santa Fe. Don't tell me they've finally got around to doing something about it."

Kissane wagged his head. "The ignorance o' folks outside Texas!"

He went on and told about it. Yes, Texas at last was about to carve out a trading route between Houston and Santa Fe, and give the cussed Missouri traders some much needed competition. Also, the new Texas Republic had always claimed the full length of the Rio Grande as her western frontier. This broad conception of the Texas boundary took in the larger part of New Mexico, including Santa Fe itself, as well as the hundreds of miles of unexplored territory lying this side of it where the Comanches roamed and held sway.

Mexico, still holding the dead hand of Spain over her northern province of New Mexico, disputed the Texas claim, but hadn't Santa Anna agreed to those boundary terms after Sam Houston whipped his Mexican army on the San Jacinto? Besides, it was said that the oppressed people of New Mexico were more than willing to throw off the Mexican yoke and come under the Lone Star of free Texas.

"That Rajimo's a bloody-handed tyrant, as everybody knows," averred Rondo. "He rules by the force of his soldiers, those murdering scum o' the land, and the people groan under his grinding heel!" The phrases sounded like pilfered rhetoric to Con. "They cry out for Texas liberation!"

But the long-awaited Expedition, it seemed, was not to be regarded as a military filibuster. Its aim was not to conquer. A body of three hundred armed men—though they were Texans—was not expected to take the whole Province of New Mexico by force after getting there, if it ever got there. Its real purpose was to open up trade and establish a regular route. Among the various civilians going with it were several enterprising and adventurous Houston merchants, taking along a string of wagons loaded with trade goods. The main force was made up of eager volunteer soldiers, for protecting the civilian officials and Houston merchants from marauding Comanches. The whole thing,

Con gathered, was looked on as a lighthearted adventure, a gay excursion through a totally unknown region where there would be plenty of hunting and, it was earnestly hoped, an occasional good brush with the warlike Comanches. The country up along Red River was reputed to abound with game, and the Indian tribes were unnumbered from there on.

Santa Fe would be the crowning climax to a grand jaunt, after all the hazards and imponderables were left behind in the wilderness. Santa Fe—golden, beckoning from beyond a thousand miles, with its undoubted welcome for the tall *extranjeros* from free Texas, its hospitality, its reputed exotic and beautiful women—Santa Fe was the happy goal.

"They'll come out and greet us as heroes come to liberate them!" vowed Rondo. "In all that country there's but one man who'll hate to see us, and that's the black tyrant Rajimo!"

Con held a slightly differing view. "His army may elect to stick by him," he pointed out. "And I never found that we Texans are so all-fired popular with any kind of Mexicans. Matter of fact, there was one Texan who had no trouble at all making himself mighty unpopular with some of 'em, up in St. Louis awhile ago. He shot and winged both Rajimo and Don Chavez."

Kissane swept a contemplative eye over him. "There's a rumor here about that. A Texan, ye say? Well, well . . . The rumor came about the same time this Tripp and his friends got here, and that was last night. They began asking for ye right away. Con, I could use a good partner. The Expedition'll be gone months, and a man could raise a fine beard in that time. He'd have three hundred friends, too, and ye know how us Texans do stick together."

Con poured himself a dram of straight Jamaica, and drank slowly. "Don't tempt me, Rondo," he muttered at last, his eyes bleak. "I can't go. I've got friends with me that I can't leave nor take along."

Kissane asked no questions. He was not a prying man. "Well, come ye change your mind, head for Austin. That's the rendezvous. Bring a good horse, guns and blankets."

"That'd bar me, alone," growled Con. "I'm broke. No, I'm not borrowing from you, thanks all the same." He drew out his watch. "Genuine Juergunsen. Paid six hundred for it. Buy it for four hundred?"

Kissane didn't argue. He went to his strapped bags. "Have to give it to ye in pigeon-feed bills. I'm taking my *dinero* along in small change for the games. If ye'd come along, Con, we'd clean up. We'd own the whole damned Expedition time we got back. Happen ye change your mind late, ye could catch up and join us somewhere along the Brazos . . ."

That was two weeks ago.

Phileda entered the room softly. She had come up from the yard for her sewing case, and didn't wish to disturb him. He was so easily irritated by small things these days. Not that he ever flared up, but his politeness then grew brittle, covering a black temper held under iron control.

He will never know, she thought, how he can hurt

me. He's hurting me now, far worse than if he beat me, because he's thinking of *her*—that girl with the look of a vivid dahlia among paler flowers. He couldn't hurt me more than this, his back toward me, not even hearing me enter, my presence not strong enough to draw his thoughts back from their far ranging. But my own thoughts and feelings are so strong, how can he not know?

There was so little release for her. Old Nick and Abel had their eternal card playing, though Abel played a bad game and didn't keep his mind on it, from what Old Nick said. Rael had his reading, his old volume of Bacon, and he could lose himself in it while reading aloud to her. Beautiful passages, beautifully enunciated in Rael's quiet voice: " '—And because the breath of flowers is far sweeter in the air—where it comes and goes like the warbling of sweet music—than in the hand, therefore nothing is more fit for that delight than to know what be the flowers and plants that do best perfume the air . . .' "

It made no sense to her. Her mind could grasp only fragments of it. What had she to do with breath of flowers, sweet music, delight? She kept her head bent and sewed, the rhythmic stitch-stitch-stitch of the needle bringing to her a small measure of dull hypnotism. In New Orleans they had stopped off just long enough to pack a few things before slipping aboard the Galveston boat. She had brought a few dresses and her sewing case. Rael, true to his instincts, had forgotten his shirts but remembered his Bacon.

She wished she were a man. Men did not suffer like

this—or did they? *He* was suffering. She moved toward him, the thought of revelation that stirred in her an upheaval of pity for them both, and made her unconscious of herself. Con was suffering. She must do something. She touched his arm, timidly.

"Con—please—don't let it hurt so much!"

He turned abruptly from the window. His morose eyes changed oddly, growing kinder than she had seen them in days.

He mistook her meaning. "Why, now, little sister, what's the matter? What is it that's hurting you? You're trembling."

She was trembling because he had put his hands on her shoulders, because his voice was kind, because he was looking down at her with a searching scrutiny that was not mocking or cool.

He asked again, with concern: "What's wrong, Phileda?"

It was his speaking of her name that pulled the last trigger of her emotion. She was suddenly helpless and childlike, crying against his shirt and holding tight onto him while her muffled voice betrayed her over and over again.

For a long time he said nothing, his hand slowly stroking her head. She quieted, horrified at her shame, and became aware of the tenseness of his body.

"You pay me a very great compliment, Phileda." He spoke with gentleness and care. "But you shouldn't feel that way about a man like me. I'm a rascal and a blackguard, a fake gentleman, living on my wits . . ."

She was being led to the door. Her shame could not

prevent her from looking up into his face. There was a strange tightness about his mouth, and a trapped look in his eyes. She was not to know that he was desperately sorry, was mentally scrambling for some way to help her.

"Some other day when things are better," he said, "I'll come and ask you if you still feel this way." It was the best he could think of to say, and the least, and yet it was too much.

"When?" she whispered. "Oh, Con—when?"

He hesitated and kissed her quickly. Footsteps were sounding on the stairs. "In a year. You must go now."

6. MONTE MAN

WHEN ABEL CAME into the room, one look at his white face was enough to tell Con that the lad had guessed too much. Con said evenly, "Don't draw that knife, Abel, or I'll have to land on you!"

"You've been making love to her!" Abel's voice was low and shaking. "I passed her on the stairs. She didn't even notice me—like she was blind. I could see what—anybody could see she—you . . . Oh, you cur! You filthy cur!"

Con took a lithe step toward him, and paused. His movement was automatic. He was not angered deeply enough to strike the white young face. "Take hold of yourself," he rapped curtly. "Do you realize what you're saying? You young fool, you're insulting

Phileda. Coming from anybody else, that would warrant a bullet."

"You—presuming to protect her name! You!"

"Yes, I." Con turned back to the window. "It so happens," he added somberly, "I have that right. Phileda has given me that right, though we hoped to wait a year before announcing it. Do I make myself clear?"

He heard no answer behind him, nothing, until the door clicked shut, and he turned to find himself alone.

He called them together for a council that night. "We've got to get out of here," he said. "More of Tripp's tribe will be coming, and they'll smoke us out sooner or later. We've got to raise cash—enough for us all to get away on. Nick, will you step out with me tonight?"

"Sure."

Con grinned, the glint of action back in his eyes. "Good. I plan to try a coup."

"I'll go with you, too," announced Rael. "I don't know what you plan to do, but I insist on helping if I can."

Con eyed him reflectively. "It's—ahem—not exactly in your line, Rael. Ever hear of a 'capper'? No? Well, a capper is a sort of underhand helper to a sure-thing gambler on the make. Gentlemen don't usually take it up."

"I insist," said Rael again.

THE BARROOM HELD a good crowd. Two poker games were in full swing under the flaring oil lamp at the blind end of the bar, and a faro layout divided heavy business with a roulette wheel. A nice live crowd. A tough crowd, too, tough in the recklessly blatant way of men who lived high between periods of hard and dangerous work. It was common knowledge that thousands of steers were being sold by men not their owners. Wholesale rustling was the sport of the day, and cattle buyers for the big Gulf shippers paid hard cash on the line and no bill of sale demanded.

Con looked for game. His expert eye roved over the crowd, sizing up, rejecting, pondering. He finally located a prospect at the bar: A cattle buyer, obviously a kingpin in his line, drinking wine at twelve dollars a bottle. Had a large diamond in his shirt front, and wore the inevitable high stockman's boots that were the badge of his profession. Had a gun on him, too, half as long as his leg, sagging from the broad belt under his coat. Shrewd, cagey, with a cool and confident eye and a large manner about him. Just the man. Cowards and fools never made good game.

Con bit his thumb for luck. "Up an' at it, Michael!"

He watched the faro game, waiting for the right time. When it came, he strolled over to the bar and took his place by the cattle buyer. "Pretty fast game they've got there," he remarked.

The cattle buyer's cool eyes considered him. "It's fairish."

"Join me in a bottle?"

"Thanks, I just ordered one."

"Then let me pay and we'll split it." Con drew out a roll of bills, a large roll, a fifty showing outside.

The cattle buyer glanced at the roll and took a pull

at his cigar. "Suit y'self, friend. M-mm—my name's Hugare."

"Mine's Connegan. Glad to know you." Con paid for the bottle and they filled their glasses. The careless way he thrust his roll back into his pocket took the attention of several nearby drinkers.

Hugare thawed visibly and proffered one of his cigars. "You seem interested in faro, Mr. Connegan, Do you gamble?"

Con laughed wryly and shook his head. "Not any more. Took oath I wouldn't, after a fellow beat me out of three thousand dollars, on the boat coming from New Orleans. It hurt my pride, I guess. I thought I was too smart to be taken in by such a simple little game."

Hugare seemed both interested and amused. "What game was it?"

"Oh, a silly sort of game with three cards," Con replied shortly. "Never saw it played before. Fellow called it Rocky Mountain euchre. I have the cards in my pocket—gave the fellow another ten dollars for them. Going to keep them, to look at and remind me what a fool I can be, in case I ever again am tempted to gamble. No, Mr. Hugare, I shall never gamble again."

Hugare winked at some of the men who were listening and grinning near by. "Ah—I imagine that game was three-card monte," he opined. "Good old three-card monte. Could I see the cards?"

Con obligingly took the three cards from his wallet—queen of hearts, ten of clubs, ten of spades. "The fellow sort of mixed them up together very fast and laid them out face down. You're supposed to pick out the queen."

He saw, in the back-bar mirror, Old Nick drift in and move up to the bar. Rael entered next. Both stood on Con's other side, without look or greeting.

Hugare manipulated the three cards with practiced hands, making them fly back and forth, shuffling them, and smiling reminiscently. "Good old three-card monte." He tossed them onto the bar with a contemptuous laugh. "Here in Texas, Mr. Connegan, we leave such stale old bait for back-country yahoos and foreigners to bite on." Some of the listeners drew closer and laughed with him at Con's expense.

Con offendedly drew himself up. He picked up the despised cards and shuffled them clumsily. "Nevertheless, suh, it caught me," he retorted stiffly. "Could you do better?"

"Certainly." Hugare reached out and turned up the queen. "There it is. My dear man, the way you shuffle 'em, I could pick the lady every time, wager a bottle I could."

"Humph!" Con shuffled again, frowning, laid the three cards face down on the bar, and again Hugare unerringly turned over the right card.

Con muttered an oath. "Pure luck," he snapped, paying for another bottle while the group chuckled. "I'll play you for the cigars."

This time Hugare missed and turned up a ten. Old Nick reached along the bar and turned over the queen. "Thar she be," he grunted. "Coulda tol' you 'twas that'n." His thumb, damp and grimy, left a small smear on the back of the queen card.

Con expanded and remarked that he was satisfied. "It isn't possible to pick the queen every time," he pointed out. "Besides, the picker has only one chance in three. When I first played on the boat I won, but the fellow finally trimmed me." He put the three cards back into his wallet.

"You're easy satisfied, friend," observed Hugare. His glance had darted to the thumb-smear on the back of the queen card. "Would you care to back your opinion with cash?"

Con shook his head. "I've sworn off cash gambling."

"What you mean is, you've been scared off," Hugare corrected. "Here in Texas, we don't let one run of bad luck turn our livers white."

Con jerked up his head. "I resent that! I'm as game as any man. How much will you bet?" He slapped the cards back on the bar and hauled out his roll.

The group around them grew quiet. Hugare calmly produced a sheaf of bills. "How much you got there, friend?"

Con looked taken aback. "Why—ah—about a thousand dollars. But . . ."

"Put it up," said Hugare, and counted out from his own roll. "Put up, or squeal small. You're in fast company, friend, and pigeon feed don't interest me."

Con fiddled with his money. "I—er—didn't quite intend . . ." He squared his shoulders as somebody snickered. "Very well. Who'll hold the stakes? Perhaps this gentleman here will oblige?" He thrust his roll of bills into Rael's hands. Rael looked bursting to tell him something urgent, for he, too, had spotted the mark left by Old Nick's thumb on the back of the queen card.

Hugare surveyed Rael briefly and handed over his bet. "You *sabe* this game? If I turn up the queen, I win the stakes. You look honest, mister, but I want no arguments later. All right, Mr. Connegan, my friend— mix 'em up."

Con made long and awkwardly intricate work of shuffling, but Hugare didn't even look. The cattle buyer puffed on his cigar, winking at the crowd. Somebody began tugging at Con's coat tails. It annoyed Con. Devil an' all, did Rael think he didn't know what he was doing? He turned his head to frown Rael off, but he found it wasn't Rael doing the tugging. It was Old Nick, and Old Nick had his eyes fixed on the street doorway. Con looked that way and went on shuffling without a break.

Three men stood in the doorway, one slightly ahead of the others, their cold and expressionless eyes leveled at him. The man in the lead was Eph Tripp, gunman from Missouri.

Con shuffled awhile longer, giving himself time to think. Tripp might or might not elect to do his work here in the barroom. This was Texas, and he would be wary of Texas law, but a brawl would cover up that matter.

Hugare leaned an elbow on the bar. "You'll wear off the spots, you wool 'em around much more."

Con spread them out. "Pick your card."

Hugare squinted smoke from his eye, removed his cigar, and lazily touched the smeared card. "There's the darlin'," he drawled, and flipped it over.

It was the ten of spades.

Hugare straightened up with a snap and an oath, and turned over the other two cards. One of them was the queen, but it had no smear or mark of any kind on its back. He crumpled it savagely in his hand.

Con glanced at him. "I win the stakes, I believe, Mr. Hugare, my friend," he said mildly. "And now, if you'll excuse me, I'll wish you good night." He took the money from Rael and crammed it into his pocket. His mind now darted to the problem of Tripp and his two allies.

Hugare flung the crumpled cards down and stared at Con. "Why so fast?" He spoke through his teeth. "By gopher, I think you jobbed me! I think . . ."

"Mister, I'll vouch you was jobbed real neat!" broke in a dragging voice from across the barroom. It was Tripp speaking, and coming slowly forward, hands dangling close to his holster-strapped hips. "That feller's Captain Con, one o' the slickest gamblin' men on the Miss', an' the two behind him is his sidekicks!"

In the brief hush following, Tripp bent his arms at the elbows and stood slightly crouched as if gathered for effort. His coat hung wide open, exposing a pair of polished gun handles curving out from the holsters strapped to his hips. His two companions remained at the open doorway, alertly on guard. Play had ceased at the tables, and men at the bar were discreetly backing out of the line of attention, wanting no part in the coming explosion.

Hugare backed only a step. "Jobbed—me! Jobbed at monte!" Veins swelled on his forehead. He dragged out his long pistol. "Hand me back that money!"

Con said, "Sure, if you feel that bad." He reached to his pocket, but it wasn't the pocket where he had put the bills. Tripp took note of that and acted accordingly, though a shade late.

The silver-mounted dueling pistol roared its one load, and at that same time Old Nick got his hand on a wine bottle and sent it spinning at Hugare's head. With his empty pistol for a club, Con charged for the guarded door. Tripp was sinking slackly to his knees, but his two companions stood ground to shoot it out. One of them got off a hasty shot that was immediately echoed by another report behind Con. The man jerked violently and swayed. His partner back-stepped fast, fired twice from out in the street, and bolted.

Con flung his empty weapon after him, scooped up Tripp's pair of guns, and spun around to see who it might be that had fired the shot behind him. It was Rael. The saloon was in an uproar, and Old Nick had his skinning knife out, while with his left arm he supported Rael and rushed him across the floor for the door. Rael, his hat gone and a trickle of blood on his high forehead, had hold of Hugare's big pistol, and it was smoking.

As he covered their retreat and backed out after them, Con revised a previous opinion he'd had concerning a gentleman's fitness to act as capper to a gambler on the make. He shook a card out of his sleeve and skimmed it into the barroom before he left. It was the queen of hearts, with a smudge on the back. . . .

SLUMPED IN A BROKEN-BACKED CHAIR in the lodging house yard, Abel came alert as the high fence creaked. He had been sitting alone in the moonlight with his misery. He rose as Con landed lightly in the yard.

"Where's Phileda—upstairs?" Con whispered. "No, don't call her. Glad I found you out here alone. Thought I would. Now, listen. There's a ship in harbor, the *Corvette*, that'll be sailing at high tide tonight, New Orleans bound. You and Phileda get aboard her. I don't care how you do it, or what lies you may have to tell her—but do it! Get her out of this town. Go with her. Look after her. You're the only one of us that can do it now, Abel!"

"What's wrong, Con?" Abel's eyes were big. "Where's Rael and Nick?"

"Hiding in a stable, the other side of town. Rael's been hurt. Not serious, but it's left him foggy. A ball tore his scalp some. Here's money. Yes, we made the coup. Better get some other clothes somewhere, even if you have to wear Phileda's other dress. The ships'll be watched and those buckskins draw attention. You can't afford to take risks, not while you've got Phileda to look out for."

"But what's wrong? You haven't told me, Con!"

"We ran into a little trouble and there was some shooting. They're after us, and not all of 'em lawmen. That's why I had to prowl back here alone. We're known. Put that money away safe. Got any friends outside of Memphis?"

"I've got an uncle near Louisville."

"Good." Con glanced up at the house. "Make your way there, and take her with you. Watch yourself. Don't show your face any more than you have to. Don't trust anybody. Don't let any slick-talking strangers get you to gambling on the boat, no matter what kind of sure thing they offer you. I'm depending on you, Abel. It's a tough job, a job for a sharp and careful man."

Abel gained stature and stood very straight. "You can depend on me," he promised, without bravado. "She'll be safe. My oath on that, Con. When will you and the others come?"

"Not for quite a spell," Con answered. "Months. We're leaving for Austin tonight, if we can slip out without trouble—and if I can lay my hands on three good horses. And we point on west from Austin." He held out his hand. "S'long, Abel. Good luck."

Abel gripped his hand. "G'bye, Con. I—I'm sorry for—what I said. I thought . . ."

"Forget it." Con gave him a grin. "Wish you were coming along with us." He looked up at the lighted window on the second floor, and said again, "S'long—good luck."

He was climbing back over the fence when Abel asked a last question. "Con, what did you mean, west of Austin? Isn't that on the frontier? What's west of it?"

Con looked back before dropping over the fence.

His eyes danced a-glitter in the moonlight, and his white teeth flashed. "Santa Fe!" he murmured, and left Abel staring blankly after him.

7. ALL IS GLORY

THE HOT JUNE SUN beat down upon an imposing cavalcade, the like of which the fertile valley of the Brushy had never before witnessed. At last the great Expedition was rolling on its way, after many delays and changes of plan. The glorious frolic had begun.

Over three hundred mounted men; twenty-four heavily loaded wagons; a large *cavallada* of spare horses, mules, oxen, and a small herd of beef cattle for meat; and a brass cannon to scare the senses out of the Indians. All marching into the unknown, with the blessings of Texas and the hopes of winning an empire.

Nobody knew the route, for there wasn't any yet known. One of the tasks of the Texas-Santa Fe Expedition was to find one and map it out for other and lesser pioneering souls to follow. Austin lay in one latitude and Santa Fe in another, and that was the only sure knowledge anybody had about it. A few of the older hands had at times ranged as far afield as the Cross Timbers wilderness, and one claimed to have reached the Brazos headwaters and got back with his scalp, but the stories they told of limitless plains stretching westward beyond Cross Timbers only whetted adventurous appetites.

The volunteer troopers had been formed into six companies, each commanded by a captain. Each company took its turn at fatigue duty, driving the cattle, and breaking trail for the long string of wagons. The commanding officer, a Texas general whose very look was law, rode at the head of the column with the scouts.

Rondo Kissane had conceived a dislike for the trumpeter, whose task it was to rouse the encamped column every morning. "Yon damned tootler itches my ear," the old gambler grumbled, scowling back through the thick dust of the marching column. The trumpeter, a cowboy in private life, practiced recklessly on his unfamiliar instrument as he went along.

But Con was listening to Rael admiring the scenery. They rode with the advance guard, ahead of the choking dust from wagons and hoofs. Old Nick had unluckily got himself attached to a fatigue party in an unguarded moment, and was working his way today with spade and axe, helping to cut some sort of through trail for the cumbersome wagons.

"It's beautiful country," said Rael. "I'm glad we came. Abel would have liked this, wouldn't he?"

Con nodded. "He'd have enjoyed the noise, the guns, the trumpeter—everything about this fool jaunt. But this beauty won't last, Rael, so make all you can of it. This Texas country can do you tricks that'd shame even Rondo. It'll entice you on, then take your scalp."

"When did it ever get yours? Eh?" asked Kissane dryly.

Con gestured toward the southwest. "My father built a fine home down along the San Saba, and raised horses. Good country for horses, that, and pretty as this. One day when the sky was blue and everything peaceful, the Comanches came. I've always been glad my mother died the year before. They burned the place, killed the old man, and took all the horses but one—the one I rode to death getting away on. Sometime later I drifted into Galveston, and picked up tricks from a crooked gambler named Rondo Kissane."

Camp was made that night on the San Gabriel. Some of the wagons had got wrecked on the march. Fires were lighted, and beef roasted on ramrods. Old Nick found Con and the others, and squatted by their fire, smoking his pipe. "Lot o' waste in this crowd," he growled. "They cut out the best bits o' beef an' chuck away the rest. Ugh! Time'll come they'll want it."

Kissane smiled tolerantly as he tossed away what he didn't want. "Plenty more," he yawned. "We'll be in Santa Fe before we eat all those cows."

Con caught Old Nick's eye. "Nick, have you got the same opinions about this grand tour that I've got?"

Old Nick hunched his shoulders. "I don't like the route, for one. Somebody tells 'em mebby there ain't no more water beyant the Brazos head, so they change course an' strike way up for the Cross Timbers 'fore turnin' west. How they figger to git the wagons over all them big hills an' woods? How they figger there's ary water up that way?"

Somebody spoke up from a near-by fire. "Where there's standing timber, there's generally water, isn't there?"

"Not in Texas!" hooted another.

"You're dead right," corroborated somebody else. "I guess we got more rivers and less water than any other country in the world!"

A friendly argument got started. Everybody had opinions, nobody had exact knowledge, but there were men in the volunteer trooper ranks who could debate well and fluently—doctors, lawyers, merchants, all with the Expedition for excitement. And the cowboys, hunters, adventurers, soldiers of fortune, they could argue all night.

Old Nick stalked off, disgusted, and Con turned to Rael. "You know, my brother Lorin would have been in his element here," he remarked. "He was one of your starry-eyed knights. Took after my mother's folks. Lucky for him, he was visiting her people on the Georgia coast when the Comanches came to the San Saba. After that, they adopted him, and we never saw much of each other. They don't recognize me."

"You speak as if he's dead," said Rael. He and Lorin Connegan had been students together in Georgia.

Con nodded. "I think he is. Lorin was a born idealist, always seeing everything as a rosy picture, always blinded by some beautiful illusion or other. A man like that either gets himself killed while young, or lives to grow bitter and tragic when his illusions crumble. It's better if he dies young."

Rael shook his head. "You're a cynical dog, Con."

"Cynical?" Con, not offended, took his gaze from the fire. "Not at all. I try to see and accept things as they are, that's all. I like most people, and I despise only the hypocrites. But even hypocrites can be funny, and some I don't despise at all. You, for instance!"

Rael started as if slapped in the face. "I? *I*—a hypocrite?"

Con nodded coolly, "You, Rael, yes. In spite of your concern over Phileda, you've been happy ever since we joined this jaunt. Admiring the scenery. I've even heard you quietly singing as you rode. But it's not the scenery you like that much, though maybe you're fooling yourself about it. But you're not fooling me, Rael!"

"Why—I—what do you mean?" Rael was red.

"Your mind," Con pursued, "is in Santa Fe. Rajimo and his party will be in Santa Fe long before we get there—*if* we get there. It's a mighty dangerous place for us, and we've got to grow beards and keep out of the way—but *she* will be in that place. A certain more than beautiful girl. And when a man's as deep in love as you are, there's always hope. I know. Yes, dammit, how well I know!"

Rael was silent. "I suppose you're right," he confessed at last.

"Now you're being honest with yourself," Con complimented him pleasantly. "I'll be just as honest. I'll tell you I've got a wild hope or two of my own, concerning that same Santa Fe lady. And when I want anything badly enough, I generally make out to do something about getting it!"

He watched Rael raise his head. Their eyes met and held over the fire. Rael said tightly, "I'll try to stop you, Con! I'll do anything to stop you!"

"Sure, I expect it." Con picked up his blanket. "Give me credit for warning you, though. It's not my usual habit. Let's turn in now and get some sleep. Looks like a tough old road ahead tomorrow."

W EEKS LATER, the long train of battered wagons lurched and bumped through the darkness, in the broken, tree-blinded wilderness of the Cross Timbers, and the gay glamour was gone. Already the grinding journey had cost heavily in wrecked wagons, accidents, men and horses killed, injured, gone, missing. No water had been found, and back along the train the few cattle left were miserably bawling. Jaded oxen drooped in the yokes, and the horses were wild-eyed with thirst. Drivers and fatigue men were worn out, hungry, so thirst-choked that they had given up cursing. The narrow passage that they had to hack out for the wagons was stumpy, rock-studded, cut across constantly by deep gullies, and the dry beds of what once had been streams.

Three more wagons had been smashed and abandoned today, and the whole command was scattered for miles through the great woods. Here and there distant pinpoints of Indian fires could be sighted on the higher hills, mute reminders of feathered ghosts and hidden eyes that glared brooding hatred at the white invaders.

The wagons slowly crowded to still another halt, and word was passed back that the gun-carriage carrying the brass six-pounder had overturned in a gully, blocking the whole train. Long hours ago volunteer scouts had gone riding ahead to seek a passage west out of the woods. Since then, other groups had quit the train and gone in search of water. Some would not return, and only the unseen Indians would know the precise reason why. Discipline had collapsed.

Con sank down against a wagonwheel beside Rael. He wiped grimed sweat from his face with a dirty hand, and laughed. "That means we're stuck here for the night. Not enough hands left to get that gun-carriage righted, and the teams are played out. 'Lo, Rondo, how're you stacking up?"

Kissane stumbled wearily up with Old Nick. "I've seen the elephant," he groaned, and stretched out on the ground.

The expression, peculiarly Texan, was new to Rael, and Con translated it for him. "He means he's seen a-plenty and would admire to call off all bets. Rondo, you surprise me. Think of Santa Fe. Think of those poor New Mexicans, suffering under the tyrant's heel and waiting for us to . . ."

"Let 'em suffer!" mumbled Rondo. He was a very tired, dirty, hungry and thirsty man. Ingenious as he was at dodging labor, he couldn't dodge all of it. And not since leaving the Brushy had he found a chance to open up a game. Everybody was too weary each night to be interested even in gambling.

Old Nick began talking, in the way of a man who

had stored up many thoughts lately. "Shoulda begun a month sooner, before the summer dry. Shoulda gone by way o' the San Saba, then northwest to the Colorado an' straight west across the plains. But, no—they talked theirselves into this route an' here we are, lost in the Big Timbers, no water, an' most ev'ry hand gone off on his own hook. If them cussed Injuns had sense they'd jump us tonight an' roast our bones in the wagons."

But Kissane had fallen asleep, and Rael was gazing up at what he could see of the stars through the gnarled little oaks and blackjacks. Con studied Rael for a moment, with half sardonic humor.

"Care for a piece of this rawhide?" he offered.

"Pardon? Oh—thank you." Rael took the scrap and turned it vaguely over in his hand. "What's it for?"

"Chew on it. Eases thirst. Or aren't you thirsty like us poor mortals?"

"Why—yes—I believe I am. Thank you, Con."

Con went in search of his blanket. He brought back Rael's with him and tossed it over, but Rael was gazing up at the night sky again and smiling as if having a pleasant dream. Con shook his head as he crawled under a wagon to sleep. There was one man still left in the party, anyway, for whom the glamour and rich promise hadn't yet faded.

8. BEYOND CROSS TIMBERS

WHILE THE MEN GASPED in the terrific heat of the plains, the officers and commissioners of the Expedition held desperate council. They had thought Cross Timbers bad, and it had taken them two weeks to get through, but now in retrospect those weeks seemed almost a time of comfort compared with what they had gone through since.

After cutting through the Cross Timbers they had formed column and pushed on, following what they thought was Red River. The river led them far off their course and then petered out in the desert plains, so they struck northwest. Troubles really lashed them then. Water grew scarce, most of it brackish and undrinkable. Food ran low. They had hoped for buffalo meat, but the buffalo herds had migrated north this late in the summer, for the grass here was burned out.

A stampede had lost them many oxen, half their mules, and a good many horses. Comanche thieves in the night had accounted for many more—and they, being good judges of horseflesh even in the dark, had taken the best. The ever harrying Comanches had fired the prairie, too, and the dead grass became a blazing ocean. Two wagons had burned, one of them containing their store of powder, cartridges and spare weapons, and it blew up with a mighty roar.

And now, directly barring their way, stood a line of craggy mountains that some guessed might be the little known Wichita Range. Nobody knew for sure. They were lost in the heart of the Comanche country, living on prairie dogs and mesquite beans and anything else that looked edible.

Camp had been made here by a small spring that tasted bitterly of copperas and magnesia and did things to their stomachs. Hunger and sickness stalked the camp. All had grown weak and haggard, and the common denominator of suffering had brought everybody down to one undisciplined level. Their unwashed clothes hung in dirty tatters, their hair and beards were thick and matted, and the fierce sun had browned their skins to deep mahogany.

At any time, Comanche spies could be seen watching from beyond gunshot range, sitting their shaggy ponies, with their tufted lances and their insolent bearing that mutely promised murder and massacre at the first chance. The shrill, rapid-fire yelling, always startling to the pricked ears of the hearers, announced the arrival of more bands of them every hour. The camp was practically in a state of siege.

There was some talk of burning the remaining wagons and trying to fight a way back, but the commander put his foot down on that proposal.

Con, who had joined the council, rather admired the stern old soldier for his prompt stand. "We're going on!" declared the commander. "I propose to send a party ahead to find the outlying New Mexican settlements and send back food and help. We can't be very far from them now."

He ran an eye over his gathered officers, a ragged

78

and hairy group. "Captain Holland, you'll take command of that party. Eighty men should be sufficient to get through the Comanches, if we've got that many fit men left. I also detail Captain Dupratt and Lieutenant McCourtney to support you. Such merchants and private civilians who wish may join you, but they must travel light and be armed. I'll remain here with the main command, and we'll hold out until you can send back help. We'll need fresh animals for the wagons, also guides who know the country. That's all, gentlemen."

Con fell into step with Captain Holland. "I'd like to join your party, Captain," he said politely.

"Glad to have you," returned Holland.

Con walked pensively back to his horse. From the outlying settlements to Santa Fe could not be so very far. He was bearded and burned, considerably changed from the Captain Connegan of St. Louis. Given a free hand in Santa Fe, as an unrecognized stranger, he could probe the mystery of vanished Lorin and the ninety thousand dollars. And there was Peregrina. . . .

"Wild hopes," he murmured to himself.

But next day, riding out with the advance company, Old Nick and Kissane along by common agreement, he found Rael jogging steadily at the rear of the column.

THE ADVANCE COMPANY struggled on, a band of wild and ravenous men with sunken eyes and blackened, fleshless faces. Eleven days ago they had left the wagon camp at the brackish spring, and not yet had they seen a sign of the New Mexican settlements.

All around, the prairie ran to the horizon like a dead ocean. The suffering horses moved with difficulty, sore-footed and played out. The men slumped in the saddles, or staggered on foot beside them. At sunrise on the twelfth day they rested for an hour by an alkaloid pool, and the captain reluctantly ordered another horse killed for food. They shot and butchered the poorest horse. Such was their hunger, they ate all parts of it, leaving no share to a lean old prairie wolf that sat quietly sniffing them from a cautious distance.

Rael, gnawing ravenously on a strip of rubbery gristle, suddenly flung the stuff from him in a fit of revulsion. "It's—indecent," he muttered slowly. "When we started from Austin, that horse was a fine animal. He was one of us, and now we eat him. Once, I would as soon have thought of—of cannibalism!"

"Better not mention that," put in Con, tearing at a ragged bone. "Might put ideas in somebody's head! Some of 'em are already down to eating snakes and lizards."

Rael shuddered. Hair and grime could not hide the fine-drawn, delicate cast of his face, any more than dire hardship could blunt his sensitive nature. "Must we throw away all decent self-respect, merely to eat and stay alive? I think I prefer starvation." He moved his bloodshot eyes to the watching wolf. "We've sunk lower than that wolf yonder."

Con shrugged. "He'd better not come any closer, that old *lobo,* or we'll make a meal of him too!"

Years ago, as a Comanche-hunted boy, he had discarded fine sensibilities in favor of keeping a hold on life. He considered Rael, and gave him one more day to hold out. Rael had not been toughened by early hardships and so his scruples had grown up with him, deep rooted and strong. By tomorrow, Rael would either be eating anything at hand, or dying. He was trembly already, barely able to climb onto his horse.

Well, survival of the fittest—When a man let his finicky scruples outweigh his instinct for self-preservation, that was a weakness. "Let him die then, if that's his choice," Con thought with irritation. "There's no room around here for such precious self-respect!"

That evening a canny Houston merchant brought in a spotted land tortoise, alive and kicking, that he had found on the prairie. He dropped it, held the butt of his rifle on it, and inquired of an avidly interested crowd as to the best way to cook it.

"It's good eating, cooked right," he declared. "I've eaten 'em in hotels at fancy prices. Happen I hit on the right way to cook this, I'll eat it down to the shell and allow I've had a meal. Who knows how to cook it?"

"For a bite, I'll tell you," spoke up Con. "Take it to that fire there and bury it in the hot ash. Keep the fire going, but not too hot. In half an hour she ought to be done. Yes, they're good eating. Lot of nourishment in one."

He watched the Houston man bury it carefully in the red embers and cover it over. The group sighed and wandered off. "You'll never get a taste of it," remarked one to Con. The merchant was not noted for generosity.

The half hour was nearly up when Con idled over to the fire. "Better give it a few minutes more," he advised, and trimmed the fire with a stick. "She was a big one. Got salt?"

"In my saddlebag." The Houston man went off to get it. When he returned he borrowed Con's stick and began raking off the fire. "Hope you don't expect me to share. . . . Say, the damn thing's gone!"

"Gone!" muttered Con brokenly. "Well, for—! Say, didn't you kill it before you put him in?"

"Kill him? No! Terrapins are always roasted alive, I heard. Anyway, you didn't say to kill him, did you?"

Con gazed at him pityingly. "You're a mighty simple man, and you must've figured that terrapin just as simple. Why would he stay there? Don't you know they burrow in the ground? If you dig, maybe you'll catch him, but I doubt it."

Rael lay with his eyes closed when Con walked up and sat by him. Looked pretty bad and done up, Rael did, his face so drawn and thin, with those black hollows under his eyes. Con shook him by a shoulder, not roughly, and Rael wearily dragged open his eyelids.

"I hope," said Con gruffly, "your cussed objections don't extend to roast terrapin. Sit up and eat!"

Next day they came upon a deserted Mexican camp and an old dim cart road. More mountains lay ahead of them. The famished men pressed eagerly onward, following the faint ruts leading upward into the rough foothills. All order was lost, the men, as they advanced, hunting for wild plums, grapes, and any living or creeping thing that could be eaten. A raw and chill wind greeted them with higher altitude, cutting through their flapping rags and shivering them. They lost the dim cart ruts during the bitterly cold night, but pushed on over the mountains, and from the summit next morning they sighted a river far below, and white patches that some said were great flocks of sheep.

Toward evening they came up with a Mexican sheep camp, and descended upon it with hoarse cries and cheers, those on foot plodding at a run, others kicking their staggering brutes to a stumbling trot. A skinny young volunteer trooper, sobbing in weak hysteria, fell and beat the ground with his fists.

"We made it! By the good Lord, we made it!"

The frightened sheepherders shrank from the hairy, wild apparitions, tongue-tied with terror, and it was long before any sense could be got out of them.

The settlements? *Si,* yonder to the west. San Miguel lay sixty miles away, Santa Fe a hundred, more or less. They listened to descriptions of the wagon camp, the mountains, the brackish spring. The Quintufue, they said. Two of them knew that country, having worked at odd times for a Santa Fe Spaniard who traded with the Comanches. There was a pass through those mountains, if one knew of it, good enough for wagons. This river here, on which they were camped with the flocks, was the Rio Gallinas, they said.

Captain Holland hired the two Mexicans to go back to the Quintufue wagon camp and act as guides. The Comanches would not kill them, he learned, as their master had a treaty with the chiefs. The captain then pulled out gold coin and began buying sheep. . . .

That night, for the first time in months, they slept on full stomachs. Some of the other sheepherders vanished during the night, but the others explained glibly enough that they had gone to get flour from their cache, to make good nourishing *atole con leche* for those of the *Tejanos* who were sick.

Captain Holland now decided to send a small party on to San Miguel, to confer with the New Mexican authorities there and arrange to buy or borrow fresh horses for the stalled Expedition. Few of the men and horses of his party were fit to travel farther, and he wished to establish amicable relations with the officials of the country as soon as possible. There was always the risk that this Expedition might be regarded by the New Mexicans as an armed invasion, rather than a trading venture—a pardonable error, and a point upon which many Texans themselves were uncertain. The Expedition itself, weakened and in hard straits as it was, wanted no kind of trouble.

Captain Dupratt agreed to go as official courier, also Lieutenant McCourtney. The Honorable Stanley Tonsall, an English entomologist who had joined the Expedition for the experience, also volunteered to join the small party.

For a man bred to all the niceties of polished society, the Honorable Stanley had succeeded admirably in adjusting himself to conditions. An amiable man, nothing ever ruffled him. He rode a mule, a rickety brute, self-willed, lame in one leg, and with the habit of falling down when least convenient. But she was hardy as a bear, and had kept going at the same mincing gait while fine horses broke and died around her under the prolonged strain. The Honorable Stanley swore by her and called her Lucrezia. When in full travel array, with a big smooth-bore on his shoulder, and a general assortment of a little of everything strung from the saddle, he and Lucrezia made a picture. Books, various scientific instruments in cases, a teakettle and tin cup, a gourd, a pair of pistols and other articles all swung and jangled in unison to the limping shuffle of long-eared Lucrezia.

Kissane nudged Con. "How could we rig it to go along with 'em?" he muttered. "I want to get to a town, any damned town. I want to get my feet under a civilized table, and a cold sherry cobbler in my hand . . ."

"And a good Havana," Con appended. "I'm just as hurry minded as you are. More. But we're not officers, nor are we civilian guests of this great and glorious Expedition." He looked around camp. Rael slept peacefully on the riverbank in the shade, his fair hair long and tousled, looking like a poet or a child despite his untrimmed beard.

An hour after the select little party of three left, Con approached Captain Holland. "Well, we can expect 'em back any minute," he remarked. "Tonsall left his microscope behind. Here it is. You know how he is— he'd turn back from the pearly gates to get his 'scope. Eh? Well, all right, I'll ride after him with it. Yes, my horse is in fair shape."

Shortly after that, Kissane hurried up to Holland.

"That Connegan—he means well, but he goes off too sudden," he grumbled. "Look here—Tonsall's little case of spare 'scope glasses and slides. Connegan ought've looked around more. Eh? Well, if you say so. . . ." He rode after Con and caught up, out of sight of the camp.

They shook hands gravely and rode on together. When they overhauled their party, both saluted casually. "It's been decided we should go with you, gentlemen," said Con blandly. "Tonsall, you lost your 'scope outfit. Here 'tis. Better tie it on tighter."

That afternoon the five Texans came upon a Mexican muleteer. The peon nearly swooned with fright, but grew obsequiously talkative after discovering that the wild-looking strangers didn't intend to murder him right away. News that the *Tejanos* had reached the Rio Gallinas, he said, had been spread by some sheepherders who came hurriedly through the night before. Fast horsemen were carrying word of it to Santa Fe. It had been rumored for a long time that a Texas army was gathering for the purpose of coming to conquer, rob and pillage New Mexico, explained the muleteer. The great General Don Rajimo himself had heard of it, while far away in the foreign north, and he had hastened back to Santa Fe to mobilize his army.

The two officers, Dupratt and McCourtney, conferred together. Dupratt waved the muleteer away and rode on. "These people always exaggerate," he commented. "There's probably a little excitement, but nothing more."

"A little excitement goes a long way with these

people, too," Con put in dryly. "There may be some *verdad* in what that mule-skinner said. Rajimo's no fool, and he'd naturally guess we hope to see him kicked off his throne. And we *Tejanos* never have been popular, even before we handed Santa Anna his whipping on the San Jacinto. These New Mexicans are sort of isolated, and they've likely heard some wild tales about us. We don't look any too gentle, either—more like a gang of bandits. I favor we step light and look well ahead."

Dupratt, an unbending man of no humor and considerable belief in his own ability, sent him a frosty stare. "When I desire your undoubtedly expert advice I'll ask for it!" he snapped.

The Honorable Stanley grinned wickedly at Con and winked. As an independent traveler with the Expedition, he knew his place, but his serene blue eyes were often eloquent. It had become the general opinion that Captain Dupratt was a big gun of small caliber.

Soon they sighted a miserable village that they knew must be Anton Chico from the muleteer's directions, overlooking the Pecos. As they entered it, a splendidly mounted Mexican, armed with gun, sword and lance, rode off at a dashing pace toward the northwest.

Anton Chico was the first sign of human habitation they had seen in months, but they were keenly aware of a hostile lack of welcome. Women and children were in hiding, and the few men in sight huddled in silent groups, sullenly alarmed. Dupratt asked in his fluent Spanish to purchase fodder, bread, and lodging for the night. The Honorable Stanley flashed his engaging grin at a little brown *niño* peeping from a doorway, and spun him a silver coin. Con bowed from his saddle in fine style to a remarkably pretty girl gazing wide-eyed at him over an adobe wall, and doffed the rakish remains of his hat with a flourish. The girl dimpled, smiled back full and warmly, and her candidly coquettish eyes said these were men, after all.

Soon the women and girls began coming out, shyly proffering *tortillas* and *miel.* The Honorable Stanley remarked on them. "Dashed good-looking, what? Nice ankles. Natural grace."

Con agreed with him. "I've seldom heard anything but good of Mexican women, except from stiff-necked Yankees who like to be shocked at the way they dress. They're kind and warm-hearted, and they'll be your friends for life. Sure, they're coquettish, but that's their natural way. They're women and proud of it."

He calmly stared down a swarthy villain who glared at him. "But the men—the low-class peon men," he added, and spat. "That's a different matter. But, then, I'm a Texan. I saw the Alamo, and I fought at San Jacinto. I could be prejudiced."

9. DEATH AT THE 'DOBE WALL

IN THE MORNING the Texans rode out of Anton Chico, followed by the farewells of the women, who seemed sincere in their calls of *Adios, Caballeros,* and the simpler, deeper *Con Dios.* The men of the village were more reserved, their eyes furtive as if with secret knowledge.

Pushing on toward San Miguel, all that morning the Texans sighted armed horsemen watching them along the route. "They act like damn' Comanche spies," grunted Rondo. "I'll be right glad to get to Santa Fe. Wonder if these heathens know how to mix up a tall sherry cobbler for a thirsty man?"

"There's no doubt we'll be questioned in San Miguel," Dupratt admitted at length, "but we can easily convince them of our peaceful intentions. We must show respect for their laws, and discuss matters in a strictly reasonable spirit. We will avoid all cause for friction. In short—" He glanced doubtfully at Con—"we will behave as gentlemen."

It sounded fine and rather noble, and the Honorable Stanley was politely complimenting the spirit of it when his Lucrezia tripped her lame leg and fell with him, strewing her whole establishment in nice confusion. That raised the usual laugh, but the eccentricities of Lucrezia were too common to cause a halt. The Honorable Stanley had become expert at putting his household together, and he never lost patience. Kissane stayed behind to help him while the rest dawdled on.

McCourtney, an Irishman and an English-hater on principle chuckled. "Tonsall's one Limey who can take a joke, I got to admit. I'd have shot that mule months ago."

They were still smiling when they topped a rocky bluff overlooking the valley of the Pecos. Upstream they could see the village of Cuesta. The road into the valley ran so rough and steep down the bluff, they dismounted and led their horses. At the bottom they called a halt to wait for Tonsall and Kissane. McCourtney studied the crooked path down which they had come. "If I didn't know Lucrezia, I'd swear she'll never make it," he remarked. "But that mule only falls when she . . . Hello, what've we got here?"

Down from the village came an ill-formed troop of more than a hundred mounted men in ragged uniforms, armed with swords, lances and *escopetas*. Con ran a swift glance back up the crooked path, and caught Dupratt doing the same. For once they were in mute agreement. That path was no handy return route for men in a hurry.

The soldiers came on at a swinging lope, accouterments jingling and flashing in the bright sun, and drew up all in a jump at a barked word of command. Their officer rode forward.

"*Hola, amigos!* Permit me—I am *Capitan* Dimasio Salezar, at your service."

He was cordial, this Captain Salezar, for all his hawkish cast of face and narrow eyes. With a queer feeling, Con recognized him at once as the Mexican officer who had acted as General Rajimo's second in the St. Louis duel. Con folded his arms and hoped for the best, grateful for his beard, dark tan and rags.

Dupratt at once went into his prepared speech, telling of the Expedition, its peaceful purpose, its misfortunes, of the main command holding out on the Quintufue and the advance company on the Gallinas, and of his desire for an audience with the illustrious General Don Manuel Rajimo, military governor of this great Province of New Mexico. He was flustered, and that made him stammer and talk too fast.

Captain Salezar bowed, cool and self-possessed by contrast. The Texans, he said, would be required to give up their weapons before he could escort them to Santa Fe. A mere formality only, he made haste to add assurance, and bared his teeth in an apologetic smile. The weapons would be returned later. He deeply regretted the necessity, but the *señores* of course knew that they could not enter foreign territory with firearms in their hands. It was contrary to the usages and laws of civilized nations, not so? All foreigners checked their weapons when entering New Mexico. For the Texans to comply also would be proof of their peaceful intentions.

There was a frankness and a polite plausibility about the man that completely won over Dupratt. The Mexican soldiers moved up closer, but with no appearance of hostility. Dupratt returned the *capitan's* bow. "Naturally, we shall comply with your laws. Gentlemen, kindly give up your weapons. It's perfectly all right, of course."

"So?" murmured Con.

Dupratt frowned. "It is my order that you disarm!" he snapped, and handed over his own weapons without any further delay. McCourtney, as his junior in rank, followed suit, but with obvious reluctance. Captain Salezar, smiling deprecatingly, passed them to the soldiers behind him. Slowly, Con gave up two pistols and a Harper's Ferry rifle, and felt uneasily naked without them.

As the last weapon passed through his lean brown hands, Salezar abruptly changed demeanor. His smile faded. His polite murmur became a harsh bark. "Tie the prisoners!"

Some of the soldiers advanced on the disarmed Texans. Others began pointing upward and shouting. Rondo Kissane and the Honorable Stanley, just coming in sight down the steep bluff, halted. Salezar muttered an imprecation and motioned to his soldiers. Half of the squad, led by a sergeant, spurred headlong at the path and went tearing up it. Even in this moment Con could marvel at such horsemanship. He wouldn't have believed it possible to ride up that perilous ascent at faster than a cautious walk.

His arms were seized and tied. The last glimpse he got of the path, Lucrezia had fallen asprawl of it while trying to turn, pinning the Honorable Stanley. Rondo, unable to force his horse past, had abandoned it and was fleeing on foot with his gun in his hands.

A hand grasped Con by his piratical black beard and jerked his head savagely around. He glared into the dark face and narrow eyes of *Capitan* Salezar. Salezar showed his teeth in a different kind of smile, thin and triumphant.

"I have good eyes, my friend, and a good memory." He spoke slowly, with deliberation. "General Rajimo will be pleased to find you among the prisoners—so very pleased—Captain Connegan!"

THE BITTERLY COLD NIGHT in the dirty little San

Miguel prison shrank to early dawn. Con sat up on the hard-packed earthen floor, looked around at his three companions, and began binding up the broken blisters on his feet with torn strips of his shirt.

All were awake and shivering, their haggard and grimed faces ghastly in the early light. They had been marched afoot from Cuesta to San Miguel in ropes, forced along at a rapid pace by Salezar and his mounted dragoons. Everything had been stolen from them, but a compassionate woman of the town had brought them a buffalo robe and a tattered blanket, and cried softly because she had nothing more to spare. Other women and girls had brought tough *tortillas* and mutton broth to the jail, defying the growled protests of the guards. A priest had sent over some hot coffee.

Con said, "Wonder if Rondo got clear? If he made it back to the Gallinas we might get help."

The Honorable Stanley shook his head dubiously. He had a wrenched ankle and had suffered agonies on the march, but he mourned most the loss of his precious books and entomological equipment. McCourtney, trying to ease his boots back onto his swollen feet, cursed everything New Mexican with a quiet and concentrated virulence.

Captain Dupratt, close-mouthed, still tried to appear the infallible leader whose reckonings had gone wrong only because of a terrible error on the part of somebody else, which he would rectify in due course.

With daylight the women of San Miguel began coming again with more food, and the guards grudgingly allowed them to come as far as the little hole that passed as a window. A soft-eyed girl, with as much distress on her face as though the captive *Tejanos* were her own brothers, thrust bread to Con, whispering rapidly to him in Spanish as he took it. Con couldn't catch all she said, but he got the general drift. Rajimo was coming from Santa Fe with his army, and he would surely shoot the prisoners.

"Pobrecitos!" ended the girl pitifully.

They ate. *"Pobrecitos*—'poor fellows,'" murmured Con, and hunched his half-clad shoulders. "That's us, all right. Damn you, Dupratt, I wish I'd kept my guns and joined Kissane on the run! It would've anyway been a livelier end than kneeling against a 'dobe wall while they plug me!"

"You really think Rajimo will execute us?" inquired the Honorable Stanley. "I can't agree with you. I think, when he examines us and learns that we came quite openly and honestly into the country, he'll apologize and set us free."

"Keep on thinking that—it'll help you in your last hours!" Con encouraged, between bites of bread. "Personally, I've got no doubts. Unless Rondo made it back to the Gallinas and gets back here with the company ahead of Rajimo's army, I expect to die. I'm gambling big hopes on old Rondo, I swear."

Throughout the day they waited, hoping and listening for a drumming of hoofs and a good old Texas yell. They heard that Salezar had left hours ago to meet Rajimo. The sun was sinking behind the mountains when a drumming did come, the drumming of a large body of horsemen, rolling down from the northwest. It grew louder, and the lounging guards took on some sort of soldierly attention. People could be heard running in the plaza. A sharp and discordant blare of trumpets rang out, and the dull roar of hoofs beat clatteringly onto the hard-baked ground of the town.

Con turned from peering through the window hole. "Well, boys," he said quietly, "we lose! Damn old Rondo's feet, they never were much use to him." He stuck a thumb over his shoulder. "Take a squint at the great and illustrious General Rajimo, damn his Injun hide—army and all!"

Within ten minutes of the army's entrance, a sergeant's guard of regular troops came marching over to the little prison, took command of the prisoners, and marched them out. The demeanor of the sergeant was grim and he would answer no questions. Con's spine prickled in anticipation. Escape was hopeless. The plaza was full of armed men. Dupratt at last showed signs of losing confidence, nervously wetting his lips and frowning.

The Texans were lined up facing the soldiers' *cuartel,* and their arms tied again. Dupratt protested and loudly demanded audience with the governor, but Rajimo did not appear. Here and there in doorways, women and girls were wringing their hands in pity, and even some of the civilian men looked uneasy. There appeared to be no great love lost between Rajimo's soldiers and the civil population.

A grave young priest came over. "*Señores,* one of your party is to be executed!" he said gently.

Dupratt started violently. "Which one?" The bald fact, stated so simply and definitely, broke down the last of his assurance. He was a brave enough man in hardship or fighting, and had proved it, but he had a high-strung stubbornness in him that made it difficult for him to accept the inevitable with any calmness.

The young priest turned, pointing. "They are bringing him. He is to die for resisting arrest. General Rajimo's order."

Soldiers were leading a bound and stumbling man across the plaza. The ragged prisoner's face was bloody from a sword slash, but as he came nearer, Con uttered a blistering oath. There was no mistaking that old plug hat, battered and shapeless but still cocked at a rakish tilt.

"Rondo!"

Rondo Kissane, shambling slowly past, turned and looked at Con. " 'Ray for Santa Fe an' a sherry cobbler!" The ruffianly old gambler managed a horrible grin. "They're dealin' me out o' the game, Con. I sent some of 'em to hell, but I had nobody around to cap for me and I ran out o' chips."

"S'long, Rondo." Con grinned back. You didn't kick when you got cleaned out, if you were a good gambler. You took it in good part, bought drinks for the house on credit, and sauntered out with much airy nonchalance to raise another stake. "Don't win all hell and the Devil's pitchfork before I get there!"

Kissane's last words came back flippantly. "You'll have to hurry. 'Bye, Con!"

The soldiers pushed him to his knees, facing the

cuartel wall. Six of them formed line and took aim at his back. A corporal barked a short command. Musketry fire crashed out briefly . . .

"Gentlemen, you have observed the penalty of resistance!" rapped a brittle voice.

Con was first to swing around. General Rajimo stood in the doorway of a small room adjoining the *cuartel,* large and commanding in long blue cape and polished boots. His dark and full-jowled face, Indian in hue, held no expression, but his heavily lidded eyes shone with the malice of a madman.

"We have observed the murdering act of a damned scoundrel!" said Con through his teeth.

The baleful black eyes rested on him. "Bring that one in to me!"

Two soldiers thrust Con forward. Rajimo turned on his heel, and as he did so his left shoulder struck a *ristra* of dried red peppers hanging from a rafter, setting it swinging. He flinched as if pricked with a knife, and for a moment he stood rigid, then his right hand flashed out from under the long blue cape. He tore the *ristra* down and stamped on it.

Con got a look at the savagely distorted face and glaring eyes. It was the face of a madman, of an intolerant tyrant and dictator made mad by pain that he could not conquer. He used only his right arm, the cape concealing his left, and Con thought of that St. Louis duel and of Peregrina's golden Cupid brooch— that pretty trinket that he used for a bullet and sent into Rajimo's left shoulder.

Con inquired deliberately, with mock concern, "You

have an injury, perhaps, Excellency?"

Rajimo's dark face was blank again, but his eyes betrayed much. "No!" The one word came like a shot.

Con allowed his hard amusement to be seen. So that was it. Rajimo, in his enormous egotism and inflated pride, would not admit that his sacrosanct body could be hurt. He had built up the legend that he was invincible, invulnerable, a godlike emperor, stern and impressive. He would allow nothing to mar that dominant pose. So he kept his injury hidden under his splendid military cloak, and covered up the pain of it behind an impassive mask, except when betrayed past bearing.

Con was not impressed, and impatience prodded him. Rajimo had said nothing more, was merely regarding him. "I presume," Con drawled with all his old arrogance, "you're waiting for me to break down and beg for my life. It happens I've no experience in begging, so you can go ahead and shoot. Or would you prefer another duel?"

If the barb struck home, Rajimo showed no sign of it. His stare never wavered. "Those I hate, *Señor,* I do not kill." His voice now was low and calm. "Death is nothing more than endless sleep. Why should I grant such a mercy to the man who . . ."

His mouth clamped shut and he did not finish. A long silence and he spoke again. "You will go with me to the camps on the Gallinas and the Quintufue. You will assure your Texas compatriots all is well, but that our laws require them to give up their arms before . . ."

Con laughed at him. "Make a lying traitor of me, would you? No, *hombre*—I'll take the 'dobe wall or whatever it is you've cooked up in your wormy mind for me!"

Rajimo snapped his fingers, and the sergeant re-entered. "Heavy chains for that one! Take away his coat, shirt, hat, boots. I shall have further orders regarding him when I return."

His stare followed Con as the sergeant hustled him out. "I anticipate with much pleasure, *Señor,* the task of teaching you to beg!"

Con looked back, and glanced pointedly at the cloaked left arm. *"Pobrecito!"* he murmured mockingly, and got some satisfaction from Rajimo's twitch of rage.

Hours later they led him clanking in chains back to the little prison. He had efficiently cursed the blacksmith, who, nervous under the eyes of the soldiers, had burned him while forging on the iron anklets and wrist gyves. The heavy chains allowed Con a certain freedom of movement, but those connecting his wrists slapped across his thighs as he walked, while his leg-irons dragged behind him on the ground. They had followed Rajimo's orders, and left him clad in little more than his ragged trousers.

The Honorable Stanley was aghast. "This is monstrous!" he burst out as Con joined him and McCourtney in the cramped cell. "It's uncivilized."

Con licked a burn on his wrist. "Take it easy. It's not a patch on what I'll do to Rajimo, come I ever get the chance! Where's Dupratt?"

"Powwowing with Rajimo," answered McCourtney. "I hope he can talk reason into that mad blackguard."

It was late before Dupratt appeared, with a guard of four dragoons. "Everything is going to be all right," he announced somewhat importantly. "General Rajimo has assured me he has nothing against any member of the Expedition—except Connegan. I'm to go with him and the army to the Gallinas camp and explain to our fellows that they're to disarm before . . . ."

"What?" Con broke in. "Why, you damned fool, it's treachery! I turned down that same filthy proposition!"

"You misunderstood it," snapped Dupratt icily. "I succeeded in convincing the general of our peaceful intentions. Naturally, he cannot allow a body of men to come armed into his province. Against Mexican law. So I am going as—ah—official mediator. . . ."

"Official stool pigeon!" rapped Con. "Are you actually swallowing his lies? Are you really going to persuade our fellows to give up their guns to his double-crossing soldiers?"

"It'd be suicide for them, Dupratt!" seconded McCourtney hotly. "You can't do it, man!"

"I must remind you that I am your superior officer!" Dupratt's jaw set stubbornly. "Also, I know best. The Expedition is almost out of powder and ball, starving, sick, and short of horses. It is necessary to avoid trouble with the general. I'm leaving at once with him and the army."

"By Jupe, I'll see you dead first!" growled Con, and leaped, swinging his heavy chains for a blow at him.

Dupratt dodged backward into the soldiers. Before Con could gather himself for another swing, a carbine struck him in the stomach and curled him up, gasping.

10. LOS POBRECITOS

ALL AROUND, the face of the land was white, and snow still fell from the starless night sky. Now it was late October, and winter was moving in on the high altitudes. Like snow-covered logs the captive Texans lay huddled together in hollows for mutual warmth and protection from the cutting wind that had preceded the snow—a scant two hundred and fifty men, ill clad and shivering, all that remained of the high-hearted Expedition that had gaily rolled out from Austin months ago. Grudgingly, one blanket apiece had been allowed them from their own robbed possessions.

They lay encamped for the night in the open, south of the *Bosque de los Apaches*. Tomorrow they would take up again the murderous trek to Mexico City and prison, hundreds of miles to the south. Here and there Rajimo's dragoon guards stamped their feet or dozed under their thick ponchos, while Salezar and his under-officers slept warmly by the fires.

Con lay listening to Rael coughing a hollow, hacking cough, and for the hundredth time he cursed because he had missed Dupratt with his chains and failed to kill him. Some said Rajimo had released Dupratt, others thought he had been quietly taken off and shot, or had perished while trying to escape after seeing the calamitous results of his own pompous stupidity. Dupratt had persuaded the company on the Gallinas to give up their arms to Rajimo's soldiers. An hour later they were being driven like cattle to San Miguel, under guard.

It had been different with the main command camped on the Quintufue with the wagons. For days they had been standing off Comanche attacks, and were in a hard way when Rajimo and over a thousand dragoons showed up. They had cheered the coming Mexicans as a rescue party—and then, after the evacuation, they discovered that their status was that of disarmed prisoners of war, and that the loaded wagons had become Rajimo's loot.

At San Miguel all the Texan captives had been herded together in the plaza. Rajimo, it was said, had ordered a mass execution by way of celebrating his glorious victory, but he fell unconscious from his horse on the way back from the Quintufue and was borne on to Santa Fe in a raging fever. A certain trouble in his left shoulder, it seemed, had been aggravated by his long ride, and his fall didn't help it. So the civil governing body of Santa Fe, which seldom had opportunity to decide anything independently of the general, took nervous advantage of the opportunity. They wanted no part in mass murder, and voted that the *Tejanos* be turned over to the Mexican Government as prisoners of war. Don Chavez, as head of the civic council, took the responsibility of hastily ordering the prisoners started south on the march to

Mexico City, two thousand miles away more or less.

The captured and smashed Expedition had now been three weeks on the march, fed mostly by the charity of settlements through which they passed, and forced to camp wherever night found them. *Capitan* Salezar had command of the dragoon guards. It was his policy to exhaust the prisoners with long marches, little food and scant sleep, so that they were in no shape to stage any desperate revolt.

Today an Apache chief with a retinue of warriors had watched the ragged and emaciated column stumble by. He had ridden all the way down from the San Andes to see the incredible sight of Texans marching as prisoners. Old and white-haired, but erect, the aged savage watched with inscrutable eyes. His warriors, in buckskin shirts, leggins and much feathers and finery, sat their wiry ponies behind him. They had all turned abruptly and dashed off as fast as they came, and many a half-dead Texan had envied them their wild freedom.

Con had spent hours in lying still, letting the snow cover his blanketed body for the sake of its enclosing warmth, careful not to move and break its sheltering crust. But Rael's hacking cough got under his skin. He had thought he was hard, had thought harsh experience had ingrained into him the elemental philosophy of every man for himself and let the weakest perish. But he finally rolled over, pulled Rael to him as if sheltering a child, and tucked his own blanket around him.

Weakly, between coughs, Rael protested. "You'll—

freeze to death—Con. You—haven't any—clothes except—your trousers."

"—And my chains," Con appended harshly. "Shut up and lie still. I won't freeze. I've got too much hate in me to let me die! Some day I'll get Rajimo—get my hands on his throat—choke him slowly. . . ."

They lay in silence, close together, and the blankets and Con's arms brought some warmth to Rael. He stopped coughing, though his breathing was rattly and labored. But he was not sleeping. His eyes were open. After a while he began speaking in a whisper, in a wandering way that Con thought might presage the edge of delirium.

"When I was a boy, back home—in New Orleans—I used to watch for a star in the evening. It shone over the bayous, very big—very bright—pure. . . ."

"Venus," muttered Con. "Uh-huh. I knew that star, too, when I was a kid on the San Saba. Yes, Venus." Curious, he thought, that he had forgotten Venus for so long. He had hung out of the window, nights, lonely with a boy's vague yearnings, just gazing up at Venus, and it seemed as if she understood. And then he'd see pictures, boys' visions.

"Did you, Con?" Rael whispered. "Did you? I—I didn't think you were ever like that, somehow. I was a shy boy, but I wasn't shy with her." He was light-headed, a little delirious. "It was hard for me to make friends—always has been hard. You're the only really close friend I ever had, Con. That's queer, isn't it? We're—so different. Con—my sister—Phileda. She loves you. Did you know?"

"Yes," said Con. "We—talked. I asked her to wait. I didn't think you knew, Rael."

"I knew." Rael smiled a little. "I could tell, at the last. She'll wait for you, Con. Con—I'm thinking of—of Peregrina."

He shivered, and Con wrapped him closer, while his own nearly naked body grew numb with cold on the surface, and his chains were like icicles against his flesh. "Venus," he muttered, and checked a laugh that hurt his throat.

"Yes—she's Venus." Rael sounded drowsy. "She's that to me, Con. I always hoped—some day—I'd find her. She's—" He sighed and his eyes closed. "She's all I live for, now. You've got your hate, Con—but I—it's worth all this, if I live. . . ."

Con, holding him, did not stir and disturb his slumbering. He lay for a long time, until he felt the cold no more and knew his own sleepiness was a danger signal. His heart beat sluggishly, fighting against the cold. Carefully he drew away from Rael and sat up, working his arms and legs, trying to quiet the noisy jangle of his chains.

A hoarse voice whispered close by, "Git your blanket an' wrap them irons quiet, Con. Let's you 'n' me make a break for the mountings tonight!"

It was Old Nick Gentry, bellying over the snow with his snow-whitened blanket over him. He crept up close. "Now's the time. Guards is dozin'. I been hours watchin'. It's tonight or never. Tomorrer we start over the *Jornada del Muerte*—ninety miles o' desert an' no water nor a town on it. Git your blanket, Con!"

Con reached for his blanket, then paused. "Where in hell could we go?"

"The San Andres," answered the old buffalo hunter. "Only twenty miles east to the foothills. It's Apache country, but I savvy Apache. That chief today—I know him an' he saw me. He's a Mescalero. Met him oncet in a Pawnee camp way north. Mebbe-so he wouldn't scalp an' roast us. It's worth the riskin'. From the San Andres we could prowl south down to the Big Bend o' the Rio an' foller the Rio back to Texas, with luck."

Con sat and said nothing. It was a slim chance, but a chance. Old Nick knew Indians, could get along with most of them, his own temperament matching theirs so closely. It meant months of winter travel through hostile Indian and Mexican country, on foot and unarmed, competing with the beasts for food on the way, but a pair of hard and tough men might make it. Tomorrow the chance would be gone. The long trek over the *Jornada* would begin, and more men would perish and the guards would be too thirsty to doze.

"C'mon, Con," Old Nick urged.

"What about Rael?"

Old Nick shook his hairy head. "He's sick an' weak. Never make it, an' you know it. They'll be after us, come mornin' an' we're missed. Got to travel fast."

Con looked again at his blanket, at the huddled form of sleeping Rael. Softly he cursed, and more profanely than was his habit. How had he got himself saddled with this burden? Why couldn't he drag off his blanket, muffle his chains, and creep away with Old

Nick? Six months ago he would have hooted at the thought that he—Captain Con, riverboat gambler and soldier of fortune—would ever live to see the day when he'd hang back for the sake of a weakling.

"Hell!" he muttered. "He's even after the girl I've marked for myself! Oh—damn!"

He turned back to Old Nick, and his lips were twisted in self-mockery. "Just call me a blasted fool, Nick, and go on alone. No, I'm not coming. Lord forgive me for a poor damned gilly—I can't make myself desert him!"

He watched Old Nick's crawling shape edge past the line of somnolent guards. Long minutes later he saw it rise and vanish at a shambling run toward the east. He had got away. Con drooped his bare head and stared down at his chains, at his naked torso and bootless, calloused feet.

"I could've gone, too. I could've got away. Oh, damn my soul!"

11. WOLF IN CHAINS

A RIPPLE RAN THROUGH THE LONG COLUMN of trudging prisoners at sound of a shot, and thin, grim faces turned to stare back toward the straggling tail-end where rode *Capitan* Salezar and his favorite under-officers.

"Cut off his ears and throw the body off the trail!" commanded Salezar, and reloaded his smoking pistol.

It was the second prisoner shot in a week—for

"insubordination." His ears, along with those of other men who had died on the way, would be kept by Salezar as proof tokens that the absent prisoners had not escaped alive.

The *Jornada del Muerte* had been crossed, with only short rests for the Texans and little food since leaving Fray Cristobal, where the settlement people had given what they could spare. As always, it had been the women who gave most, though the men too had shown some commiseration. It was very obvious that the common people hated Rajimo's brutish soldiers, and pitied anyone falling into their mercy. All shuddered to find that the notorious Salezar, most brutal of Rajimo's officers, had charge of the captive Texans.

This morning the Texans had been herded across the Rio Grande, fording the chill water on foot while the mounted guards threatened to shoot down any stragglers. Now they were in Mexico proper, and three miles ahead lay the Mexican city of El Paso del Norte. It had sometimes been said by Texas patriots that the tyrant-ruled land above the Rio Grande would some day be part of free Texas. It was even speculated that the day might come when that greater Texas would become part of the United States of America, if the people of New Mexico ever succeeded in asserting their rights to choose their own allegiance. But this was idealism.

The remnant captives of the ill-fated Expedition were now of no minds to concern themselves with potential matters of changing empires. They had shot their bolt and missed, and now were paying the penalty. Their unshaven faces were sunken, they were exhausted, in rags, vermin-ridden. They shambled along like sleepwalkers, benumbed, staggering against each other. Rael, forever coughing, tottered with the stragglers. The Honorable Stanley limped ahead of him. Con trudged steadily near by, his leg-irons dragging in the dust. He had developed a stride that compensated for the weight of his chains and kept him from tripping on them. Behind him, a Houston man named Chappell reeled weakly in the last stages of fatigue.

Chappell fell and failed to rise. Con trudged on. Rael halted, swaying, and bent to help the fallen man, but he sank to his knees and could not struggle up again. He hung there, coughing, and slowly fell over onto his face.

"March!" A soldier prodded Chappell with his carbine.

"Can't!" mumbled the Houston man. "I'm—done up."

Salezar drew his pistol. "March—or I shoot!"

Chappell, with fumbling fingers, tore open the remains of his filthy shirt. "Shoot an' be damned!"

The pistol spat.

"Cut off his ears. . . ."

Salezar reloaded, his murder-inflamed eyes on Rael. "Up, dog, and march! March! And you!" He shifted his stare to the Honorable Stanley, who had paused, shocked pale by the ruthless murder.

The Honorable Stanley was on his last legs, crippled by his wrenched ankle. It had been all he could do to keep up, but he had asked for no help from anyone. He had set his gaze toward far-off Mexico City and the resident British consul there. Blood, tradition, and a conviction of eventual triumph, had elevated him to a fine indifference over the present. Rule Britannia was on his face, and a sublime faith in the Queen's Navy lodged in his soul. But a pointing pistol could not be ignored. The Honorable Stanley hobbled on, bloody mad but unbowed.

The pistol muzzle lowered and pointed at Rael, lying coughing on the ground. "March!"

Con had turned back. He bared his teeth like a wolf at Salezar and the cocked pistol. "You murdering damn' Injun—!" He lifted Rael to his feet.

Rael was not heavy. He had thinned, and sometimes he wiped blood from his lips after a particularly bad coughing spell. But he was heavy enough to make a hard burden for a man living on the last reserves of his strength. The chains made it difficult, but Con managed to get his right arm around him. "C'mon, partner—up an' at it!"

Automatically, Rael stumblingly attempted to walk, half his weight on Con's bare arm and shoulder. "I—I can't, Con. Just—leave me."

"The devil's foot I will!" Con got a better hold on him. "Venus—partner, remember Venus? Some day you'll have her, I swear to God you will. It's worth all this—remember?"

It was then that the carriage came wheeling down the trail, with uniformed outriders and a strong guard of mounted dragoons following, and drew to a halt near the end of the long column. The whole equipage, with its heavy gold monogram and plumed horses, reeked of splendor and opulent luxury. The monogram was a royal R—for Rajimo.

A rumbling growl soughed along the tattered column, an incoherent voicing of vengeance deeply vowed against the man responsible for weeks of misery, humiliation, murder. Even the plumed horses sensed the creeping wave of intense hatred, and stamped nervously, rolling their eyes.

"*Capitan,* why are these dogs not tied in fours and made to march in order?" The brittle demand issued from the carriage. "You are too indulgent!"

Con, bearing the sagging weight of Rael, stumbled to a halt. His bloodshot glare settled on Rajimo's dark and heavy jowled face, until he grew aware of two other passengers. Don José Chavez y Salomain sat beside the tyrant. In the seat opposite rode Peregrina, her face pale but as hauntingly beautiful as ever, so arrestingly vivid in its beauty that even some of the exhausted captives stared at her.

Con wanted to curse her, but again vibrant cords tightened and hummed in him, and strong feelings raced their ways, twanging his senses. He stood swaying a little, long legs spread for balance, Rael's fair head slumped against his naked shoulder, and he regarded her. Venus. To Rael, now too far gone to see her, she was Venus, his star and his hope.

Con shook with sudden fury. Damn her, she was no white star to him, remote and unattainable. She was Woman, warm, challenging, full of guile. She was devil, angel, color, life. He knew her. He had kissed her. Venus? Yes, but not Rael's kind of Venus. Rather, Venus the prize of the Olympian gods, or of the man who could take and tame her.

She was gazing at him, and what he saw in her eyes inflamed his fury further. She could have shown triumph or even mockery, and he could have met it readily with his own sharp weapons of unspoken insult and studied insolence. That would have put him on equal ground with her as an enemy not yet so beaten that he still could not unsheathe some sort of blade.

But what he saw in her, instead of triumph, was all the compassionate pity of the softly crying women and girls back along the terrible trail—and more, much more. It was something he could not fight and it left him unarmed. Of all the weapons she could have used, her pity was the one intolerable spear that could stab through his armor.

"And she knows it!" he thought savagely. She was taking her revenge for the lashing insult he had thrown at her back in St. Louis, on the Planters' House balcony. "The beautiful damn' minx knows it!"

H E HAD NO WAY of knowing that she held a loaded pistol under her loose traveling wrap. She was cold with horror, and her pity ran so deep it hurt as a physical pain shuddering in her. Anger flared with her pity, a blinding anger that she knew could make a murderess of her. She drew back the hammer of the hidden pistol, and under the concealing wrap she lined the muzzle on the general in the opposite seat. If he began now giving his threatened order for the execution, he would die, and all Mexico would rock to the news of his assassination by the niece of Don Chavez.

Her eyes went back to the man in chains, and it was hard to hold back the hot tears.

Somehow, she had not expected to find him like this, gaunt and emaciated, encrusted with dirt and the dried blood of stone cuts, sores, insect bites—him whom she remembered so well as piratically debonair, dangerously elegant, immaculately clean. The others, yes. She knew the nature of Salezar, knew the kind of animals Rajimo had in his army. But the mental picture she had kept of this man had remained clear and never changed. And there he stood, in bare feet and chains; a wild and starving wolf of a man, supporting that other who shook weakly to a racking cough. She remembered that other. She remembered two tall heads, one dark, one fair, inclined in courteous bows to her in the doorway of the Rocky Mountain House, where the buckskinned trappers drank and roared the elemental chants of the Cheyenne and the Comanche.

They had been so courtly, these two, so clean and tall and indomitable, correctly mannered but frankly attracted by a pretty girl whom they tried politely to take in charge, and not easy to rebuff. There they were, those same two heads, one dark, one fair, still together—one the head of a dying man, the other the head of a bitterly glaring savage in chains. She did not see the rest, the long line, the mounted guards, and Salezar hurrying obsequiously to the carriage. She saw only those two. It was right that she should have found them still together.

"But not like this—oh, *Madrecita,* not like this!" She breathed the words aloud, and Don Chavez, hearing her, looked bleaker than ever.

Salezar came up and saluted. "They could not march while tied together, General," he stammered. "But I have kept the chains on that one. . . ."

"He will need them no more!" interrupted Rajimo. "Give me your pistol and bring him closer to me!"

Don Chavez coughed. "I must remind you, Don Manuel, that we have crossed the Rio Grande," he murmured. "We are now in the military department of El Paso del Norte, under command of General Vigil. He would feel strongly. . . ."

Rajimo turned on him. "Do not try my patience too far, Don José! Already you have greatly angered me by having my prisoners sent out of my jurisdiction while I lay in fever. I will have my way!"

His quick passion brought out the veins of his forehead and deepened the lines in his face. He was showing more and more the strain of constant nagging pain, and his iron self-control was breaking. Often on the journey he had openly nursed his left shoulder, his eyes glazed. His injury had grown worse. He was making the long journey down to Mexico City to engage the best surgeons to work on it. Don Chavez accompanied him because commanded to do so. Rajimo trusted nobody. He had seized command of New Mexico, himself, after faking a revolution during the absence of a former governor. The Mexican Government under Santa Anna, following its policy of allowing the strongest men to govern the provinces, had solemnly sent him confirmation and a vote of approval. Rajimo had no intentions of leaving behind him in Santa Fe anyone as popularly respected as Don Chavez, to seize possible advantage of a like opportunity.

Peregrina had experienced little opposition in convincing her uncle that she should come with him to Mexico City. Don Chavez, in the Spanish tradition, took very seriously his guardianship of her. A large branch of the affluent Chavez family resided in and around Mexico City. Peregrina would be under his eye there, and well chaperoned, better so than in the more casual and frivolous Santa Fe.

Con laid Rael down on the ground as gently as he could. When he rose, he jerked his chains free of Salezar's grasp and advanced to the carriage. He put a touch of his old swagger into his stride, despite the dragging leg-irons, and held his shaggy black head jauntily high. Devil an' all, he'd show these people whether he was beaten, or could ever be beaten.

He didn't see Rajimo's pistol until five paces from it.

The long column had moved onward, and through the rising dust the rear guards could be seen dashing about in grand and energetic fashion, fearful of Rajimo's fault-finding eyes. The last stragglers stumbled on under the shouts and crowding of the mounted soldiers. All was confusion, each guard trying to outdo all the rest in loud yelling and riding.

Salezar, left behind, fidgeted. His proper place was with his command, and Rajimo might at any moment remind him of it. On the other hand, if he rode off without waiting for permission, Rajimo would be even quicker to reprimand him. So he stood and fidgeted by his horse, impatient to see the chained *Tejano* die and the splendid carriage move on.

It was Don Chavez, his austere face white, who snatched the pistol from Rajimo's hand, "I will not sit by and see murder done, Don Manuel!" he rapped, while Peregrina leaned forward, eyes wide and blazing, her own hidden pistol ready. "This man is an unarmed prisoner of war, not an outlawed criminal!"

For a moment it seemed that Rajimo would explode in frenzy. His glittering eyes bulged. Only when the tinny notes of a trumpet rang out, far ahead, did he tear his glare from Don Chavez. Far to the front along the trail, coming from the direction of the as yet unseen El Paso del Norte, appeared a troop of horsemen, arms and accouterments flashing in the sun.

"It is General Vigil, coming from the city to take over charge of the prisoners entering his department," said Don Chavez quietly. "I have saved you much embarrassment, Don Manuel. General Vigil would have resented your action, and he is no friend of yours."

Rajimo turned from his bitter survey. "Consider yourself under arrest!"

Don Chavez rose, bowed stiffly, and alighted with icy dignity from the carriage. Rajimo moved as if to intercept Peregrina as she was following her uncle, but she brushed past and stepped out, carrying a small satchel with her. She came directly to Con, her head erect.

"I—I . . ." She could find no words. Furtively, her dress hiding the act from Rajimo, she dropped the satchel at Con's feet. "Food," she whispered.

Her pity had galled Con, but her charity infuriated him. "Salve for your conscience?" he drawled harshly. "You can't pay me off that cheap!" He dug a bare toe under the satchel and contemptuously sent it under the wheels of the carriage.

She flinched, and her eyes shrank from his. "It—it is unfortunate that you have lost your good manners along with your liberty, Captain Connegan," she said faintly.

Con said slowly, bitingly, "I'm not a begging man, and charity I don't want—not from you! Just let our account ride. Some day I'll come and collect at my own terms, and you'll pay me in full—I swear you'll pay me!"

He saw her pity give way to the look of challenge that he remembered. She was very feminine, but the more dangerous to him because of it. And she was like him, in that both possessed strong fighting wills that readily reared up when prodded. A curious admiration for her, having nothing to do with her tingling physical attraction, stirred in him. It was the healthy respect of one good enemy for another. Had she turned away crying, his respect for her would have been less. She was strong enough to sweep aside her unwanted pity, and fighter enough to meet him with a counter challenge.

"Then you expect to succeed as a desperado, where you failed as a gentleman?" she murmured, and contrived to look coolly at him though well within reach of his naked arms. "I think, on the contrary, that the day of settlement may find you more humble, Captain!"

From Rajimo in the carriage came a queer mixture of command, apology, and biting animosity. "Don José, I request that you and your niece enter my carriage. I spoke in anger. I cannot allow your niece to fraternize with these *Tejano* dogs—inasmuch as you appear to have no control over her!"

Still wrapped in his icy dignity, Don Chavez escorted Peregrina back into the carriage and entered after her. A barked command from Rajimo, a cut from the quirt of a liveried postilion, and the matched team lunged forward. The heavy equipage got moving, outriders at correct distances on both sides and the dragoon escort following in the rear.

Con dropped his eyes to the satchel lying in the dust. He discarded his lofty pride, now that Peregrina couldn't see him, and practically dived at it. A hind wheel had crushed over part of it, but he wasn't fussy. He hurried back with it to Rael, who was struggling to sit up, and knelt by him.

"Food, partner!" He drew out a handful of broken *dulces,* small cakes spiced and sugared. The satchel evidently held the remains of a generous lunch. "Here—eat. Hope there's meat." He groped fast, his hunger overpowering at the nearness of food, and spilled out the bag's contents. She wouldn't forget meat. Surely she wouldn't forget. . . .

"My good abundant Lord—look! Look, Rael! Why, bless her heart—a flask of brandy."

A shadow fell over them. "You thieving *picaro,* give me that satchel!" rapped Salezar, and jumped back with a hand to his holster as Con rose crouched and growling in his throat like a trapped wolf defending its last cub.

12. A THOUSAND MILES TO TEXAS

THE CARRIAGE had halted again, halfway to the receding end of the column. One of the outriders came loping back.

"His Excellency has further orders, *Capitan* Salezar."

Salezar muttered an oath, mounted, and rode back with the messenger. Con sank to his knees again, watching him go. He looked beyond to the halted carriage, and caught Peregrina peeping out over the carriage door. She withdrew her head so quickly he couldn't be sure whether she had seen the satchel. Well, he had made his grand gesture, anyway. What was it she had said? "On the day of settlement, you will be more humble."

"Devil I will!" He shoved food at Rael. "Hurry and eat. That damn' Salezar. . . ." He uncorked the brandy flask. "Take a drink, all you can swallow. Three miles yet to Paso, and we sure need nourishment. Wish they'd overlook us back here. Still, where'd we go? Thousand miles to Texas."

He drank, talked, ate, asked and answered his own questions. The brandy was good, and it stopped Rael's cough so that he could eat. Con drank some more, his eyes on Salezar at the carriage. That coffee-colored dog! Take away his scummy soldiers and what did you have? A coffee-colored dog, not fit to swamp out a good Texas saloon.

Surprisingly, Rael reached for the flask and took another drink. He began evincing signs of coming out of his sick daze. "I thought—I dreamed—Con, was that—?"

"Venus," Con nodded gravely, and took back the brandy. Time was when he could have drunk six times this much and not shown it, but he guessed then he'd been in better shape than now. "Venus in a gold coach, partner, with food and brandy, bless her wicked little two-timing heart. Y'know, when I do get to Santa Fe . . ."

"Santa Fe?" broke in Rael, munching bread and young lamb. He was befogged, what with sickness and the brandy. "I thought they were taking us to Mexico City."

Con waved the emptying flask airily. "I mean after that. Y'know, Rael, I've never seen a more beautiful girl. And when she's mad, I swear . . . Another drink? Well, then I might's well finish it."

Draining the flask, he distinctly heard in the still air Rajimo talking to Salezar. The column was now far ahead, and lack of noise made the harsh voice clearly audible.

"Remember, *Capitan,* you are to remain in command of the prisoners until they are delivered to the fortress in Mexico City. I shall so inform General Vigil of my wish. And that one in chains back there— I shall accept your explanation that he died of sickness, should you arrive in Mexico City with only his ears. You understand, *Capitan?*"

The *Capitan* understood and said so. He remounted his horse as the carriage rolled on, and came riding back.

Con tossed away the empty flask. "Hear that?"

Rael blinked sleepily, shook his head, and searched around for another *dulce.* "Hear what?"

"Oh, just a noise—one of those things you hear in these parts." Con found a cake for him. "This what you want? That's right, partner, lie back and eat comfortable. I always did think those Roman fellows had a right good idea in table manners. Or was it the Greeks? Anyway, they just sprawled round, served by pretty girls, while they watched another Christian get tossed to the lions. I'm no lion, and Salezar is no Christian to my notion, but . . ."

When he saw two Salezars riding toward him he knew the brandy had been good. This idea of hiking down there to Mexico City, it was just plain silly. But Rajimo, burn his black soul, had talked of his ears, and that wouldn't do. He had to look after Rael. Had to get to Santa Fe some day. Had to look into that matter of Lorin and the ninety thousand dollars in Mex gold.

And there was Peregrina.

"Lovely minx," he yawned. "I swear, if I didn't hate her so much, I'd love her. Maybe I do love her, at that. I wouldn't have a girl who couldn't make me mad enough to . . ."

"March!" came the familiar hated command.

"Eh? Oh, hello, Salty." Con shook Rael. "C'mon, partner. Well, now, he's asleep. What d'you do in a case like that, Field Marshal?"

Salezar drew his short sword and nudged his horse forward. "He is dead—his ears go to Mexico City!"

Con got to his feet. "So? Why, you—!"

He leaped, and the sword was useless against the swing of his heavy wrist-chains. He struck again as Salezar fell out of the saddle. The horse kicked in all directions and took off at a head-down bolt back toward the river, dragging Salezar by a stirrup and spur, and stopping every so often to kick frenziedly at it.

Con was sorry about the horse. He could have used it. He stood and thought about things. Here they were, he and Rael, and away yonder went the column. There, too, went the carriage with Rajimo, to meet General Vigil and his staff coming from El Paso. And there, bumping in the general direction of the Rio Grande, went *Capitan* Salezar, dead enough to bury.

"Now, if I had that horse. . . ."

A thousand miles to Texas. A thousand miles to Texas. Seemed to him there was a song like that. If not, then he'd make up one, on the way to Texas.

"C'mon, Rael. Up an' at it, partner."

"Con, we're going the wrong way—we're going north."

"That's the right way!"

He hoped to catch up with that horse somewhere along the river. The animal would tire out sooner or later, trying to kick loose of that frightening dead body.

Rael became deathly sick, his long-starved stomach revolting against the solid food and brandy. Con couldn't hold him up, much less carry him, and his own stomach felt filled with cold stones and vinegar. He let Rael sink down, and sat by him, spent and shaking, and reality hammered clarity into him with brutal blows. He was chained and afoot, with a sick Rael, and Texas was as far off as the moon. It was with no great interest that he raised throbbing eyes to a group of horsemen pulling up around him in a boil of dust.

"March!"

"They cannot march," spoke another voice. "Two of you dismount and lift them onto your horses. The rest ride on and search for your *Capitan.*"

GENERAL GUSTAVO VIGIL, *comandante* of the Mexican military department of El Paso, stood in the crowded yard of the *cuartel* inspecting the prisoners. "Officers and civil gentlemen will please step forward and introduce themselves," he requested. His eyes were inscrutable.

Con thought he might qualify as an officer, if not as a gentleman, banking his claim on his old rank of captain in the Army of the Texas Republic. However, after a good look at the general he chose modesty and stayed with the rank and file. General Vigil did not present a prepossessing appearance, aside from his splendid uniform and medals. He wore an enormous pair of whiskers, split like those of a Turk, and a huge pair of drooping mustachios, coarse, grizzled, and evidently of virgin growth untrimmed through the years of his manhood. He was not a big man, but his hoary head and whiskers made him look big, and he wore his military hat low as if to conceal any sinister expression that the whiskers might fail to cover.

So far, his manner had been that of the seasoned officer, noncommittal and curt. It was plain that he looked with contempt on Rajimo's provincial soldiers. Rajimo and his entourage, it was learned by the Texans, had dallied no longer in El Paso than was necessary to change horses and pay respects to General Vigil. He was possessed by an obsession to get to Mexico City, where famous foreign doctors worked miracles. He feared blood poisoning.

General Vigil exchanged bows with the Texan officers, and made a statement. "General Rajimo has expressed to me his wish that his own troops, under *Capitan* Salezar, retain command of you."

It was impossible to tell from his tone or expression what he might be thinking. He was a soldier. "However, since General Rajimo's departure, *Capitan* Salezar has been brought in dead. This leaves me no alternative but to take command. You will therefore consider yourselves as temporarily in my charge, until

I deliver you to the proper authorities at Mexico City. Am I understood, gentlemen?"

The group murmured understanding, but the Honorable Stanley took it upon himself to try drawing out some light upon the unknown future. "General, may we ask what sort of treatment we may expect?"

Some sort of quiver crossed the general's hairy face. "I shall try to base my treatment of you upon a precedent already established," he said enigmatically. "You gentlemen are Texans. You may be interested to learn that I fought your rebel army in the battle of San Jacinto, as a colonel under Santa Anna. I was wounded and captured with two of my staff, by the Texans."

The Texans gulped. Con scratched his bearded jaw and wondered whether to say something or keep quiet.

"And—ah—how were you treated, General?" inquired the irrepressible Honorable Stanley.

General Vigil looked reminiscent. "The Texan who captured us was a young cavalry man who had pursued us for two days after the battle. While taking us back, he taught us a card game and won everything we had, even our spurs and saddles. Later he conducted us into Galveston, demanded the best food and hotel quarters for us, and paid our bills."

Con thought it might be safe enough now to speak up. "You're wrong, Gus!" he called out. "I sent the bill to the Texas Government, and quit the army before they could argue it!"

Later, as host at his own table, the general ordered more wine. "Gentlemen, I am a soldier of Mexico," he stated simply. "It is my duty to see that none of you escapes before reaching Mexico City. However, it is in my power to see also that you are fed and treated fairly on the way. At the expense of the Mexican Government," he added dryly with a glance at Con.

"I shall arrange for carts and wagons for the sick," he went on. "You officers and gentlemen will be furnished transportation in accordance with your rank." His eyes rested again on Con. "Why was a captain put in chains?"

"A whim of Rajimo's," murmured Con modestly.

"I shall take the responsibility of ordering them removed from you," said the general. "I have never favored heavy manacles. A dangerous prisoner could possibly use such things as a weapon." His eyes were inscrutable again. "You will travel with the other officers. I presume you have no illusions as to what may be waiting for you in Mexico City? General Rajimo is influential. It is considered a great misfortune to become his enemy."

Con nodded. "I'll appreciate getting rid of these irons. Thanks. But I guess I'll stay with the rank and file, if you don't mind. I've got a sick friend among 'em."

"As you wish." General Vigil raised his glass. "Gentlemen, I have met Texans on the battlefield, over a card game, and at the dining table." His fierce mustachios blew to his short and gusty laugh. "I much prefer the dining table!"

Leaving that evening, Con felt the old soldier's hand on his shoulder. "I am sorry, *amigo*. . . ."

13. LITTLE GOLD CUPID

ENTINELA ALERTA!"

C The hourly cry of the sentinel rang mournful and eerie against the hush of night, moving feeble echoes to whisper uneasily down in the empty yard of the huge old prison. Another voice took up the cry, then another, and another, each from a different point, repeating the wakeful call required every hour from the night sentinels. Sentinel alert! I am awake— I am alert! Each voice hung lingeringly onto every syllable, distorting it, stretching the call to a long-drawn wail.

"Centinela alerta!"

The last wailing voice released its hold of the last note. The last whispering echo faded from the high walls and crumbling buildings. Chains clanked on hard stone floors, a few curses were muttered from drowsy habit, and the prisoners of the Santiago went back to sleep. The disturbed flow of other sounds crept back into the still and moonlit night. Here on the fringe of Mexico City such sounds were muted and mysterious, the more intolerably enticing because the sources of them could not be seen nor known. From somewhere floated the faint and delicate music of harp and mandolins, sometimes distinct enough so that the exotic tempo could be caught for a moment. Winter had come and gone, and Spring was here. The Forty Days of Fast were over, bringing release of restraint and the restless sense of new growth, new life, and a gaiety that met quick response from Latin temperaments.

Mexico City, old as her ruins and young as a sweetheart, throbbed to the fresh season. Moonlight softened her signs of aged decay and brought out the silent grandeur of her great palaces, broad streets, splendid old buildings. Robed monks, veiled women, swaggering dandies and the ever-present ragged beggars, all took on an air of mystery and carnival. Parties and fandangos were in high season, prolific of coquetry and worried chaperons, and lights shone till early hours through cracks in shuttered windows.

But not in the prison of Santiago.

Con, his elbows resting on the sill of a barred window and gazing out onto the blank yard, restlessly tapped a foot on the stone floor and thought of the Planters' House farewell ball last Spring in St. Louis. Always, when music reached into the prison, he was unable to sleep. Behind him, in rows along the damp walls, over sixty Texas prisoners lay sleeping—each, like himself now, with a single manacle riveted around one ankle, and a six-foot heavy chain attached. During the day they worked in the streets, chained in line and under guard. At night they were uncoupled, but the manacle and chain were never removed.

In the months since they had been here, hopes for release had faded. President Santa Anna, remembering his disastrous defeat on the San Jacinto, held on tight to the prisoners, and let it be known that they would be executed if Texas ever tried to stir up New Mexican rebellion against the Mexican Government.

They were permanent hostages, given the prison treatment of criminals.

The Honorable Stanley Tonsall's unshaken faith in the Queen's Navy had been rewarded, however. The resident British consul, after learning of his identity under all the grime and hair, had promptly set off some diplomatic explosions under Santa Anna. Was his Excellency aware of the fact that to mistreat an English gentleman was not conducive to British goodwill and cash loans? Also, four visiting British men-o-war happened to be riding at anchor in Vera Cruz. . . .

But even the Honorable Stanley, armed with shining new monocle and Malacca cane, discovered to his indignation that he could do nothing for his imprisoned comrades. The Mexican authorities tried tactfully to point out that though the Texans spoke a certain brand of English, they were not British subjects. But the Honorable Stanley brushed that aside as a technical trifle and probably a lie at that. They spoke English and that was sufficient. Be damned to your history, gentlemen! He had finally sailed home for England, vowing to take the matter before Her Majesty the Queen, God bless her, egad.

The Santiago had once been a monastery. A few monks still had their quarters on the second story of one wing, and kept themselves aloof, meek and dignified in their cowled robes and tranquil-eyed silence. The rest of the walled and gloomy old pile contained a soldiers' barracks and the prison. The high wall ran along two sides of the yard, the crumbling old buildings enclosing the square.

Con turned his head from the barred window and glanced down at Rael, lying on his tattered blanket in the favored corner that Con had permanently won for him by beating up another man who thought he had prior claim to it. Rael wasn't asleep. The moonlight slanted in on his fair head and hollowed face. He was gazing past Con at the moon, as if seeing pictures in it. A dreaminess had settled over Rael lately, and he didn't cough so much. Often he wandered a little in his speech, but he seemed not unhappy in his daydreaming.

"Can you hear that music, Rael?" Con asked softly.

Rael's eyes slowly found his face. "Yes. Spanish. Beautiful." He spoke in a whisper, and smiled. "I was dancing to it. . . ." His eyes drifted back to the moon, grew absorbed and far away.

Con stared back through the bars. He knew with whom Rael was dancing in his dreaming. Peregrina. He had been dancing with her himself, and her lips had been warm, her eyes challenging, the way he remembered her when—how long ago? A year ago. It had been Spring in St. Louis. Now it was Spring again. He wondered what she might be doing now, this minute. Dancing, perhaps, at one of those gay parties. She was here in Mexico City, he knew. So were Don Chavez and Rajimo. It was said that Rajimo had undergone an operation on his shoulder, had fully recovered, and was expected to start back to Santa Fe as soon as the snow cleared off the mountain passes in the north.

Con touched a hard little object in his trousers

pocket. It had been slipped into his hand weeks ago by one of the younger officers of the prison guard, easy-going Lieutenant Navarro, as he came in with the chain gang from work.

"I have a message for you," Navarro had whispered. "From a certain unnamed lady. The message is: 'If humility has replaced arrogance and you desire a favor, return this token in the same way that you now receive it.'"

In the scant privacy of the big crowded cell, Con had examined the token. It was the tiny Cupid, badly scratched and marked, with broken wings and a scarred leer on its chubby face. He glared at it—the trinket that had played its part in putting him where he was now. And yet, ironically enough, it once had saved his life.

So the surgeons had finally dug the thing out of Rajimo, and Peregrina had got it back and now she . . . Why, that beautiful little hellcat! So she expected him to return it to her again, as his token of humble surrender, and beg for her help.

"I'll rot in the cussed hole fist!"

Rael grew weaker every day, so that Con took to feeding him goat's milk that he robbed from the other prisoners' rations. The prison doctor came and looked at Rael, and spoke of trying to get him moved to the hospital quarters.

"Don't bother," Con discouraged him. He knew something of the prison hospital, with its smallpox patients and crowded conditions. "He's better off here with me. If you're inclined to help, just fix it so I don't have to go out with the chain gang and leave him all day. Eh? No, he's not out of his head. Just dreaming, is all. Let him dream. He's been through a lot."

Lucid intervals became rare. Rael grew childlike, smiling a great deal and murmuring with the ghosts of his fancies, vaguely troubled and uneasy only when Con wasn't by him. His labored breathing and occasional dry cough told their own story. A Texan who had been a doctor gave it as his opinion that the end wasn't far off.

"When you begin hearing a sort of whistling in his breathing, that'll be the end. Damned shame. I guess he never was very strong, was he?"

Con kept his eyes on Rael's face. "Strongest man I ever knew—in one way," he said. "And the best. Wish I could give him half my heart and a lung."

Once, Rael said clearly, suddenly, "Con, when you find Phileda, tell her—tell her all this wasn't bad. It's true, Con. I haven't minded much. Enjoyed a lot of it. It's been good—you and I—friends. Worth it. But she'll need you. You'll find her? Look after her?"

Con said steadily, "I'll marry her, Rael, if she'll still have me."

Rael smiled again, and the childlike quality crept back into his face. He couldn't swallow the goat's milk at noon, though Con held his head up and tried to feed him. By evening he was out of his head, his hands working fretfully, and a frantic despair seemed to have hold of him. Con, attuned to all his moods in health and sickness, guessed the reason. Rael had somehow lost hold of his dreams, couldn't conjure them up again, couldn't find them.

Con went to the locked door of the big cell and banged on it, and begged for Lieutenant Navarro to come. Navarro came, his good-humored young face inquiring, and Con handed him the battered little golden Cupid. "Tell her—the lady—right away. Thanks."

She came after dark, cloaked and veiled. She could have come in a winding sheet and Con would still have known her. Navarro displayed some nervousness. He was taking chances. If the prison *comandante* heard of this there would be the devil to pay. But he was young, reckless, and his pay was meager.

Con said soberly, "Thank you for coming. It would have been too late tomorrow."

Peregrina drew aside her heavy veil. "Then I am glad, too, that I came tonight." Her eyes played over his face, and he sensed an eager excitement in her. "It has taken you a long time to send for me, Don Desperado—and to ask for favor. Or are you still of a demanding mind?"

Her nearness had the same strong effect upon him as ever, her eyes even more brilliant than he remembered, her skin finer and whiter, her lips warmer and more provocative. And the laughing mockery and challenge were still there, shaded over by something that reminded him of her pity for him months ago on the murderous San Miguel trail.

He held himself in and answered quietly. "No, I'm not demanding. I'm asking a favor. It's for Rael. He's dying. I've done all I can, but now I'm helpless. He—

he's been living on dreams for weeks."

It was difficult to say like this, baldly, trying to keep Navarro and the others from overhearing. He muttered the rest hurriedly, almost ashamed, not meeting her eyes. "He wants you. If you could just sit by him—let him know—let him think you—you . . ."

He was begging, the best he knew how, humbly and without pride. "It wouldn't be for long," he pleaded. "He—he hasn't far to go now."

She slipped past him, so swiftly that he never saw the effects of his pleading on her face. Navarro uttered a shocked exclamation, while the startled prisoners stared at her as she hurried along the untidy rows of pallets. Con caught up with her and touched her arm. "There, over in that corner."

But she had already located Rael by his mumbling and tossing. She sank down beside him, and the mumbling ceased. A great sigh came from Rael. His fair head was cradled in arms that he had never known in reality, yet which were as familiar to him as Con's.

Her voice sounded, so soft with pity and compassion that Con suddenly felt the full loss of Rael's going.

"*Pobrecito!* Oh, my *pobrecito*—my loved one. . . ."

Con wheeled abruptly, barred Navarro's way, and the young officer came to a quick stop at the look in the *Tejano's* eyes. The prisoners, one by one, turned away from the scene in the corner, awkward and embarrassed. Those nearest, by common consent, quietly picked up their blankets and drifted to the farther end of the long cell.

Navarro, at first undecided and aghast, at length

shrugged nervously and turned his back. He drew out a couple of *cigarritos,* offered one to Con, and they smoked. Only a low murmuring came from the corner, Rael's whisper broken and eager, incredulous, happy, the girl's soft and reassuring.

Rael's whispering ceased, but it was long before a hand touched Con. "He's—all right—now."

He wanted to stop her, thank her, but he couldn't speak, and she was hurrying out, almost running. The scent of her perfume remained, and slowly mingled with the rank odors of the cell.

"I must arrange for the funeral," muttered Navarro, and left.

They came for Rael a bare three hours later, and in Mexican custom the funeral began at once. First the ringing of a bell and the subdued tramp of feet. The door swung open and they entered, monks bearing lighted candles, and a boy swinging a small silver bell. Then a half-dozen soldiers carrying the empty coffin. Lastly, the prison *comandante,* a dour and elderly man. While the body was placed in the coffin, low prayers continued, and the monks knelt.

The touching solemnity of it caused Con to grow cold and critical. Death and burial, he considered, were greatly overrated. All this impressive gloom— there was no reason for it. Rael wouldn't have wanted it. Rael had gone out happily, smiling, his dream an amazing reality.

"I'm glad I could do that for you, partner. They can't take that from you, nor touch you with all this spooky damned . . ." It was no good trying to fool himself.

Con found himself praying. "Oh, God, look out for him! I did my best for him while I could."

With incense burning and the little bell ringing, the candle-lit procession filed slowly out with its burden. The Texans stood at attention until the door closed, and Con walked slowly back to a corner that was queerly hushed and lonely.

14. ESCAPE

PEREGRINA VISITED the prison again a week later, this time without being asked. She came as before, at night and heavily veiled, and Navarro allowed her and Con the privacy of the *castigo* cell, the grim little punishment room.

She showed a cool self-possession, and her first question took Con off guard. "Do you intend to sacrifice all your companions, for the sake of your pride?"

"What do you mean?"

"I mean that it is mostly because of you that they are being held," she stated. "Representatives from the United States and other governments have expressed disapproval of this imprisonment. But General Rajimo has some influence with President Santa Anna, and insists that none of the Texans be released. I think you can guess his reason."

Con nodded. He tried to read her eyes, without much success. "He'd have the whole bunch of us kept in prison to rot, just to make sure of me, eh? That's a right nice *hombre* you're betrothed to!"

Peregrina did not attempt to elude his probing gaze. "Our betrothal has been broken. My uncle no longer insists upon it—which is fortunate, for I never intended to allow myself to be wedded to Rajimo. After Rajimo found what it was that you shot him with, he flew into a rage." She smiled as though facing Rajimo in one of his rages was a matter for humor. "It then was easy for me to break off the betrothal. But this situation we spoke of—as long as you are alive and one of them, Rajimo will fight against release of the Texans."

"Sure," Con agreed. "Well, I suppose I could hang myself some quiet night."

He saw her smile vanish. "No." She scanned his face candidly. "But could you not ask me for help in escaping?"

Now that Rael was gone, nothing but pride remained on which to base refusal. Pride was a small thing, weighed against the lives of the Texans. Con knotted his fingers behind his back. "You win," he said at last.

Impossible to tell whether her involuntary little sigh sprang from relief or triumph. Her smile returned in all its frank charm. "It will not be easy, but between us we should accomplish it, you and I—yes?"

"Maybe." It was pleasant to feel that they were fellow accomplices, working together. "Navarro?"

"No," she rejected. "He is reckless and in debt, but he has his limits. No, we must do it between us."

"Could you smuggle me in a file, so I could loosen the rivet of this leg-iron?" Con asked. "And could you get me a monk's robe? We might do it that way."

Trouble is, it takes a funeral to bring the monks into the prisoners' quarters."

They pondered. "The monks would come to your quarters," Peregrina said slowly, "for any celebration of which they approved—such as a saint's day fiesta. Perhaps the *comandante* would grant permission for such a fiesta, too, if he thought it a proper occasion. This is the month of April. Let me see. . . ."

Con grinned faintly. "What about the 'Glorious Twenty-first'?"

"What is that?"

"Anniversary of the Battle of San Jacinto," Con explained dryly. "Two days from now."

Her eyes shone, matching his humor. "Why not? People here in Mexico do not remember such dates— and of course you will not enlighten them as to the real significance. A proper gravity must be observed by the Texans, so as not to arouse any suspicions. I can easily arrange anonymously for money to be provided for whatever you may need in the celebration. It will be thought that some foreign sympathizer sent it. And tomorrow I shall bring the file and the monk's robe."

Con took her hands in his own. They were small, and lay in his without struggling, and high temptation ran through him. "Why are you doing this?"

For once her eyes eluded him. "Did we not agree that we had an account to settle between us?" she reminded him demurely, and though the light was dim he knew she flushed.

After she had gone, Con gazed out through the bars, still with the feel of her small hands against his palms, and her nearness. "She'd be a girl to have. I swear, if I . . ."

A sharp memory intervened—of Phileda, and of his promise to Rael. He looked at Rael's blanket, lying unused in the familiar corner. "It's all right, partner. Just dreaming, is all."

THE MONKS WERE GRAVELY SURPRISED to learn that the foreign barbarians actually had a patron saint, and they were intrigued by a solemn occasion that required such things as *chinguirita* rum and *vino del pais* in its ceremonies. The *comandante,* in reluctantly giving permission for the celebration, had insisted that he and several of his under-officers must be present. Con privately cursed that condition. The dour old *comandante* had a stern and eagle eye, and never allowed anything to be put over on him. The Texans, asking no questions, unanimously approved of the whole idea, and all vowed to make it a howling success.

Someone with artistic talent got some paint, and on one cell wall sketched a fair likeness of General Sam Houston, adorned with a red-white-and-blue halo and the Lone Star of Texas. Tastefully spread out on the floor were the purchased fruits, food, *puros, cigarritos,* and the generous array of bottled goods. The bemused Mexicans elevated their eyebrows at such strange preparations, but wholeheartedly fell into the spirit of the affair when the feast began. With the Texans, they solemnly and repeatedly drank toasts to the picture on the wall, and even the *comandante* thawed, visibly impressed by such congenial ardor.

During the height of the festivities, when the Texans had got around to teaching the Mexicans to join in a Texas song to the tune of "Old Hundred," Con unobtrusively slipped off to his shadowy corner away from the yellow light of the candles. The *comandante* was accepting another drink, his dourness temporarily liquidated.

Some of the abstemious monks were leaving in their silent-footed way. They took no special notice of one of their number, who walked with hooded head bent, evidently in profound contemplative mood. The guards at the door, furtively getting their share of drinks behind the *comandante's* back, paid no heed at all.

Outside, groups of soldiers lounged along the flagstone walk, and the big gate had been shut. Con followed the monks with whom he had left the cell, pacing slowly and letting them get well ahead of him. The flagstone walk became a narrow passage between buildings, dark and unlighted, and he lost sight and sound of the monks. Feeling his way, he almost sprawled on stone steps, and began mounting them. Lightly as he stepped, his rustling echoes stirred hollowly in the deep stair-well, and his own breathing sounded loud in his ears.

A weak and flickering light appeared up ahead, and he made out the somber figures of two monks wending their way somewhere with a lantern. They vanished and all was dark again before him. At the top of the steps he paused to look about him. He was on a long gallery that formed part of the great surrounding wall, with the low doors of the monks' quarters lined along his left. On his right shone the scattered lights of Mexico City, with nothing imposed against him but a low parapet and a long drop.

He moved noiselessly to the parapet. Below was the street, silent and deserted at this late hour except for a public coach temporarily abandoned by its *cochero*. He eased himself over the parapet, hung stretched out, and let go, legs bent. He landed on his feet, but rolled over. When he rose, his ankles stung. They would be sore tomorrow, and . . .

"Coche, Señor!" growled a low voice. *"El coche—pronto!"*

Con whirled. The *cochero* had appeared from nowhere and was beckoning. Con got an impression of a swarthy brigandish face under a towering sombrero, and looked instinctively for sign of a weapon before he remembered that all *cocheros* had that villainously dashing air. They knew more secrets than did the police, and for pay would connive at anything. Con moved over to the coach without a word. It was of the common type, a covered hackney body mounted on a cumbersome frame, painted and elaborately carved, drawn by a team of good mules.

He made to enter, and drew back swiftly, ready to fling off his voluminous robe and fight or run. The coach already had an occupant, a lean-faced man with deep-set eyes, who held a pistol in his lap. The impersonal black eyes flickered over Con's face.

"Enter, *Señor*—we must hurry!"

Con climbed in beside him, with a queer feeling of being the only actor in a play who didn't know his lines or what was expected of him. The *cochero* sprang up onto the off-wheel mule, postilion fashion, and the heavy conveyance lunged into motion. At the second turning two mounted men caught up from behind and fell into pace alongside, exchanging no words with the *cochero* nor with the man who still held the pistol in his lap.

The coach rumbled through one street after another, avoiding the heart of the city. Several times the man with the pistol peered back through the rear opening. The two horsemen constantly reined aside and disappeared, to appear again farther along the route, their horses blowing from running. Once they came up in a hurry and conferred briefly with Con's fellow passenger, who muttered a rapid command to the *cochero*.

The coach lurched and came to a sudden halt in an alley barely wide enough for it. In the strained silence about him Con caught a coming clatter of hoofs. The two outriders dismounted, and now each held a carbine. The hoofbeats passed along the street, made by a detachment of mounted dragoons muffled in yellow military cloaks against the cool night air. The sound of them had not yet died away when the coach started on again, the scouting outriders ahead.

Soon the city lay behind, and the road grew rutty. The outriders fell back and trotted in the rear. The lean-faced man ceased peering rearward, and put away his pistol after carefully uncocking it. Abruptly he spoke to Con for the first time since leaving the Santiago:

"I am Jesus Bustamente."

He looked more a man of the country than a city dweller. There was a solidness about him and a blunt manner that marked the outdoor man. Yet he wore an air of some authority. The two outriders had spoken to him with respect, and his commands to the coachman were brisk and decisive. He obviously was not a man of idle talk and superfluous courtesies. His deep-set eyes were intelligent, cold, neither friendly nor hostile.

The coach bumped its way through open country. Con dozed, content enough for the time being to ask no questions as long as he was being borne steadily away from Mexico City and the grim old Santiago. He woke to find the coach halting. They were in a courtyard. Through a gaping hole in a time-gnawed wall he saw open plains, and what appeared to be a lake. The likeness of this gaunt old building to the Santiago brought a tight readiness to him. A few bats whirred, disturbed.

"What place is this?" he queried sharply.

"The ruin of the old San Cristobal Palace," replied Bustamente, getting out. "Be pleased to alight, *Señor.*"

Con climbed out, and was surprised to find men and mules in the yard. Bustamente muttered a few words, and coins clinked. The *cochero* mumbled a blessing upon all, jumped to his team, and the coach rolled out of the yard. The men and mules moved into orderly formation. Everything evinced previous careful plannir

Two of the largest mules bore a *litera,* while the rest were saddled for riding. Bustamente motioned Con to the *litera.* "We have far to go, *Señor.* Should we pass anyone on the road you will please to remain hidden."

A silent Mexican helped Con up into the *litera.* It was in the shape of an oblong box, with a covered top and side curtains, built on two long poles that were strapped onto the saddles of the two mules. There were no wheels, and the mules bore the full weight. Con climbed in and found it more comfortable than any bed he had slept in for the better part of a year. A mattress had been fitted into it, with pillows and blankets, so that he could lie full length or sit up, as it pleased him. He chose to stretch out and luxuriate. It was good to relax body and mind, to give himself utterly over into the capable hands of others, after all the struggle and grinding hardship, and the responsibility of caring for Rael.

The party started off. The easy swing of the *litera* lulled him to sleep. He did not know how much later it was when he woke, shivering, and pulled the blankets around him. They were in the mountains and climbing higher, he thought drowsily, and warmth returned and he slept again.

15. HACIENDA

ON THE LONG MARCH DOWN from San Miguel, Con had seen a few of the great private estates of Mexico, each a miniature kingdom with its own village and church, so he could judge with some accuracy the comparative importance of this *rancho* of La Caleta, where he had now for three days been a guest.

The big residence, unlike those of most *haciendas,* stood well off from the village, surrounded by trees and a flower garden. The church, most prominent edifice of the village, was of stone, and boasted a silvery bell. Hard by it was the *tienda,* the commissary, and around this central point clustered the houses of the peon workers. *Señor* Bustamente was the superintendent.

It was a large *rancho,* well managed, and the big residence had many servants. Con had the run of the house, himself its only tenant except for the servants, but lately he had begun to suspect that he was more a prisoner than a guest.

"You will please to remain inside, *Señor,*" Bustamente had told him in his coldly polite way, the first time Con strolled out to the village.

"Why?" asked Con.

Bustamente volunteered no explanation. Perhaps it was accidental that he allowed his leather jacket to fall open, exposing a pistol stuck in his belt. Some of the male servants, Con noted, also carried pistols. Henceforth he found one or more armed men loitering at the front and rear of the house whenever he wandered downstairs.

"Dammit, what's her game?" he muttered, restlessly pacing the small gallery outside his room. He had not seen Peregrina since his escape, and he had quit inquiring about her. All his questions elicited the same response—the eternal and infuriating *"Quien sabe, Señor?"*

He was comfortable enough here, his every want supplied lavishly. A close-mouthed *criado* had shaved him and trimmed his hair, laid out clean linen and new clothes for him, and never grumbled at the astounding number of baths he was required to arrange. Food and cooking were excellent, and very fine wine was plentiful. There was even a box of long Havanas in his quarters.

And the view from his gallery was superb. He judged the location of the *rancho* as somewhere on the eastern slope of the mountains surrounding *Cofre de Perote.* Far below, to the east, lay the *tierra caliente,* hot and jungly, and farther east would be Vera Cruz and the Gulf of Mexico.

But this matter of being practically a prisoner—*her* prisoner—galled him. It was disturbing, just as she was disturbing. It held too many unknown possibilities.

"Beautiful minx! What's she rigging up on me?"

A vision of Rael came to him, as it often did. Rael's thin white face and the eyes of a dreamer. Rael's calm faith that all eventually would be well. Rael's idealism.

"Wish you were here, partner. Damn' shame you had to go."

On the fifth day Peregrina arrived in a light carriage with an escort of outriders, and the big house immediately hummed alive. Servants ran out to attend their mistress even before the carriage wheeled to a halt. Con, on his gallery, restrained his first impulse to go down right away and greet her. He compromised by bowing to her when she glanced up at him as she stepped from the carriage. Her eyes danced, and she arched her brows at his changed appearance.

"Join me downstairs—but not for an hour yet. I must make myself presentable for such a handsome desperado!" she called, scandalizing her servants.

Later, walking with her in the garden as the sun went down, Con inquired after Don José. "Didn't he come with you? Nor your redoubtable *doña*—to guard you from the perils that beset the path of beauty?"

She laughed softly. "Perils? Ah, but our bandits rarely harm ladies, and I had a strong escort."

"I wasn't thinking of bandits."

She laughed again, and stooped to touch a pink mimosa guarded by thorns. Con had never seen her so lovely, so utterly feminine. It was difficult to couple this carelessly gay girl with the keen intelligence that had planned his escape from the Santiago, or with the woman of deep compassion who had held Rael in her arms while he died in a corner of the prison cell.

She tilted back her head and looked up at him, tall and lean and immaculate above her. "No, my uncle did not come. He is busy preparing for our journey back to Santa Fe with General Rajimo, and I did not tell him I was coming here. And the good *doña*, sad to say, has broken out with what she fears is smallpox— though I think it is nothing more than a result of eating too many *chirimoyas* which I bought for her. So you see I am a truant and a very bad girl. This *rancho* is mine. My father left it to me."

Con restrained another impulse, looking down at her. "I like it," he said. "But not enough to enjoy being held prisoner on it."

She rose, her smile fading at his tone. "I am sorry, but it was necessary. They have placed a price on your head. Rajimo swears he will have you tracked down, and I did not know how much he might suspect. I gave Bustamente his orders."

Con bowed. "Excuse, I beg, my vile suspicions," he drawled gravely. He had in mind the occasion when each had vowed to humble the other. "I have a low type of mind."

Her eyes grew brilliant and her color came high, and he knew she suspected him of irony. "You thought— you think—? Oh! Captain Connegan, you are not a gentleman!"

"No," agreed Con, and this time he did not restrain his impulse.

She struggled in his arms, then grew quiet as he kissed her. Her hands, first pounding against his chest, slid over his shoulders. . . .

"*Señor*—be good enough to release my niece!" rapped an icy voice. "I do not wish to shoot while she is in your arms!"

Bitter-eyed, his mouth pinched in, Don José Chavez regarded them. They sprang apart, and Con looked first at the pistol before raising his stare to the narrow patrician face of the Spanish aristocrat.

"You fly off easy, friend," said Con, and meant just

that. These highly strung Latins were altogether too impetuous about gunplay, and too apt to jump to conclusions where a girl was involved. He took a casual step, and tensed when he saw the bitter eyes. Dammit, the fellow was going to shoot, sure as his word.

"Don José!" Peregrina, not making the error of running at him and hastening the trigger, spoke from where she stood. "I forbid it!"

The bitter eyes whipped to her, acid in their haughty scorn. "You—forbid? You forget yourself!"

"I forbid it!" repeated the girl, and her tone was as haughty as his. "It is you who forget yourself, Don José. This is my *hacienda*. I resent your trespass upon my privacy! I resent your attempt to override my inherited authority here! And I resent, sir, your insulting attitude!"

At any other time Con could have fully enjoyed Don José's stunned discomfiture. The Don was taken all mentally a-sprawl by the girl's counter-charging attack. Possibly he had expected shamed contrition, perhaps some defiance. Most certainly he hadn't been prepared to find her a furious-eyed girl who not only defied him but condemned him and pointed out his serious transgressions.

"I demand your apology!" added Peregrina, either as an afterthought or a final thrust.

Con admired that. Devil an' all, she was a fighter from way back, ready and wicked as they came. No frantic seeking for defense, but a swift charge to the attack. Meet 'em halfway. Up and at 'em. Lord, what a girl!

"My—my apology?" stammered Don José, and looked almost foolish despite the pistol. He drew himself together, gathering back his sternness. "I followed you here on horseback, Peregrina, to protect you from your own indiscretions. I suspected from the first that you aided this man's escape, and I had you watched. I find him here, in your *hacienda*—without a chaperon—you in his arms—! And you have the impertinence to demand—!"

"I do demand it," returned the girl. "And Captain Connegan also warrants your apology!"

Con thought that was pushing the Don a little too far, but he played up to it and nodded gravely as an injured party. For the moment, anyway, the danger of a bullet was set aside. It had become a battle of wits, and he backed Peregrina to win.

"And why," demanded Don José dangerously, "should I apologize to this man?"

Well, now, that was a point. Con couldn't think of any suitable answer, considering the circumstances, and he began to doubt whether Peregrina could do any better. She appeared to be debating it in her mind, and she gazed at him as if not quite sure of herself. Con flashed her an encouraging look, and then she brought out an answer that was simple and definite.

"Because, sir," she said clearly, "Captain Connegan is my betrothed!"

Con stood stunned.

LATER, IN THE HOUSE, Don José said unemotionally, "I do not pretend to approve. You are not the man, Captain Connegan, that I would have chosen for my niece. In my opinion, sir, you are a penniless adventurer and a desperado!"

Con bowed. "That opinion, sir, has been shared by others." He glanced at Peregrina.

Don José stiffened a little more. "However," he went on, "in view of the—ah—circumstances in which I find you both, I have no alternative. My niece, in this strange mood that possesses her, has taken from me the pleasure of shooting you, which I regret. Therefore I do more than give my consent to this outrageous betrothal. I desire—insist, rather—that the wedding take place immediately!"

He stalked out and left them, on his way to the church to apprise the *hacienda* priest of the coming ceremony.

Con inclined his head to Peregrina. Anger smoldered in his eyes, and his mouth was hard. "You make me very happy, my dear," he drawled harshly.

She flinched, her eyes clouding. "Would you rather have been shot?"

He shook his head. Her frank distress hurt him, and he placed his hands on her small firm shoulders. "No," he said slowly. "I've wanted you from the first minute I saw you. But not this way—not pushed and jockeyed into taking you. It's a humbling experience to be driven into marrying a girl—even though you happen to love her—and I'm not a humble man, as you may have discovered in the past."

"Yet you wanted to humble me!" she charged, but her shoulders trembled under his hands.

"I wanted to win you," Con corrected. "I still do. I always will. We're pretty much of a kind, you and I. We can hate, love, fight—and have fun doing all of it. Maybe we're too much alike, too tricky and domineering to get along together. Lord knows we've been good enemies! Do you realize what this marriage means to me? It means becoming an unwanted and despised poor relation of the Chavez clan. The penniless husband of a wealthy girl, dependent for everything . . ."

"Always your pride comes first!" she flashed at him.

He held her, and grinned down at her without hardness. "You look more natural to me when you're mad. Yes, I reckon maybe it's pride. A man likes to hang onto that if he can. But, Lord, you're a temptation! I wonder did my brother Lorin love you that much?"

"Perhaps." There was defiance in her, and a desire to hurt him. "I think he did—and more nobly. He was a gentleman!"

"And he died for it." He shook her gently. "You minx, if I could get the truth out of you—! Who killed him? Rajimo?"

"No."

"Who got the ninety thousand dollars he had?"

She made no reply to that, and Con shrugged, still holding her. "I've half a mind to—well, let it go." He laughed shortly. "Now you see how we'd be. Here we are just betrothed and the wedding in the offing, and already we're at each other's throats!"

He kissed her quickly, before she could duck her head, and released her. "But I'd rather fight with you than own a harem!"

Don José entered. "The church is being prepared," he said, looking at neither of them. "The wedding will take place in an hour. Captain Connegan, I shall use all possible influence to have charges against you dropped. Santa Anna, I believe, will soon release your companions."

"Thank you."

"I desire no thanks from you," retorted Don José. "As the husband of Peregrina you will become entitled to the protection of the Chavez family, little though we may wish to extend it to you. Please excuse my bluntness—I find it necessary in my dealings with you."

"You're excused," murmured Con.

Up in his room again, Con stepped out onto the gallery and peered down into the garden. One of the armed *criados* lounged beneath, arms folded. Over in the village, lights shone from the church, where the priest made ready for the wedding.

Wedding. The word, in Con's mind, sounded strange. He—Captain Con—walking out of a church with his bride. Well, it would be a zesty joy to be wedded to Peregrina, and life would never be dull with her in it.

"If it were that, and no more . . ." He recalled Don José's cold promise. "'As the husband of Peregrina, you will be entitled to the protection of the Chavez family, little as we may wish . . .'"

The husband of Peregrina. That was putting it correctly. The consort of the queen. The secondary element. Despised as a penniless foreign adventurer who had somehow caught the fancy of a rich and beautiful heiress. Peregrina's trained bear. She would own him. Dammit, she had won him!

He stood stock-still. Now, had that little devil deliberately rigged this up on him? The thought brought no animosity, but rather an added respect for a clever and determined opponent. "If she did—Lord, what a gambler she'd have made!"

Tardily, remembrance came to him of Phileda, of what he had promised her, and his added promise to Rael.

"I've got to get out of here!"

He took another look over the gallery rail, and found the *criado* still there below. Somewhere over there to the far east, beyond the jungle of the *tierra caliente,* lay the Gulf coast and the Vera Cruz seaport. There would be a foreign ship or two swinging at anchor under the old Castle of San Juan de Ulua, maybe an American trading cutter bound for New Orleans or Galveston, or calling in at some of the little anchorages around Matagorda Bay.

He noiselessly swung his legs over the railing, got poised, and dropped, keeping his heels together. His boots struck the unsuspecting *criado* squarely on the head. . . .

At the far edge of the garden he paused to look back at the lighted house. Behind one of those lighted windows Peregrina would be dressing for her wedding. A sense of shame rose in him, and hard regret. It would take all her splendid young courage to face Don José alone and admit that her betrothed had slipped his leash. There would be furiously hurt pride in Peregrina's secret hours tonight. Tomorrow she would start back with Don José to Mexico City, and then to Santa Fe, instead of remaining here in her inherited *hacienda* as a bride.

Con looked to the east, then back at the house, and for a moment balanced in hesitation. "No, I can't stay and see it through, girl." He shook his head. It wasn't just pride. They both were wrong about that. He had promised Rael he'd find Phileda, take care of her, marry her.

"A man's got to keep some sort of respect for his word," he muttered, and ignored the fact that he could have broken it had he given it to anybody else but Rael. "I'm sorry, girl. I wish to God it didn't have to be this way. Maybe we'll meet again—maybe in Santa Fe."

He turned and hurried on toward the east, avoiding the village.

16. WHITE APACHE

THE ADOBE-WALLED CITY of San Antonio de Bexar still bore the scars of siege and cannon shot, reminders of the Texan war for independence against Mexico. Above the ruins of the old Alamo the Lone Star flag had now fluttered for seven years, proclaiming this hard-won land as Texan. But the city's ten thousand inhabitants remained mostly Mexican and Indian, and *siesta* still ruled the days.

Always the sun shone by day, cool breezes brought comfort in summer, and the air stayed dry and healthful. If a man wanted to die here, said the white *Tejanos,* he had to go somewhere else to do it.

But night brought a stir to life, and the whine of a fiddle might be heard anywhere until near dawn. On the plaza lighted doorways enticed the wandering citizen to wine and fandango, while dark side streets became the roving grounds of *ladrones* and *picaros* loitering about with furtive eyes to nefarious business.

Con entered the plaza by night, and for a while leaned against the old stone gateway of the Alamo, listening to music from half a dozen sources. He had been here before, seven years ago, but under somewhat different circumstances. He had ridden in then with the hard-bitten Texas troops under Cooke and Milam, after the siege. Well, the fortunes of war ran to extremes. Tonight he entered as a fugitive afoot, with only the saddle blanket left of the pony and saddle that he had borrowed without leave two hundred miles back. He was hungry, tired, dirty, and his clothes were in sorry shape.

"I wonder, now," he mused, "where I'll sit me down to eat tonight? H'mm—sounds like a game going on over there."

In a side street just off the plaza the noisy clink of coin and slap of cards bespoke a gambling house. Some horses drooped outside, wearing Texan cavalry saddles and faded troop insignia on the blankets. Well, well, so Texas still maintained the San José garrison, couple of miles down the river, eh? Con cast back in memory.

"Let's see, now. Would that be old Pablo Maria's den? Seems like it was—why, sure, that's it. So the fat old scoundrel's still doing business! Seems like I recall pulling some kind of rig over on old Pablo before I left here. I sure wouldn't have passed him up, the fat thief. Well, I can take a bath in the river, anyway. After that we'll see about eating."

Pure curiosity led him to cross the plaza and pass by Pablo's on his way to the river. He passed on the far side of the street, just as an unwanted bundle of humanity got thrown out of the place. That, too, struck a familiar chord of memory. It was a dull night when somebody or other didn't leave Pablo's a deal quicker than he had entered. Pablo himself, fatter than ever, waddled out, aimed a kick at the ejected one, and retired with dignity.

The derelict sat up dazedly, groping for his hat. He was barefoot, covered with hair, rags and dirt, and Con paid him scant attention. Drunken beggars, degenerate Indians, white men sunk low, they were common enough in the frontier towns. He grinned at Pablo's enormous back, and speculated about his prospects.

Prospects, he concluded as he bathed in the river, were none too good. "Still, seems like I ought to be able to think up something," he muttered.

A small fire sprang up along the river bank. He eyed it idly while drying himself with his shirt, his mind still occupied, and recognized the old derelict squatting by it, warming up something in a broken pot. The wretched scene intruded into his thoughts, and he frowned. Poor old devil. Age without honor. That was what you came to when you let go and admitted yourself whipped. Looked more like an Indian now, squatting there, but no Indian ever had whiskers like that. Hadn't even a blanket. Nothing but his tattered rags.

Con dressed and picked up his saddle blanket. He held it out and looked at it. "If I hang onto you, blanket, likely I'll persuade myself to curl up in you and sleep out. But if I get rid of you, then I'll damn sure find some way to sleep in a bed tonight. Yes, and eat before bed. Besides, when a man's as busted as I am, best thing he can do is give something away. It's lucky and makes him feel rich."

With which logic, to explain away his reasons and outwit the charge of foolish charity, he advanced on the miserable little fire. The derelict shrank like a cur that had been kicked too often. Disgust rose in Con, but he flung the blanket down. "Here's something I don't need, old-timer."

The derelict mumbled something, staring at him over the fire as if seeing ghosts. What could be seen of his face through the matted hair was haggard and had a sick hue. The eyes were bloodshot and dazed. It seemed to Con, as he turned away, that he caught his own name in the mumble, and he swung sharply around.

"What? What's that? Do you—?"

He stepped closer and bent down, staring into the sick face. "My—good—Lord! *Old Nick Gentry!*"

Old Nick put out a trembly hand. "Sure—sure! It's

me, Con—it's Ol' Nick. Where you been, boy?"

Con gripped the hand. He had never in his life felt so shocked. Old Nick had always been a rough-hewn man, more Indian than white in his ways, but a self-sufficient man, tough and powerful and lawless, truckling to nobody and standing square on his feet like a chief. This was a poor shadow of him, pitiful and beaten and beggarly, no strength to his hand and with that bleared glaze in his eyes.

Con sat down by him. "What in the hell have they done to you, Nick?" he demanded gruffly. "Was it the Apaches?"

"No—Apaches was all right." Automatically, Old Nick stirred the greasy mess in the pot with a stick. "Mex woman gimme these *frijoles,*" he husked. "Mex women is all right. I allus claimed so. Mutton fat is here. Yeah, Mex women is all right. So's Apaches. I hunted buff'lo with 'em along the Bayou Salade last winter. If I can swaller this . . ."

Con took the pot and set it down. "Dammit, tell me what happened!"

Old Nick reached vaguely back for the pot. "They robbed me."

"Who? The Apaches?"

"Naw. Apaches is all right. That fat Mex—what's his name? Pablo somethin'." Old Nick went back to his stirring, holding the pot over the fire. "I sold my buff'lo hides an' come in. That fat Mex—what's his name? Seems like I can't 'member nothin' no more. He done it. Likker tasted queer. I went back awhile ago an' tol' him he done robbed me, but him an' some more Mex, they . . ."

"I saw it," broke in Con. "So you handled the Apaches, cleaned up on buffalo, and then let a fat Mex pull a rig on you. I be damned! Nick, I'm glad it's nothing worse. Gave me a turn, finding you like this. Thought you'd cracked."

The fire began dying. "When did it happen, Nick?"

"Couple days—mebbe a week—I dunno." Old Nick passed a gnarled hand over his face. "I been sick, Con. Ain't et nothin'. They took my knife too, an' my lance, an' my bow'n arrers."

"Did your buffalo hunting with an Apache lance, eh?" Con studied the hairy face. "You sure go Injun when you get out!" Some filthy herbal concoction had done this to the old hunter. Pablo was expert in such arts, and this time he had pretty nearly ruined a good man for his money. "How much cash did they get?"

"Sixteen hunnerd dollars." The old hunter was positive on that one point. It was one thing that had stuck in his drugged mind. "'Twarn't a good year, an' buff'lo cows was scarce in the herds." He began eating, using his fingers.

"Sixteen hundred dollars, and it wasn't a good year." Con pulled at his chin. "Nick, I need a stake bad. Got to find Phileda. Promised Rael I'd look after her. Rael died in the Santiago. And then there's Lorin— remember? I want to get to Santa Fe, somehow, some day."

Nick remembered. He stopped eating. "Santa Fe?"

"Sure." Con was glad to find that his talk of things familiar could ring response from the sick and clouded mind. "That's part reason I came back. I jumped the Santiago, after Rael died. Rest of the boys are getting out, I hear, soon. Nick, you'll never know how hard it was to quit Mexico. I took ship at Vera Cruz, left it at Matagorda Bay, and rode up here on somebody's pony. I'm broke again and there's a whole lot I want to do."

He watched Nick eat for a while, and said suddenly, "Let's go hunt buffalo, Nick. What you need's a horse under you and a *cibolero* lance in your fist, and some red meat in your stomach!"

Some of the old gleam crept into Nick's eyes, and faded again. "Ain't got no outfit. Need wagon, good Injun-trained ponies, guns, bow'n arrers, knives . . ."

"We could buy our outfit, here and there," Con remarked, "with your sixteen hundred dollars."

Old Nick raised his head. "He won't give it back. That fat Mex—he won't give it back."

"I didn't figure he would, just for the asking," Con agreed dryly. "Not Pablo Maria!" He picked up and folded the saddle blanket. "First we'll trade this somewhere for a drink. A dram or two of rum will pull you together some. Come on."

Half an hour later, sitting in a side-street *cantina* with an emptied mug, Nick hit his chest and swore deep in his throat. "That fat Mex! I'll scalp him!"

Con grinned. It was a satisfaction to see some of the old savage fire creep back, though it had to be lighted with a half pint of raw rum. Pretty soon Old Nick would be letting out a war whoop and scaring all the women to fits.

"You feel like getting that money back, Nick?"

The old hunter worked his hands. "If they'd left me my knife—if I had a gun—!"

Con leaned across the table. "Listen. There are four good horses outside Pablo's place. Cavalry nags, but Texas is rich and we'll turn 'em loose after we make our getaway. All four have got army carbines in the saddle boots. We only need two—and we both shoot well when we have to, don't we?"

He slapped the table and rose. "Well?"

Old Nick rocked to his feet. "I'll hang his hair on my belt!" he growled, and together they left the *cantina*.

Minutes later a scream and a shot shattered the mingling music of the plaza to abrupt discords, followed by a wild whoop. An explosive fusillade crashed out. Two men burst from Pablo's place, smoking carbines in hands. They jumped to two of the startled horses, flung themselves into the saddles, and beat up dust across the plaza while cavalrymen and Mexicans piled out in pursuit and somebody inside went on yelling.

Two carbines thumped back into saddle boots. Two pairs of heels drummed against the ribs of the galloping horses. Con shifted the weight of a crammed cash-filled hat under his shirt to a more secure position. Old Nick tucked a hank of coarse black hair tighter into his belt, flung back his shaggy head, and whooped again.

"Wa-a-h—ha-ha-ha—hoo-ee!"

17. THE BUFFALO HUNTERS

THE DARK MASS OF THE BUFFALO HERD was at halt on the prairie, feeding on the sun-dried grass and rolling in the dust, but at the approach of the hunters a shaggy bull turned and pawed the earth in majestic challenge, angrily tossing his horns. Others near him threw up their massive black-maned heads and stood statue-still, scenting, their fierce little eyes glaring. The two hunters came on, riding without haste and saving their wiry ponies for the headlong dash to come.

Somewhere a pair of belligerent young bulls settled grievances, oblivious of all else, while uneasy silence rippled over the rest of the herd. Broad and matted foreheads met with thudding impact, and then began the death contest of straining muscles, each stubborn battler seeking to topple and gore the other. They were lusty with good grass, furiously jealous of their cows, and the old bulls had long been driven out of the herd. Fights had raged all through the mating season and far into the summer, as the wolf-gnawed bones scattered over the prairie bore witness.

Con, with four of the new Colt's dragoon pistols stuck in his belt, veered off to take the left flank of the herd, while Old Nick swung over to the right. Both had discarded hats and wore only a rag knotted around hair that had grown long. Both rode stripped nearly naked, their bodies browned and glistening with sweat, each absorbed in the task ahead, unsmiling but eager. Their split-eared ponies, Indian-trained, wore the same air of sure confidence in themselves, leavened with a respectful regard for the element of danger. They knew their business.

Old Nick, as Indian-trained as his pony, rode bareback for lightness' sake and used a rope halter, trusting to the good sense of his pony to bring him alongside the kill. He favored also the Indian shortbow for hunting—fashioned from carefully tapered horn—and he could let loose an arrow with enough power to bury it up to its feathers in a buffalo, one every four seconds while riding at top speed. But he didn't brag of that. There were Indians who could throw four arrows to his one, and as accurately.

But then, as he remarked to Con, "Injuns was runnin' meat long afore us whites, an' they savvy how better. Same thing with stalkin' an' fightin'. Give an Injun a blade o' grass fer kivver, an' he'll slip an arrer 'twixt yore ribs whilst you cock your smoke-gun a-lookin' fer him. Yeah, an' two more in you whilst you fall. You gotta give Injuns credit. They make the most o' their op'toonities."

The herd remained passive, though with growing unease, while the sentry bulls flung up showers of dirt with their angry pawing. A half-grown calf bawled its premonition and sought its mother, creating a stir. Still the hunters came on, now apart and taking different directions. Con drew a Colt's pistol, smacked the others more firmly in his belt, and cocked the hammer. Old Nick went through the swift jugglery of fitting an arrow to his bowstring in a single smooth movement, and jabbed the belly of his pony with his toes.

The raging bulls whirled and charged off in their rolling gallop, ungainly but fast, sudden alarm pricking them. The fright spread at once and the whole mass of the herd got into thundering motion, heads lowered, tufted beards and frontlets waving, the short and wicked horns thrust forward as a menace to anything in their way.

In the boil of dust the confused roar sounded like a rumbling explosion, gathering greater momentum as it went on. Half blinded by the smother, Con gave rein and let his pony have full headway. He rode with shortened stirrup leathers, knees bent and sitting lightly, prepared for the necessary leap clear in case of a spill.

But the racing pony, with ears flat and eyes alert, had the wary suspicion of a cat. For this kind of work a pony was picked for its brains as well as for speed and stamina. It dodged the swift side-lunge of a slashing horn, fell back a step, and spurted up abreast of the kill that it had marked from the first. To take any sort of steady aim from the jouncing saddle was impossible, yet to miss the vital mark—the hairless spot just behind the buffalo's shoulder—might mean a lightning whirl, a gored pony, and disaster. Con brought down the pistol and fired. Sights on a short-gun were never of much use to him at any time. He was a snap shot.

The buffalo ran on as if unhurt, but Con and the split-eared pony knew better. A buffalo had a tenacious grip on life, and could run fifty yards with a bullet or arrow in its heart. The pony flew on through the wild stampede, gave its attention to the next kill, and Con did his part again. It was a matter of teamwork, a perfect understanding between man and pony.

Somewhere in the dust and clamor Old Nick was getting in his work with his silent arrows, dropping buffaloes faster than Con could with his four pistols. Con took a quick look back, and through the wild haze in the rear saw black dots marking the gouged-up course of the herd. Tonight the wolves that always haunted the buffalo herds, dragging down calves when they could, would gather and quarrel over the skinned carcasses, and the herd would gain a respite from their predatory hunting. The far-off wagon, already loaded to creaking with hides, would strain the mule team to bring it up for yet another load. Con smeared grimed sweat from his eyes with a hasty swipe, and made another clean kill.

That night, filled with dark red meat and fried *boudin,* Old Nick stretched out and lighted his pipe. " 'Twas a good run," he allowed. "We've had right good luck since we partnered. Pity we ain't got 'nother wagin. Them mule'll earn their feed pullin' this'n. Sure is plenty buff'lo on the plains, an' gettin' more ev'ry year, seems like. Some day they'll fill the hull damn country."

"I doubt that," Con disagreed lazily. "More hunters are turning to buffalo every year, and that'll keep the herds down. Right now we could take a million hides and they'd never be missed. But if every hunter turns to buffalo it's going to kill the business. The price of hides will fall, and they'll kill more to make up for it. There's no crop of anything that'll stand that. It's like cutting down a whole woods for timber, or trimming a sucker out of his last dollar. There's nothing left for seed, and the time finally comes when there's nothing left to cut, trim or hunt."

"You feel sick or somethin'?" grunted Old Nick.

Con loosened his belt. "No, I feel fine. Maybe I've eaten so much buffalo meat I'm beginning to see their point of view!"

After the skinning, they had butchered the youngest and fattest, cutting out the tender tongue, chopping off the hump ribs, and slicing off the back-fat which Old Nick called "Injun bread." Old Nick could pretty nearly eat his weight in buffalo meat, but he didn't stop at that. He ate the liver raw, and fried other tidbits that Con had always considered should be decently left to the wolves. Among the many things that Old Nick had learned from the Indians was that buffalo gall, taken before eating, was a stimulant that lent to life a more than usually rosy glow. Con took his word for it without personal experiment. He liked his own stimulants labeled, sealed and aged, when possible.

Right now, Old Nick was a stimulated man, mumbling a Cheyenne chant in his beard and cocking a satisfied eye at the loaded wagon. "Where'll we sell out, Con?" he asked.

"Not in San Anton', anyway," Con yawned. "Might be well to sell to the first dealer we run across. Sell the wagon and outfit, too, unless you want to hang onto it for yourself."

Old Nick, on his back, rolled over and peered at him. "You aim to quit me?"

Con nodded. "I'm heading north soon's we cash in. Last I saw young Abel Fonley, he said he had an uncle near Louisville and he'd take Phileda there. May take me some time to find 'em. After that I'll see about taking another crack at Santa Fe. Sorry, Nick, but you see how 'tis."

For awhile Old Nick smoked in silence. "Gonna miss you, Con," he decided finally. "I never had a better partner since Chief Wolf Runner got hisself killed in a Cayuga fight, twenty year a-gone. He war like you. When he got sot on a notion, nothin' would do till he snagged it down or broke up all hell a-tryin'. 'Twas his ruin in the end, an' nigh mine."

Con had a suspicion that a sermon of sorts was in the offing, and was curious to hear it. "How'd it happen?"

"Wimmen!" pronounced Old Nick heavily. "Wolf Runner, he war a cagey cuss in a fight or hunt, but one day he saw a Cayuga gal he wanted bad, an' I couldn't do nothin' with him. About forty Cayuga fightin' men jumped us when we prowled into their camp one night to steal the gal. Wolf Runner's big medicine run out on him an' he knowed he was killed. He had a lance stuck right through him an' a leg nigh chopped off."

He shook his head at the memory. "I was in bad shape, but they let me crawl over an' hold him up, an' he sung his death-song whilst they listened respectful. Then his leg give way an' he fell dead on me. He'd killed seven of 'em, so they give him proper burial next day, an' the gal she carried on fierce. She run naked through the cactus to show her grief."

" 'Twould appear," Con remarked, "that the damsel wasn't averse to being stolen by the right man. Well, that'll tempt any man with red blood in him. How'd you come out?"

"I married her," answered Old Nick simply. "Seein' as how they'd killed her man, an' I was his friend, she claimed me—an' they 'lowed she was right. Injuns is diff'rent from whites, an' a lot more reason'ble in some ways. After she nursed me well, I went off an' stayed drunk for a moon, all the time thinkin' o' Wolf Runner. It hit me kinda bad. Him an' me got along like brothers, an' he was all man."

Con studied the lawless old renegade. "Why not come north with me?" he suggested.

Old Nick sat up and tapped out his pipe. "Why the hell didn't you ast me? Sure I'll come—north, Santa Fe, or both. It's only decent you'd oughta have a friend around to hold you up, time comes you sing yore death-song!"

18. NEW KENTUCKY HOME

THE KENTUCKIAN was keen-eyed and taciturn, a long and lean man in coonskin cap and leather shirt, with a hunting gun under his arm. "Fonley?" he said, and his eyes searched the two strangers. He was of guarded ways and distrusted all outlanders. "Naw, I reckin I never heerd of him."

"He's a nephew of Talton Fonley, who lived along the Ohio near Louisville," said Con. "Old Man Talton died recent, folks say, and left Abel Fonley a piece of land out this way. Abel'd want to see us," he added. "He'd thank a neighbor to point us the way."

The Kentuckian spat the juice of his leaf chew. With no change of expression, he pointed. "Yonder up the valley to the big bottoms," he said. "B'like he'll be clearin' timber."

He stood watching after them as they rode on, and was still watching them when they took the gradual descent to the bottomlands. Everything about them, their clothes and the way they rode, made them unusual in this land of farms and homespun.

"Shy-tongued folks, these," commented Old Nick, and they fell silent, both settling their eyes on a cabin below. It was tiny, dwarfed by the large spread of the landscape. The smooth green hills ran off to both sides, heavily timbered in the folds, and ran higher to the friendly mountains. Down on the bottomland a plow had turned over the rich soil in a clearing. The furrows were new in the clearing, but over toward the cabin lay a square of what last year had been grass-land, now gold and green with growing corn, high and tasseled. Tree stumps fringed the plowed section, telling of the slow spread of cleared land, enlarged doggedly with axe and bucksaw.

The sight and significance of it drew both riders to halt. "The like o' that takes work," observed Old Nick succinctly, and shook his shaggy head in wonder that anyone should choose such a life task.

"Takes courage," Con amended. He spoke musingly, his brows drawn. "What is it gives a man that kind of courage? What makes a man . . ."

He paused, his eyes caught by a slim and bonneted girl emerging from the cabin, and Old Nick grunted sagely, "Mebbe there's your answer!"

The slim figure took seat at the door in the shade, and went to work grinding corn. Once the girl stopped, brushed back a stray strand of hair from her forehead, and sat quietly as if listening for a familiar and comforting sound. It came, the ring of a striking axe somewhere in the clearing, and she resumed her task.

Con heeled his horse down the gentle slope, Old Nick following, and at the drumming of hoofs on the sod the girl rose with the startled motion of one to whom the coming of horsemen was rare. She was standing, wide-eyed, when Con and Old Nick drew to a halt before her.

Con doffed his broad-brimmed hat as he dismounted, and suddenly he felt strangely out of place here. He had chosen his new outfit with his usual fastidious care, reveling in good clothes after so long in rags. His long coat was of fine broadcloth, and under it a wide black silver-buckled belt was stretched across his lean middle by the weight of two hanging objects that the coat partially hid. Tailored pants were neatly tucked into the high riding boots of soft leather, strapped across the arches and ornamented with the single silver star of Texas. The flaring gauntlets of his buckskin gloves were fringed and hand-worked. Tall, sleek, with his dark elegance and immaculate cleanliness, he looked as if he'd never in his life soiled himself with honest labor.

Old Nick, prevailed upon by Con to don at least the semblance of civilization, had gone whole hog. His bushy gray head gloried in a tall beaver while his feet suffered inside real boots.

"Hello, Phileda!" Con murmured, and found it needed an effort to flash on his old easy smile.

"Con!" She ran to him, took his outstretched hands in hers, and stood on tiptoe to kiss him. Con bent and kissed her before sudden embarrassment flooded her face. "Oh—hello, Nick!" she stammered.

Her face was flaming, and Con caught his breath, marveling that he could ever have thought her merely quietly pretty. Why, she was almost beautiful. Her eyes—what had she done to them? They were the eyes of a lovely young woman, full of deep feeling and an awareness of life that she had not yet revealed when he thought her a child.

Old Nick grinned through his whiskers and shook her firm little hand. "Moughty glad to see you, missy, lookin' so peart an' all. Con an' me, we done consid'able huntin' for you, ain't we, Con?"

Con didn't answer. He had happened to glance through the open doorway into the cabin, and now his eyes were on a hickory bark cradle. A baby lay sleeping in it. He could see a tiny hand. "Where's Abel?" he asked.

"He's working in the clearing. I'll go and . . ."

"No. Nick, you go call him, huh?"

He went into the cabin, and stood gazing down at the infant. "A boy. Fair hair. Handsome boy," he murmured, and raised his eyes to Phileda.

She met his steady eyes, the hot flush still on her face. "I—we were married in Louisville, Abel and I," she whispered.

Con queried bluntly, "You love him?"

"Yes—oh, yes, Con!" Her reply came swiftly, earnestly. "Can you forgive me? I—I know now that I must have loved him from the first. But I thought—oh, I can never explain, Con. I thought it was you. But after you went away, then—without you—I could see him. And soon I knew. Can you understand, Con?"

"Sure." He touched the pink palm of the sleeping baby, gently, with one finger. "It's all right, Phileda."

Queer, now, that he couldn't say what he wanted to say. This was what he had hoped—hoped desperately—to find. Forgive her? Why, bless her, he had given her into the hands of young Abel, with a prayer for luck. But now a voice inside of him kept whispering, "This could have been mine . . ."

"We named him Michael," said Phileda, and her eyes were on him, and he wondered with a start if she could tell what he was thinking. Women had such instincts. That would never do.

"I'm glad for you and Abel," he said, a little huskily. "I'll always be glad it turned out this way. Now sit down. I want to tell you about Rael."

"He—died?" she asked, and her eyes filled.

Con looked away. "He died happy, Phileda, with all that he wanted. Believe that. It's true. He asked me to tell you—'It's been worth it,' he said. Yes, he died happy. I swear it. The other prisoners were released awhile ago."

"Yes, I know," she answered. "And I knew Rael must have died, when he never came to find me. I thought you must have died, too—or joined those Avengers."

"The what? Oh—the Texas Avengers, you mean? I've heard about them. It's all over the country. Yes, some of the Expedition boys have formed a brother-hood of vengeance against Rajimo. I doubt if they'll get far with it. Probably make raids against the New Mexican wagon outfits along the Santa Fe trail, and knock over a few of Rajimo's dragoons."

"I'm glad you haven't turned to that, Con. It sounds like banditry."

"That's what Rajimo will call it, anyway," Con hedged. "There's going to be a lot more trouble down that way before— Well, now, here comes Abel running. Hey, Abel, *amigo!*"

LONG INTO THE NIGHT, over a fire outside the cabin, young Abel Fonley talked eagerly of his plans for the future, after Con brushed away his halting young explanations. Come winter, he'd have a good piece of land cleared for planting, and corn was selling high. Maybe he'd have enough to make a small cash crop, and then he could buy a cow. He badly needed a mule, but little Michael would have to have milk next year.

"He's going to be a fine big boy," he said proudly,

and smiled across at Phileda, whose glowing face reflected his pride.

"He will that," agreed Con, and leaned back from the light of the fire, gazing at the pair of them. So young they were, and so confident. Gone was all Abel's flighty fofuraw. He had grown steady and tough, with browned skin and hard hands. Thinner, but his eyes shone deep contentment. The boy had become a man, a man with a young wife and son to care for.

Next year, Abel went on, he'd build another room onto the cabin, and dig a well over there—right there where it was shady and close to the house. He was sure he could strike water at thirty feet. The ground was stony, but good soil. Grow anything. He had about sixteen hundred acres. Some day, when he had it all cleared, this would be the finest farm in all Kentucky. Couldn't they just see it?

Sure, they could see it—in his shining eyes. A fine big property with a tall white house, a big stable, a herd of cows, and children playing on the wide green lawn. . . .

Con met Old Nick's eye, and knew that his own thoughts were shared. There sat the cabin, a single room of hewn logs chinked with mud and straw. A puncheon floor and a sod roof. No well. No cow. No mule. Just an axe and a handmade plow, a borrowed nag—and a world of hope.

Phileda rose to retire. When she said her good-night, Con caught an expression in her eyes that brought a feeling of cold guilt to him. She was gazing at him, and it was as if his own inner doubts had reached her, for a shade of his doubt had clouded her eyes. She was a level-headed girl and could see more clearly than could Abel, blinded by his constant work and visions of the future.

Con called after her, almost roughly, "Wait, Phileda, I've got something for you and Abel." He rose, but Old Nick got up ahead of him and moved off.

"I'll git it, Con." He returned with one of Con's saddlebags and tossed it over.

It felt heavy when Con caught it, heavier than his one sack of gold warranted. Con felt inside, and again met Old Nick's eye and his brief nod. There were two sacks in the saddlebag, his own and Old Nick's, their shared profits from the long months of buffalo hunting.

"Abel," he asked, "how much did my brother Lorin borrow from you? Two thousand, was it? And Rael lent him three, didn't he, Phileda? That's five thousand, all told."

He plumped both heavy sacks into Abel's lap. "Here it is, more or less. Buy your cows and mules, hire your clearing done, and build your house. Next time I come, I want to see that big farm you've been prancing so gay about. Eh? Aw, run inside, the pair o' you, and do your crying together in the dark! Nick and I, we'll curl up here by the fire. Got to make an early start in the morning."

It was not yet morning when they quietly saddled. The murmuring inside the little cabin had aroused a baby's cry, but now all was silent in there.

"I'd like to've seen the kid awake," Con muttered. "Oh, well, it doesn't matter. Let's go, Nick."

They walked their horses away and mounted in the dark. "Where to, Con?" queried Old Nick, and grinned, knowing the answer.

Con sighed once, but he felt good. Rael would have thanked him in his gravely earnest way for what he had done tonight. He grinned back at the old hunter.

"Y'know, Nick, it's my opinion those Texas Avenger boys have got a right good idea!"

19. THE TEXAS AVENGERS

ALONG HERE, where the Arkansas River ran east from its meanderings down the Rocky Mountain slopes, the rutted tracks of the Santa Fe Trail were filled over by the ever-shifting sand dunes. North across the river rose the high terrace of the Great Plains, the underlying sandstone of the bluffs laid bare, carved by erosion into gaunt palisades, but the top as flat as a table and stretching into the barren distance. Lonesome country.

The forty-odd heavily armed and travel-worn men waited in ambush with their horses in one of the deep sand basins overlooking the bottomland of the river. Unofficial guerrilla warfare, epitomized by the Texas Avengers, was in full swing between Texas and the Mexican province of New Mexico.

Some three hundred miles to the southwest, below Spanish Peaks and over Raton Pass, lay Santa Fe.

East, some five hundred miles, at the American end of the trail, was the frontier town of Independence.

Lately, certain wealthy and powerful citizens of Santa Fe—after having looked covetously on the profits of the Missouri traders—had formed a syndicate and entered into the business. Rajimo, himself, was reputed to be its head. They were sending their own caravans over the trail of the Americans, and had begun a campaign to corner and control the rich trade, by means of exorbitant taxes imposed upon American goods brought into Santa Fe.

Along this eight-hundred-mile trail, at this time of year, a mule train or two from Santa Fe could reasonably be expected to pass on its way to the States, loaded with Mexican silver with which to finance the purchase of goods in Missouri for the Santa Fe syndicate. Usually they were guarded by a troop of Mexican dragoons until over the Arkansas Crossing and sometimes beyond. The forty-odd men waiting in the sand basin expected such a mule train to appear today. They expected, too, the accompanying hundred dragoons. The Mexican muleteers, scouts, hunters and *ciboleros* with the train would perhaps number another fifty, all armed. Forty against a hundred and fifty wasn't such bad odds, they considered, and the silver made it well worth the game. Somebody had suggested hopefully that perhaps Rajimo himself would be commanding the dragoon company. It wasn't likely, but the hope took hold and added a blazing eagerness to the waiting men. They were gaunt from short rations and long riding, but they had come hundreds of miles for a fight, and hunger only keened their savage edge.

Once they had had a leader—McCourtney, the Irish lieutenant. He had resigned his commission in the army of the Texas Republic, in favor of leading this guerrilla band of Texas Avengers. But McCourtney had got too far away from the bunch one day, while scouting for a crossing over the Cimarron, and a gang of Comanches jumped him.

They had only their horses and their guns. Nothing to lose but their lives, nothing to slow their free and fast travel but the demands of exhausted nature. There were men among them who had been hungrier, on the way down to the Santiago. There were others who had never seen Mexico, but who were just as tough and several shades more predatory. McCourtney, before he got himself killed, had given careless assent to a dozen bad-eyed Kansas rovers who asked to join his guerrillas. Most of the Texans had since regretted it. The Kansans did them no credit, were outlaws pure and simple, and wanted to do things their own way.

"I reckon," said Con, with a glance up at the sun, "they'll show up in an hour or two, unless they stopped for siesta. You say it was only ten miles up river where you spied 'em, Nick?"

"More or less," answered Old Nick, lying by him and squinting along the bottoms. "But they war takin' it easy. You know how they are—all holler an' no git-up. Good string o' mules, but overloaded as usual. A Mex jest can't git it through his head that— Say, do I see their dust?"

"It's them! Keep low, boys—here they come!"

The dragoons rode in squads along the mule train, the flat crowns of their high shako hats shining like bobbing discs in the sunshine, and the whole company making a brave show of military might. The heavily laden mules plodded along in a string, and in the rear rode a group of *ciboleros,* gay in stiff hats and tight leather pants, tasseled buffalo lances held upright in saddle sockets. In the lead of the column rode the dragoon officer, looking uncomfortable in his hot tunic and plumed hat.

Some of the crouching Texans cursed softly as they gave their weapons a last hasty going-over, and their eyes began to glare at sight of the hatedly familiar uniforms. Con thought of Rael dying in the Santiago, and of Rondo Kissane shot to death in the San Miguel plaza. Yet somehow he could rouse no sharp lust in himself. It was Rajimo he wanted to get his hands on.

Yarnell, blond giant leader of the Kansas rover gang, had ambitions to take McCourtney's vacant position as captain. He called out, "Soon's they pass that gritstone outcrop yonder, pour all y'got into 'em, boys!" His dozen followers had already spread out, nestling their rifles in grooves scooped in the sand.

Con whirled on the man. "We're no damned bushwhacking jayhawkers!"

He looked around at the Texans. "Boys, did we come all this way for a fight or a massacre? Are we Texans or just dirty renegades? Both, maybe!—but I say let's make a square fight of this. Let's get on our horses and rip into 'em with a bang and a holler. Hell, it's only four to one!"

Yarnell reared up, massive and truculent. "You crazy? We can lay here an' pick 'em off like . . ." He cursed as the Texans ran to their horses. "Four to one! They're crazy!"

In the confusion of untying horses and springing up into saddles, noise was not absent, and bridle-bits rang out clearly in the dry air. Somebody shook out a faded Texas flag and hoisted it on his rifle. Down on the bottomland a voice that was tinny and urgent barked a quick command.

Con, as he put his horse over the hump, saw the faces of the Mexican party turned upward toward him in alarm. Carbines were being brought into readiness and some of the dragoons were hastily dismounting to fire from behind their horses. The dragoon officer flung a glance backward along the column and called another command, anger in his tone, but the shouting of his own men drowned him out.

Discipline, Con thought as his horse slid and floundered down the sand hill, was a mighty fine thing if you could make it work when needed. He saw the officer rein his mount half around and with deadly calmness sight a pistol. The pistol spat dry bursts of sound, and a horse and rider crashed with snapping noises close behind Con. The yell of the Texans wailed high and wild, pierced by the staccato notes of Old Nick's ear-splitting war whoop, and the halted line of nervous mules flung up their heads and crowded into a tangle. Horses danced in fright and the shouting swelled to a panicky babble. Here and there along the disrupted column carbines cracked, but the firing was ragged and unorganized. The officer gunned his weapon empty, stood up in his stirrups, and drew his sword. He drew it with something of a challenging flourish, and Con lost all half-reluctance for this business as he lined straight out for him.

The two horses were meeting almost head on, but the officer scorned to rein aside. His stare settled on Con's head with the fine calculation of an expert butcher planning his initial cut at a carcass. It was a temptation to shoot him and avoid running under that long blade, but the gameness of the man demanded clean fighting. Con, bearing down on him at a dead run, estimated that the horses would hit right shoulder to right if neither shied off. At the last instant, with his eyes on the slender length of steel, he whipped his right leg free of the stirrup to save it from a mashing in the coming collision, and leaned far over to the left.

The sword flashed in an arc, and Con threw back his head, but the point ripped his face. The blade thudded solidly into the rawhide of his saddle. Then the impact of the colliding horses flung him forward and he lunged with his pistol at the tight-fitting tunic. The muzzle struck so hard it drove the butt past his palm, the hammer digging into his hand. The horse under him rebounded heavily from the impact and went to its knees, and Con completed his headlong spill.

The column was a column no longer, but a disorderly jumble of shouting men, rearing horses and scared mules. The Texans closed in with another yell, and as hand-to-hand battle flared up and down the bottomland, Yarnell and his Kansas rovers came charging belatedly down the sand hill to join in. Con rolled over on the ground, smothered with sand and his face running blood, and looked to see how things were going. The coming of the Yarnell bunch on the heels of the Texans had made it look as if the hills might be full of raiders. Without an officer, the dragoons reverted to their first instincts for self-preservation.

The officer sat up, one hand against his chest where the pistol had jabbed him, the other searching about for a weapon. He'd lost his sword and pistol, and his horse had bolted, but he wasn't yet through with fighting. His expression was of deep annoyance rather than fear. A horseman drew up near by, kicking sand over him, and he looked up. Con looked up, too, at the horseman. He still had his pistol in his hand, and he cocked it as he swung it up in line with the horseman's yellow head.

"Leave my man be, Yarnell, and go get one of your own!"

Yarnell sat still. His eyes were pale blue and bloodshot in the corners. He very slowly lowered his rifle. Without a word, but with his eyes distended, he whirled his horse and took off into the fight. A lot of the dragoons were strung out along the river bank, riding back westward in full flight, but some of them still held out and the *ciboleros* were putting up a scrap.

Con said, "Now, *Teniente,* use your head. Happen you find your gun, I'll for a fact have to shoot you."

The dragoon lieutenant met his gaze with black and acrimonious eyes, but ceased his groping search. He was a very much upset man, and the horrible indignity of his position plainly galled him. It was one thing to die as a soldier, but it was quite another to be knocked alive off his horse and see his command scattered while he sat sprawled here with a pain in his chest.

Con pulled out a handkerchief and wiped sand from the thin gash in his cheek. He and the *teniente* sat on the ground facing each other. "How're folks in Santa Fe?" he inquired. "Rajimo there? And Don Chavez?"

Stiffly, the officer inclined his ruffled head. He found his plumed shako and clapped it on firmly. "You will learn, I trust, from General Rajimo himself the excellent state of his health—when he catches you!" he retorted acidly. "He is the owner of this mule train!"

"No!" Con exclaimed. "That a fact? Well, well, now that's good news! Did I hurt you with that poke in the chest?"

"Very little," lied the officer. "Possibly less than I hurt you."

They rose and eyed each other. Con grinned amiably. "There's my horse. You ruined the saddle for looks with that cut, but it's still good enough to ride. Take the horse and light out, *amigo*. When you get back to Santa Fe give my regards to Rajimo, and tell him thanks for the silver. Yes, and remember me to Don Chavez and—uh—to his niece, the *Señorita* Peregrina."

The officer moved to the horse, concealing his feelings under a cloak of frigid unconcern. "And from whom shall I say the messages come, *Señor?*"

Con patted the nose of the horse. A good brute and it had held up well. "Oh—just say Don Desperado. They'll know. She will, anyway—the *señorita*. Tell her I'll be seeing her one of these days!"

"The young lady whom you mention," replied the officer icily, "is not in Santa Fe. She is in France—in a convent—where her guardian committed her for private reasons of his own!"

Con suddenly had a sick sensation of loss, even keener than he had experienced at the death of Rael. The blow came so unexpectedly that he could not at first gather his forces to take the hard hurt. Among all the possibilities that he had figured upon, this one had never entered into his calculations. She was so alive, so real and tangible in his mind. He could no more envisage her as completely lost to his reach than he could think of her as dead.

"Damn him!" he muttered, and again, "Damn him! When did he do it?"

Curiosity stirred in the officer's eyes. "Don Chavez did not bring his niece back to Santa Fe, but sent her to France from Mexico City," he replied. "It is presumed that she was sent against her will."

"I'll bet on that!" growled Con, and anger flooded him. "That prim old goat! What part of France?"

The officer elevated his shoulders. "That I do not know." He narrowed his eyes and added with malice, "Beauty and youth, *Señor,* are not always discreet— and indiscretions must be paid for, is it not so? The rule applies to all. A faraway convent for the indiscreet *doncellita. Si.* And death to the desperado!"

The tag end of his glib discourse stood by itself as a vow and a threat, meant as such. Back in Santa Fe, disgrace awaited an officer who returned in defeat. He flicked a salute and mounted quickly.

"*Adios, Don Desperado,* and may I live to see you hang!"

He was off in a gallop, making for the river, and Con watched him go. The fellow had nerve and defiance.

Poor Peregrina! Con had an acutely painful vision of her confined behind foreign convent walls, all her movements under the watchful eyes of black-robed women. So that was what he had sentenced her to, when he jumped the armed *criado* at La Caleta and fled through the *tierra caliente* to Vera Cruz. Why, she'd never stand it. Tame and monotonous days were not for the like of her. There were birds you killed by caging, and she was a light-winged young golden eagle if there ever was one, glorying in high flight and a full life.

"By God, I'll not have it!" he swore. "I'll not let 'em do that to her—she's mine!"

He had been watching the *teniente,* but not seeing him. Now he saw the fellow swimming the horse across the river and fighting the current. He'd better go easy there, or he and the horse would be sucked under. A little plume of white water rose and fell just beyond the swimming horse and rider, then another, closer in. Most of the firing had stopped, down along the bottomland, and the last dragoon had joined the rest in rout.

Con snapped around, scowling, and found the

source of the bullets that were whipping up the water. Yarnell stood by his horse, some of his Kansas rovers watching him critically as he sighted his rifle for his next shot.

Con started toward him. "Lay off, you!"

Yarnell turned his big yellow head without lowering the rifle. He stared briefly at Con, muttered something, and rested his cheek again at the butt. Con brought up his pistol and fired once.

Yarnell's rifle went off, but it was pointing far off the mark when the hammer fell, and the stock was splintered. The blond giant looked at it, and his followers looked at him. He turned and stared again at Con, dropped the rifle, and came walking at a slow gait. The walnut butts of his holstered pistols bobbed and shone in the sunlight as he paced his deliberate way, and his big hands hung just below their level.

They met and paused, a dozen yards apart, neither man showing much expression. Yarnell said heavily, "Ain't room for you'n me both in this outfit, Connegan!"

Con nodded. "That's my opinion, too!"

Some of the Texans drifted over and stood around, eyes still aflame with the aftermath of violence. Others, jockeying with the captured mule train, left off and watched. The Kansas rovers drew closer in behind Yarnell. Tension gathered swiftly, and suddenly they were not one party but two.

Yarnell dropped his stare to Con's pistol. He moved his hands without haste and unbuckled his gun belts, and Con did the same for his own. Each matched the other's movements, watchful and untrusting, until both stood stripped to pants, boots and shirts. The old scars on Yarnell's head, Con figured, proclaimed him a butter. One good butt of that hard head, with all that weight and muscle behind it, would end the fight, and then the boots would get in their work.

They advanced on each other squarely, and Yarnell's first blow came like a streak, a long and powerful drive that Con evaded with his chin but caught on his shoulder. It spun him around and sent him down. He rolled twice over, fast, and leaped up before Yarnell could get in a kick. Yarnell drew up, took a raking right in the mouth, and came on. Con got in another right and a left, and then Yarnell's fingers got a grip on his shirt. The scarred head came slamming at Con's face like a battering ram. Con twisted, swung Yarnell off balance, and got clear with half his shirt gone. He whipped his left at Yarnell's thick neck as the big man lurched by, but the Kansas rover was quick, amazingly quick. He whirled, and his hand clawed on Con's hair. There was no wrenching free of that grip. He kicked at Con's legs and again his head ducked to butt.

Con let himself go before the yellow head reached his face, and dragged Yarnell down with him. He struck three times before the agonizing strain on his scalp loosened and was up on his feet first, in time to use a knee that sent Yarnell down again before he had half risen. Yarnell rolled, bounded up, and came on with one eye watering. This time he tried to butt at once, without grappling first, and Con's vicious drive at his stomach brought a grunt. The next sent the yellow head up, pain straightening the snarling mouth, and Yarnell tripped to his knees.

"Y'got him, Con—y'got him!" sang out Old Nick. "Give 'im yer boots now—quick!"

Con wiped his face and stood out of reach of the long arms, waiting. Yarnell remained kneeling, watching his feet and ready to dodge. When the kick didn't come, he lunged, arms shooting out to grasp, and again Con used his knee. Yarnell gasped and rested on his hands. His head reared up slowly and he stared around at his Kansas men. One of them put a hand to his belt and began sliding out a knife to toss to him. Promptly, Old Nick's long skinning knife dropped at Con's feet.

"Save me his hair, Con!"

Yarnell shook his head. His bleared eyes followed the long knife as Con picked it up. "I'm through," he mumbled. "Next time . . ."

They broke up the mule train and split the silver by rough guess, and by night Yarnell and his rovers were gone with their share. Old Nick caught up the *teniente's* runaway horse and presented it to Con, and made an announcement loud enough for all to hear.

"I figger yo're *jefe* of this outfit, Con, ain't it so?"

"You figure wrong, Nick," said Con. "I'm quitting. This was Rajimo's mule train, but it's not likely we'd have the same luck again. Keep on, and the day will come when we'd be raiding everything along the trail. You know how it goes. Anyway, I've got business elsewhere."

Old Nick sighed but said nothing. Later, though,

riding with Con while the sky darkened overhead, he swore mildly at their two loaded mules for lagging and ventured a question. "Santy Fee?"

"Sure—Santa Fe," Con nodded. "We've got our stake, enough to buy a smallish wagon outfit and load. We'll join the next caravan pulling out of Independence."

"Kinda chancy, ain't it?"

Con ran a hand over his face. "Might be. But if I trim this beard right and shave my eyebrows, I could get by, don't you reckon? This cut on my face will leave a scar, and that'll help too. Yes, and I could wear specs."

Old Nick sniffed. "I'd still know you."

"Yeah? All right. I'll wear a patch over one eye. That ought to do it."

"You'll look like Cap'n Kidd then, sure 'nuff!"

"And after Santa Fe—if we're' still alive," Con ended, "I figure to head for France and break open a convent."

Old Nick stared silently ahead. After a while he hunched his shoulders and spat. "Go to France an' bust open a convent, huh?" he muttered dazedly. "By gopher, that even beats ol' Wolf Runner!"

20. THE SANTA FE TRAIL

TURN OUT!" roared the omnipotent Caravan Captain, and in the early morning light three hundred men tumbled out of their blankets, jerked on boots or moccasins, and rolled up their bedding.

The caravan was two months out from Independence, and just ahead lay the toughest part of the trail—the high mountain route to Santa Fe. Tonight, with luck, they would make camp at Hole-In-The-Rock on the Timpas, and there repair wagons and harness in preparation for the straining haul over Raton Pass.

"Catch up!" sang out the Caravan Captain. By virtue of past experience and the fact that he owned more of the loaded wagons than any other five men combined, Dall Burgwin had again won leadership when the caravan organized at the Council Bluffs rendezvous. Though domineering and officious, he was generally conceded to be as good a man for leader as any.

For a while the wagon corral presented the usual seemingly hopeless tangle of men, mules, oxen and horses, all lively and truculent in the cool morning air. Mules tried to dodge harness. Horses bucked saddles off and kicked at all four points of the compass. Oxen stubbornly refused to get under their yokes. But finally the last cursing teamster got his animals hooked up, vowing he'd shoot that off ox if 'twas his'n, and called out, "All set!"

Burgwin rose majestically in his stirrups and waved an arm. "Stretch out!"

The massive wagons began rolling toward the west, breaking corral formation and slowly reforming into a long double line until they stretched out, over a hundred, lumbering along behind plodding oxen and eight-mule teams. Off to the right and out of the dust rode Burgwin and the elite of the other trading proprietors, and far behind shuffled the *cavallada* under the eye of the wrangler.

One of the wagons swung out of line and drew to a halt. Unlike the majority of the proprietors, its owner rode beside his teamster on the wagon seat, his saddle horse hitched to the tailgate. But then, this trader hadn't mixed much with the others since joining the caravan, and his manner did not encourage casual familiarity. He was tall, black-haired, with a wide spread of shoulders and a flat waist that was seldom without its pendent pair of Colt pistols and a knife. His short black beard, cut in imperial style, and his slender line of mustache, gave him the stamp of a Frenchman. His remarkable eyebrows, pointed slightly upward at the outer corners, gave him an expression of faintly satanic inquiry and made his lean brown face seem long. A thin scar ran aslant his right cheek and he wore a black patch over his left eye. Altogether, he was marked by the caravaneers as a man of mystery, an enigma, an adventurer of the world with a dark past. His one unshaded eye had a disturbing trick of pinning an unwinking stare upon the too inquisitive. His teamster, a thickset ruffian with only a grizzled stubble of beard, matched him for spareness of speech. A hard pair.

Burgwin came riding over to the halted wagon, frowning in his oppressively officious way. "Hey, get back there in line, Nagennoc!"

The single unwinking eye rested on him with the

impersonal regard of a microscope turned upon an insect. The one-eyed man voiced a gentle correction, with a touch of foreign accent.

"*Monsieur* Nagennoc, if you please—*Mister* Burgwin!*"

Burgwin flushed dull red. He had had a few little skirmishes with this sinister-visaged Frenchman already since leaving Independence, and had not come off best. It was not that Monsieur Nagennoc openly flouted his authority. Nothing so tangible. Just a sort of knowing and contemptuous amusement veiled behind polite words and that cool stare. Burgwin shifted his attention to the teamster.

"What're you stopping for?"

The teamster dropped unhurriedly from the wagon and tied his lines before making reply, and then he wasted no words. He merely jerked a thumb in the general direction of the team and began hauling on the tug-chains. Burgwin looked as if he wanted to make one of his famed sarcastic criticisms, but thought better of it. He snorted and rode on to his group.

Monsieur Nagennoc stepped around to the off side of his wagon. Here he was fairly well shielded from sight and the dust of the passing *cavallada* made a curtain. He drew a small mirror and a razor from his pocket and examined his pointed eyebrows. Stiff little black hairs were beginning to show themselves just below the sharp upward slant. He shaved them off carefully. It was a nuisance, but it was not a task that he could attend to under the gaze of the camp.

"Y'know, Nick," he murmured pensively, "I'd like

to give Burgwin another whipping some time, as good as I handed him that day in St. Louis!"

"Go easy, Con," growled Old Nick. "We're sittin' on gunpowder as 'tis. Ain't no sense to light a fire on it. Burgwin don't like us, nohow. I've see'd him eyin' us like he's studyin' did he ever see us afore. Folks don't fergit you easy, Con. Sure, you look changed a heap—but you can't change what's inside you. Folks kinda feel it."

Old Nick, himself, had shaved off his whiskers and cut his hair short. He was letting it all grow out again, but it would be years before even his various Indian wives would know him, if he ever ran across any of them in the meantime.

They got started again, caught up with the train, and took their places in the rolling lines. Their wagon was not overly loaded, and they had a good mule team. Most of the traders' wagons carried precious loads of velvets, fine cambrics, silks, woolen goods, ribbons, bombazines, crepes, iron hardware, hand-forged axes and hatchets, knives, traps, powder, and a multitude of other merchandise. Con carried baled linen, which had been the best he could do with the finances at hand.

Toward afternoon the wrangler let out a hail, and word came along that they were being overhauled by the Mexican caravan that had followed them steadily all the way from Independence. The Mexican outfit had kept within sight of the big Missouri wagon train for protection through the Pawnee country along the Arkansas. Now that peril was passed they were speeding up to beat the rival *Americanos* in to Santa

Fe. It was ethical, as trader ethics went, but Burgwin could be heard bedamning and cursing. The first train in would skim the cream of the market and get the best prices. Not only that, but Rajimo would see to it that the Missouri traders were held up and delayed by interminable customs house inspections until all the Mexican goods were sold.

"By thunder," bellowed Burgwin, glaring back along the trail at the coming pillar of dust, "in the old days I'd have known how to stop 'em! Jump 'em, burn their wagons, and . . ."

He broke off when some of his group slyly grinned. Nowadays he was a respectable and wealthy merchant, having no truck with such brigandish methods, but there were those who remembered that he had once called himself a fur trader and lived with a roving band of Comanches who got his skins for him without traps, in return for whisky and guns.

The Mexicans overhauled and passed with ease the plodding oxen and creaking wagons. Their train was a motley collection of pack mules and carts. They couldn't carry as much as the big Conestoga wagons, but they could get over the country quicker. There was even a light Jersey hack in their train, a spindly wheeled thing with rolled side-curtains, driven by a ragged boy and used as a private carriage. A fair-skinned youth rode inside, and he evidently had no liking for the thick dust. He was enveloped in a traveling cloak buttoned up to the neck, and breathed through a kerchief tied around his mouth and nostrils. Another large silk kerchief was tied around his head, with a soft black hat pulled down over it, in the style often affected by the more fastidious travelers.

By afternoon the Mexican train had pulled out of sight, and it was not camped at Hole-In-The-Rock when the Americans circled their wagons there just before nightfall. Teams were unhitched and turned to graze, men took their stand on night guard, and cookfires sprang up. Groups gathered around the big kettles and coffeepots and a measure of contentment descended upon the camp after hunger became satisfied. Tongues loosened, pipes were lighted, men laughed again. The fairer-minded traders allowed that maybe the cussed Spaniards had only done the natural thing, pushing ahead when they could. And that gave rise to a swapping of yarns, wherein each narrator told in lusty detail just how he or his trader boss had outsmarted his rivals in the past.

Con grinned at Old Nick in the flickering light of their fire. "A crowd of Mississippi gamblers would sound like honest men here!" he murmured. "Hello, who's coming?"

Running hoofs beat up from the south. Somebody rose and shouted, " 'Ware the guard!"

A guard outside the ring of wagons called his peremptory challenge. "Who comes?" The talk broke off, every man on his feet and listening.

The drumming of the horse continued, and its rider could be heard screaming words in Spanish. Soon he was up with the wagons, surrounded by men, still screaming in a mad hysteria of fear. *Los Tejanos! Los Vengativos—!*

They dragged him into the firelight. He was a ragged Mexican boy, the same who had driven the Jersey hack. His mount was a mule without a saddle. He either knew no English or had had it scared out of him, and few of the Americans knew more than a smattering of Spanish. Con shouldered his way through the crowd to the boy. His own Spanish was more comprehensive than faultless.

"*Que tiene?*" he queried. "What is the matter?"

The shivering boy gulped and poured out his story. *Los Tejanos*—the dreaded and terrible Texas Avengers—they had come swooping down upon the Mexican train but a few hours ago! *Si*—near the Rio de las Animas Perdidas. First a horrible blast of gunfire from hidden places that dropped men without warning, then they came, charging and making hideous noises, and what could the muleteers and drivers do but flee? He, himself—Vicente—had leaped to a runaway mule and so escaped, but lost his way. The boy rolled his eyes. *Por Dios,* but he had looked back at terrible things done. He had seen a great giant of a *Tejano* knock down a fleeing muleteer and then shoot him as he lay. That one, of course he was the fierce Don Desperado—the same one who had led the attack months ago on the great Rajimo's mule train— did the *señores* not think so?

Yes, the *señores* thought so, all but one who nevertheless made no comment.

Burgwin said in a strangled voice, "This'll ruin us! Rajimo will swear we were at the bottom of it!"

"That's right for a fact," muttered somebody. "We

won't be tradin' in Santa Fe this trip, nary one of us. Lucky if Rajimo don't use this for an excuse to confiscate our goods!"

That was Con's first thought, too. Whether he believed them guilty or not, Rajimo would seize this chance, and accuse them of having instigated a murderous raid upon their Mexican rivals. The circumstances were too propitious for him to pass up. Here was his opportunity at last to declare with much self-righteous wrath a ban against the Americans, and to take over full control of the trade. Con swore to himself. It did begin to look to him as if all his efforts to enter Santa Fe were cursed.

The boy Vicente was babbling again. His *muy grande patron*—the handsome young *caballero* who had hired him as coachman—he had not escaped. He had snatched the reins and tried to drive away, but the savage *Tejanos* overhauled him. Vicente sobbed. What would they do to his gentle young master? Such a kind young *caballero,* and of the Chavez family.

Con caught the familiar name. "Chavez, you say?"

Vicente nodded vigorously. Of the family of the *grande* Don José Chavez, no less. From Spain. His name was Don Patricio and he had come to surprise Don José with a visit, he had told Vicente. He was traveling alone. Ah, but Don José would be prostrated when he heard of this.

The Americans looked at one another. Burgwin for once forgot to curse. "That settles it!" he declared heavily. "When this news reaches Santa Fe—!"

"We better make up a party and go see what's left,"

put in Con. "Might be some wounded lying around."

He had forgotten his accent for the moment, and became aware of Burgwin's quick scrutiny. An observant man, Burgwin, at all times. The others didn't notice the slip. Men ran and caught up their horses. Soon the party was made up and they moved out of the camp, the boy with them.

It was midnight before they caught sight of glowing ashes and a few dying flames. Here the trail ran along the foot of Spanish Peaks to the swift-running Rio de las Animas Perdidas, called the Purgatoire by the far-roving French-Canadian trappers, and known as the Picketwire to most Americans. Giant cottonwoods lined the course of it, and the trail approached it over and around a rolling succession of shrub-dotted hills.

"Good spot for a *'boscada* all right," allowed Old Nick from the depths of his Apache experience.

They rode into the hollow where the smoldering remains of the carts glowed. A few bodies lay here and there. Con looked down at powder marks that blackened a hole in the forehead of one. The Mexican had been shot to death at close range while he lay wounded. Con brought his eyes back from their somber inspection and met Old Nick's bleak look. "Is this what they've come to—the Avengers?" he muttered. "Shooting from ambush—murdering the wounded! It's senseless! Damnable! What goods they couldn't carry off on the mules, they ruined, then they set fire to the carts. I swear, Nick, if Texans did this I'll never again brag I'm a Texan!"

The boy Vicente ran about searching. He came up to

Con, as to one who could understand. *"Mi patron no aqui! Cocha no aqui!"* His young *patron* was not here, dead or alive, nor the Jersey wagonette.

Con and Old Nick scouted for sign while Burgwin and the rest grimly went over the bodies and searched the charred remains of the carts. Old Nick was first to halloo a find, and Con joined him.

"Here y'are." Old Nick was on his hands and knees. "They took off east after they finished. Took the mules an' that dinky wagin. Here's the tracks. That wagin won't slow 'em if they hitched extry mules to it—which they did." He ran his gnarled, wise hands into the ruts. "Deep. They loaded it up. I reckin they musta took that young Don along."

Con nodded, speculating. "They could see he was a rich somebody. Likely took him along for hostage, happen they need one. If they were Comanches, now, I'd say they took him for ransom."

"They was Comanches—white ones!" grunted Old Nick. "That's wuss. You see what they did to them muleteers they catched? Me, I've did consid'able fightin' in my time. I've fit Injun style an' white style—killed 'em brown, red an' white—but I never yet massa*creed* a man when he war down on his back. Ugh!"

Con swung back onto his horse. "I reckon I'll follow those tracks," he said quietly. "No, Nick, you stick with our outfit. Eh? No, I'm not hunting suicide. If that *'boscada* bunch are some of the Avengers, they'll listen to reason when I make myself known to 'em."

"What if they ain't Texans?"

"That'll call for something else," Con admitted. "But you see how it is. We've got to do something to counteract this dirty business or we're all blowed up. If I can save that young Don it'll give us a clean bill— and Monsieur Nagennoc will be riding high in Santa Fe!"

"Or dead on the Cimarron desert!" growled Old Nick.

Con leaned over and slapped the old renegade on the back. "Lay your bets on the M'sieur, old-timer!"

He heeled off, following the tracks, knowing they would lead to the river. The raiders would ford the Purgatoire at its nearest point. If they were Texans they'd then swing southeast for home. If they weren't Texans they'd probably strike out for the desert route to the Cimarron. The tracks would tell, later on.

21. CAMP ON THE CARRIZO

THEY WERE CAMPED in an arroyo when Con rode up within sight of their fires the next night, and it looked as if they had chosen the site with care for secrecy and defense. The stream ran low and shallow, little more than a trickle, leaving a wide and level bed exposed, and here they had made their camp. They were sheltered by the high banks, their fires reasonably hidden, and they had staked their horses out to grass above the bank. Off to the south, seen clearly by day, rose the straight-topped mass of a long mesa, high above the surrounding desert plain.

Con thought the arroyo might be the Carrizo, running into the Cimarron sixty miles or so farther to the southeast. The mesa, that he had steadily approached all afternoon while following the tracks, resembled descriptions he had heard of Mesa de Mayo. He drew rein on his tired and drooping horse and took survey of the situation. From the drift of the trail, the raiders were not lining for Texas, but for the Kansas badlands.

"Got to get it out of my mind that they're Avengers," he mused, "though it might be a bunch of the boys gone bad and strictly on the loot. You don't run with the wolves and not learn to howl sooner or later. I wonder, now, how edgy on the trigger they might be if a man let out a real polite squall and rode in a-visiting?"

He could see the outline of the Jersey wagonette. It was drawn up on the near bank, its team unhitched. The pack mules had been unloaded on the bottomland and the men used scattered packs to sit on while they ate around the fires.

Con bit his thumb for luck. "Only one way to find out."

His tired horse, smelling water and its own kind, grew festive. Con nudged it on, but held it down to a walk. That the encamped raiders were jumpy had to be taken into account, and a proper etiquette had to be observed in the approach. He sent out a low halloo. The sitting men had their moment of alert stillness, before they rose and crisscrossed in swift activity, slipping out of the firelight. Yes, they were jumpy,

Con decided, very jumpy, but one lone figure remained seated as he drew closer. He had covered half the distance to the arroyo and was wondering uncomfortably how many gun-sights were seeking him in the darkness, when an answering curt hail rapped at him.

"Que es?"

Playing Mex, eh? Well, he might as well let 'em know it didn't catch. "Just one lone white *amigo,*" he called, and uttered a short laugh. "Don't shoot, boys— I'm too tired to duck!"

He passed by the Jersey wagonette and reined in on the bank. Here some of the firelight reached him, but the raiders stayed in cover. He leaned on his saddle horn wearily, and ran an eye over the camp. "Boys, I smell coffee and fried meat. Where's your manners?"

A shadow lengthened behind a pile of packs and a man slowly rose, rifle in hand. Others rose with him and more drifted in from the outer darkness. The lone seated figure hadn't stirred, and its face was turned toward Con. The clothes—the traveling cloak and black fedora pulled down over the kerchief-wrapped head—were those of the youth, Don Patricio, who had ridden in the wagonette, but the face was dark now, darker than the shadows warranted. Con rested his attention on the first man who had risen into sight, and he leaned more lightly on his saddle horn. He flicked his lucky thumb with the forefinger, condemning it for letting him down this badly. The man was Yarnell, big and blond, with a twist to his nose and a dent in his upper lip, mementos of his fight on the Arkansas.

Some of the others Con recognized as Yarnell's rovers, but the rest were strangers, and not all of them white men.

"Who in hell might you be, an' where'd you come from?" Yarnell questioned, and his eyes were restless. He stood with head cocked, listening. They all were listening, keyed to catch sounds that might betray the coming of other riders in the night.

Con gave thanks to his black eye-patch, French beard and shaved eyebrows. They had got him by Burgwin for two months, and it seemed reasonable to hope they'd get him by again in this poor light. He eased his horse down the bank.

"The name's Nagennoc." He bared his white teeth in a grin at Yarnell, and dismounted. "I'm with the *Americano* wagon train. The boys sent me to talk to you. You've put us all in mighty bad with that raid."

Yarnell grounded the butt of his rifle and folded his hands over the muzzle. "We're right busted up about it."

"I can see that," Con returned equably. "Now, there's nothing personal about this and there's no need to go on the prod. A man's got to make his living the best way he can, and I've made mine in ways I don't talk about in strange company. I trailed you here to talk business. There's nobody behind me. I came alone."

"You take a fool's chances!"

"Chances, maybe, but not a fool's," countered Con. "I take you for *hombres* of my own kind. I wouldn't say we're fools, any of us. Am I right?"

Yarnell stuck a toe at a fire blackened pot. "He'p y'self to coffee." The others relaxed and settled around the fires, their eyes on Con.

Con poured hot coffee into a tin mug and speared a slab of fried meat from the nearest pan with his knife. He played for time while he sought inspiration for moves ahead. Eating, he let his glance travel to that lone and silent figure in the cloak, and he jerked the point of his knife that way.

"What d'you aim to do with that?" he asked.

Suspicion reappeared in Yarnell's steady stare. "What's your guess?"

Con shrugged. "I might's well admit he's the reason I'm here. We traders need proof we didn't set you boys onto that Mex outfit. He'd do, if I took him safe and sound into Santa Fe. *Sabe?*"

He saw Don Patricio look up swiftly, and caught a better glimpse of the face. Its darkness came from smeared dirt, through which the skin showed pale and white in places. The shine of the dark eyes under the hat-brim held an anxious urgency. Strangely stirred, Con had to force himself to snatch his attention away and wait patiently for Yarnell's comment.

Yarnell said slowly, "I *sabe*. That's reason'ble. Mebbe I'll 'blige you. We didn't trove so much out o' that Mex outfit—mostly cloth an' stuff. That's why we brung him along. He looks like he oughta fetch ransom."

"Five hundred in gold?" Con suggested. He had that much in his money belt, held in reserve for the payment of customs duties on his goods in Santa Fe.

Yarnell looked interested, but shook his head. "His name's Chavez, he says. I've heard that's a powerful rich Santa Fe family. They'd pay more. Ain't he the lily-fingered young macaroni, though! Y'oughta see his hands—whiter'n a burro's belly. I done tol' him if he made a move to run off I'll strip him nekkid an' tie him to my horse's tail. He's been good as a woolly lamb since."

"How would you collect ransom on him?" Con asked. "Those Santa Fe folks will cross you up on that and take your hide. Better take my offer."

"No." Yarnell's scarred mouth set stubbornly. "I've got my mind on five thousand. Got to split with my boys, here, an' five hundred wouldn't spread far. I'll collect—or stake him out for the Comanches to find! Can you read Spanish? I want him to write a paper for his folks, an' I want it to read right. Mebbe I oughta rough him up some first, an' put him in the right mind."

The bent head of Don Patricio lifted again, and again Con caught the urgent flash in the dark eyes. Con finished his coffee and rose. "Might not need to. S'pose I talk to him?"

"Sure." Yarnell stared after him. "Say, you got that five hundred on you?"

Con looked back. "No." His spine tingled a little as he walked on to the seated Don Patricio.

"I am trying to help you." He spoke in Spanish, pausing over the cloaked prisoner. "Would your relatives in Santa Fe pay five thousand dollars ransom for you? Young fellow, look up at me—I'm talking to you!"

The head rose hesitantly, half defiantly. The kerchief was pulled down low over forehead and ears, and the brim of the soft fedora was bent down all the way around. The cloak still was fastened up to the chin, and what could be seen of the face was as dirty as if purposely smeared. But Con stood paralyzed, staring down at close range.

It was the face of Peregrina.

Yarnell called out, "Hey, what d'you see so queer about him?"

Con straightened up, dove into his chaotic mind for a plausible reply, and ended up by waving a gesture that could have meant anything. He sat down, blinking at the head that now was bowed again. Like different cards being turned over rapidly, reasons and explanations became plain to him. The kerchief and big fedora—to hide her head of hair. The voluminous traveling cloak—to hide the lines of a body that could never otherwise be mistaken for a boy's. The smeared and dirty face, that she must have done hastily at the last minute when she knew disaster had struck the caravan.

Yet, with all these tricks, how had she fooled them? Con was astonished. He would have known, himself, that this was a girl. Why, even at a distance he had felt a strange sort of . . . Hell, no, it was because it was she—Peregrina! Something inside of him had known at once that it was she, dirty face and all. But she couldn't fool Yarnell and his crowd much longer. They had been busy today, on the jump and driving the captured pack mules. They wouldn't give her anything like the respectful privacy that she had enjoyed as a private traveler in the Mexican caravan. Con recalled Yarnell's casual threats, and a blazing rage ran through him. He spoke, holding his voice to a low pitch and still speaking in Spanish.

"You've got to get away from here!"

"Si, Señor!" came the whispered response.

Her tone, and the formal term, brought to Con a mingling of surprise, relief and some chagrin. So she hadn't recognized him through his disguise, though he had recognized her through hers. Well, that was a woman for you. A man, now, knew his woman no matter how she dressed or how dirty her face might be. He felt disappointed in her for the first time, though he knew he should be glad that she had not recognized him. He moved closer to her, so that the left holster under his coat pressed against her.

"That's a pistol," he said softly. "Can you hook it out without being seen? I've got another."

He felt a movement of her arm, then the sliding touch of her hand. She trembled a little. The weight of his left holster lightened, and her hand vanished under the cloak with the pistol. Con felt better then. He didn't know what sort of shot she was, but he knew she'd have the nerve to use the pistol the right way if she had to. She raised her head a little and glanced sidelong at his face.

"Gracias!" she whispered. Aloud, she said, as if in reply to a query, "Yes, my name is Don Patricio Chavez. Don José is my uncle."

Con rose. *"Alerta,* Don Patricio!" he murmured, and

walked back to Yarnell.

"Five thousand, h'm?" He met Yarnell's speculative scrutiny. "No less?"

"Not a cent less!"

Con spread his hands. "You win. We traders need that youngster to put us in the clear. I'll pay it."

Several men stood up, their eyes on his hands, and Yarnell questioned gently, "You got that much cash?"

Con grinned companionably at him. "A man picks up habits, here and there, and one of 'em is to bury your gold before riding into a strange camp."

Yarnell nodded his comprehension. "Good habit. I'll go with you an' get it." He put on his leather coat.

"Might's well bring the youngster, too," Con suggested. "Save me coming back here. How about throwing in a horse and saddle for him?" The thing was shaping up very well. Yarnell had taken the bait. With just him to attend to, away from his bunch . . .

Yarnell quirked his scarred lip in peccant humor. "Why, sure," he agreed affably. "We'll make it a party. Boys, some o' you saddle a horse for our young macaroni an' bring him along!"

It was dark away from the campfires. Con's grulla horse, rebellious at leaving the water and grazing, fought the bit and attempted to turn back. Yarnell swore when it bumped into him for the fourth time, and dropped behind.

"I swear, sometimes I think I'll take to riding a mule," Con grumbled, yanking his mount's head forward again. "Say, can any of you see the tracks I made coming in to your camp? I've lost 'em, fooling with this damned jughead. I made my cache in the roots of an uncommon big mimosa, somewhere along here. Maybe we better turn back to camp and wait for daylight."

His suggestion was ignored. Yarnell had brought four of his crowd along. They spread out and began searching for the tracks and the big mimosa, bending low from their saddles and peering down at the ground. Yarnell turned and beckoned curtly for Peregrina to come up ahead of him where he could keep an eye on her. She had been riding with his rovers. Con circled about, aiding in the search, but having more trouble with his fractious horse. The exasperated grulla finally threw a hump in its back and bucked in a tentative attempt to unseat him. Yarnell snickered as Con loomed up in the darkness with one arm wrapped around the brute's neck. Con swore convincingly, got his seat back, and lashed with his rein ends. The grulla bawled, leaped, switched ends, and fetched up heavily against Yarnell.

It had all the appearance of accident, and it was in the nature of things that Yarnell's horse should promptly spook and rear up, pawing. But Yarnell piled out of his saddle and took the reins with him. He lit on his feet on the wrong side, with his right hand jabbing under his coat, and Con knew that the man's instincts for danger had given him warning.

One of the searching men called through the darkness, "Who got spilled?"

Con spent two seconds he couldn't afford in aiming a kick at Peregrina's mount. The horse blew a snort and took off at a run, its cloaked rider bent over and tugging at the reins. Con brought his heel back against his grulla's ribs, but the animal's temper was up and it went into a dancing spin, and Con dug for his pistol.

Yarnell's gun exploded its brief flash and roar. Con whistled an involuntary "Umph!" in an escaping rush of breath, hit hard in his middle, and sick agony interfered in his nerves. At the second jolting whirl of his horse he fired, and Yarnell's horse broke away, leaving Yarnell standing with one hand outstretched as if blindly groping. Con chopped down the Colt's pistol and fired again.

"Hell take you, there's all the ransom you get from me!" he swore, and shifted heavily in his saddle to meet whatever might be coming from the others.

They were heading in, calling through the darkness to Yarnell, who wasn't standing any more, but the next move of the grulla put Con's back toward them. Somebody rode up in a stamping smother, shooting, and Con leveled the Colt. He almost pulled trigger, but changed his aim fast to another who charged in. The first rider, now halted and shooting, wore a cloak tangled by the wind, and was not shooting at him.

The oncoming horseman let out a yell and swerved, and caught two shots broadside. His body lost rhythm with the rise and fall of his horse, bumping, and fell backward while the horse ran on. Two more riders showed up dimly, warily circling, shouting to Yarnell. The darkness made them unsure of anything, until Con got off another shot that turned one of them off in a straight run back for the camp, where commotion sounded faintly. The grulla took it into his head to follow. Con hauled its head around and got it straightened out the right way. As he got back to where he had started, somebody rode across his path, and he saw it was Peregrina.

"Get that damned nag going, you!" he called, and pain put savage temper into his voice. "I don't want to pile up on you—I'm having it tough enough as 'tis!"

In the darkness it was not possible to see much of the terrain, and they had to trust to their horses' sense. Peregrina's mount was fresh, but the grulla wanted to quit. Con looked back, wincing as he turned, but he could see nothing now of the camp. Yarnell's crowd might or might not be pounding along in pursuit, but if so they were too far behind to be heard. "See if you can find a place to cross the river," Con called out. "My horse won't last, and we've got to hide out."

Peregrina veered close over to the high bank. Where a cave-in had cut the bank she wheeled and put her horse down the soft-sand slope. Con followed in her tracks. He heard the sand suck at the grulla's hoofs when he reached the bottom, and yelled a quick warning, but too late. Here the bottom was low and the river spread out in shallow streaks. He drew up to turn back, recognizing the danger of quicksand. Peregrina had evidently recognized it, too, for she sawed reins, but her horse was plunging in too fast and the footing was too treacherous. The animal slithered, went in up to its belly, and floundered headlong into the shallow water. Its rider kicked clear, threw herself backward, and hit the wet sand with a soggy smack.

"Good Lord of Texas—what next!" groaned Con, and began tearing loose the short catch-rope tied to his saddle. The grulla snorted and backed as it felt itself sinking, and all Con's kicking couldn't stop its wary retreat.

The need for the rope was made unnecessary. Peregrina crawled out, wet sand clinging to her, and reached his side. Her sinking horse squealed its terror, and Con exchanged the rope for his pistol. After the single shot the horse sank over and ceased its vain struggling.

"That," said Con, "leaves the two of us with one played out nag! Don't you know any better than to barge into a thing like that?"

"I'm—sorry," came the halting reply. "You had best ride on, and—and I'll . . ."

Con reached down and hauled her up by the bedraggled cloak, and she scrambled behind him. She had lost her hat, and the kerchief was all awry, letting wet hair tumble down, but Con passed no comment on that. He forced the grulla to climb back up the bank and pointed it away from the river.

"We won't try that again," he growled. "Better we swing south around that mesa and see can we strike the desert route to Wagon Mound. Have to risk Indians. Have to do some walking, too. This horse won't go far, carrying double. Don't hold me so tight—I got a stomach ache!"

She quickly changed her hold on him for a grip on his coat. "How far are we from Santa Fe?" she asked, and from her movements behind him Con guessed she was tucking the betraying hair back under the kerchief.

"I don't know exactly," responded Con. "Should be more water south of the mesa, and maybe a stray buffalo or two farther on down. We'll need to eat, and we've got to keep from ruining this horse. With luck we might make Santa Fe in a week."

"A—a week?"

"Maybe, I said. Have to travel nights awhile and hole up during daylight, 'count of Indians. Quit wriggling around with your hair—I know you're a woman! Incidentally, happen Apaches catch us alive, you're my wife, understand? Apaches have some morals. Sometimes they sort of halfway respect a married woman, I've heard, but they got none at all for the—uh—for what they figure is the other kind. And what they'd do to a gal wearing man's pants, I swear I can't guess. They'd figure she was a hussy for sure!"

"Oh!" she said faintly.

"Sure do hope we strike water again," pursued Con. "Not that we can't do without drinking for a day or so, but we both need baths—you particularly. Your face was dirty enough to begin with, and then you had to go fall in that sludge. You're a sight!"

She said nothing, stiff and trembling behind him, and even his pain couldn't keep him from grinning into the darkness, enjoying her speechless wrath.

A T SUNUP they stumbled upon a spring south of the mesa. It flowed into a ravine, forming a stream and a natural oasis of greenbriar thickets, wild berries and good grass. The grulla, plodding at a walk, halted on the rim and Con eased sorely out of the saddle after Peregrina dropped off.

It took some search to find a path down to the water. Once on the bottom they drank, and Con had to drag away the grulla to keep it from foundering itself. He off-saddled, staked the animal to grass, and then lay down wearily with his eyes closed. When he grew aware of silence he opened his unshaded eye and found a forlorn and muddy figure sitting on the grass.

"Take your bath," he muttered, and closed his eyes again. "You're safe. Right now I wouldn't raise my head to look at Cleopatra splashing in the Nile. I'm too done up. Better wash your clothes, too, while you've the chance."

He rolled over on his face, struggled out of his coat, and tossed it aside. "You can wear that while they're drying. Wake me up if you see anybody—but not for less than ten Indians or three white men. Less than that you can well handle!"

He did not know how long he slept, but when he woke the sun was high and his body felt as if it had been kicked around. His first look was for Peregrina. Her clothes hung drying over a wild currant bush. He turned his head, seeking her. She sat huddled in his coat, asleep sitting up, beside her the pistol he had given her. The coat was big around the shoulders, but she had had to curl her legs under her in order to make it do as a robe.

There she sat, in the only position compatible with modesty, like Buddha turned young and beautiful. Con wondered why she hadn't taken the saddle blanket, until he discovered he had it over himself. He didn't recall taking it. Her face was clean and she had done something to her hair. Con didn't know just what, but it wasn't in a tangle. It lay spread out over her shoulders, the ends still wet, but the rest in smooth waves, drying.

The old strong stir rippled through him. "Never saw anything so perfect. Still the fighter, too. I might've known they couldn't keep her shut up in any French convent! Wonder if she's got any suspicion who I am? Hard to fool the minx, so it is, and well I know it!"

He sat up painfully and looked down at his shirt. Surprisingly, he saw no blood. He peeled off the shirt and a gold piece fell out. The long pouch of his leather money belt, worn next to his body, was burst open as if hit with a blunt hatchet. His right side and part of his stomach were badly discolored by the spread of an angry bruise.

"Well, devil an' all!" he said aloud, and looked up as Peregrina moved. "Excuse my partial undress," he drawled, seeing her startled eyes. "I've just found one more proof that hard cash is a man's best protection. I could've sworn I was bleeding to death all night, but Yarnell's bullet only smacked my—uh—financial standing. Cold water might help this bruise. A dandy, isn't it?"

Passing her, he gave her the blanket. "I doubt you're as comfortable as you look. Roll up in this and stretch out. Cover up your head, too."

She tried to wither him with a haughty glance. "Why should I cover my head?"

"Because," answered Con primly, sitting by the spring and pulling off his boots, "I like privacy in my bath!"

Her head was under the blanket when he got his second boot off, and the gasping sound he heard under it could have come from shocked modesty, anger or laughter.

T HEY LEFT THE RAVINE at sundown and pushed on toward the south. "Not much nourishment in those wild berries, is there?" observed Con, digging a seed out of his teeth. "Tomorrow we'll eat meat if I have to run down a jack rabbit."

He walked while Peregrina rode, and he noted that she was candidly studying him. She'd soon be asking questions, he felt, and he decided to beat her to it. "How did you happen to be with that mule train?" he asked, as she opened her lips to speak. "And what made you wear pants?"

She flushed at his second question, and Con was amused at her. He had noticed before that there was a natural modesty in her, a maidenly delicacy that remained unblunted by her other qualities. "I joined it at Independence," she replied. "No other women were with it, so I posed as a young man traveling privately. Your name is Nagennoc? You are French?"

Con gravely inclined his head. "Yes. But why are you traveling alone? The circumstances must be—ah—unusual." He fixed her with his unshaded eye, smiling gently, but not innocently. His narrow mustache and jaunty beard did not lend themselves to innocence, and his upturned eyebrows and black patch looked more sinister than harmless.

"I ran away from a convent in France," she explained calmly, and smiled. *Votre France, elle est très belle, M'sieur—n'est-ce pas?"*

That stumped Con. He knew no French; hadn't the remotest inkling of what she had asked. But he slid out of the dilemma as best he could. "You will please forgive me if I refrain from conversing in what was once my native tongue," he apologized with cool gravity.

"There is—uh—a tragedy in my life," he added after some swift inventive thought, and sighed heavily for her benefit. "Powerful enemies conspired against me, and I was banished from my lovely France. On the day that I became an exile, I swore an oath never to speak my native tongue until the unjust disgrace is lifted from my name. Nor—hem—do I wish to hear it spoken."

"How terrible for you," murmured Peregrina softly. "It must have been a bitter experience."

Con shrugged tragically. "Yes. Er—your family is in Santa Fe? Will you not be sent back to the convent?"

Peregrina shook her head. "I think not. My guardian—my uncle, Don José—will wash his hands of me after this. I am a very disobedient girl."

"Your true name is—?"

"Peregrina."

Con bowed, congratulating himself for having slid past the knotty point very neatly. "A lovely name. But perhaps I should call you Don Pat, and try to think of you as a young man. I confess it will be difficult—but safe."

"Oh, I feel very safe, *M'sieur,*" she assured him, a trifle breathlessly. "I still have your pistol."

"H'mm—yes." Con sent her a suspicious glance, not quite certain how she meant that. "But don't be too ready to use it, please. In feminine hands a loaded pistol can be an—er . . ."

"Argumentum ad hominem?" she suggested helpfully.

Con frowned reproachfully up at her. He had never seen her look so utterly guileless and sweetly innocent, and that should have warned him. "I have already mentioned, I believe, that I do not desire to converse in French," he reminded her.

She smiled a secret little smile. "That," she murmured demurely, "was Latin—*M'sieur* Nagennoc!"

On the ninth day Con got his first glimpse of Santa Fe.

There it lay, cuddled by the bold and rocky Sangre de Cristo range—*La Villa Real de la Santa Fe de San Francisco de Assisi*—Royal City of the Holy Faith of Saint Francis of Assisi—once the royal city of haughty Spain's Kingdom of New Mexico, now a far-flung outpost of the Mexican Republic. The Golden

Thebes of the Yankee traders. Santa Fe!

City of color and strangeness, romantic, fascinating, where the influence of old Spanish culture remained a living tradition. City of charm and courtesy, hot blood and frivolity, dark intrigue and quick death, pomp and poverty, gay freedom and savage tyranny. City of somnolent ease and sparkling passion, *siesta* and *fiesta,* mystery and candor, Santa Fe! Westward away from it ran the great plateau, the strong sunlight gilding the pointed hills, the far bottoms purpled by distance, and the colors running together to form a thousand delicate hues. The Sangre de Cristos were near and hovering, but the faraway mountains of the Sandia and Jemez hung blue and mysterious against the sky beyond the plateau.

Con turned his face to Peregrina, and she, who had been watching him, grew still-eyed at his smile. His smile was wicked, predatory, and his unshaded eye glimmered like a diamond. For an instant the workings of his mind were flashed on his face. He was thinking, "I've brought you here—but when I've done what I came to do, I'll be taking you away with me!"

Peregrina said quietly, "That large long building you see on the plaza is the Palacio, executive offices of General Rajimo, the governor. The Casa de Cabildo—offices of the civil council—is on the east side of the plaza. My uncle's house is on the Camino de Chimayo, a little west of the plaza. I should tell you that all foreigners must report their presence immediately upon entering the city."

Con thoughtfully adjusted his eye-patch, fitting it

closer. "First I'll take you to your uncle's house."

For two days they had been following the regular beaten road that connected the villages of Pecos and Cañoncito with Santa Fe. Mexicans riding little gray burros had eyed them curiously. Pueblo Indians, friendly and cheerful, had waved to them. Peon women, bare-legged but graceful, had smiled upon them. This morning a small detachment of dragoons had passed at a trot, going toward Santa Fe. The officer had peered closely at them and kept looking back until out of sight.

Con punched the grulla on, and they descended the road into the city. "Your caravan has not yet arrived," remarked Peregrina. "If it had, we would see the wagons outside the old *londiga*—that building on the northeast corner of the plaza. It is used as the government warehouse where goods are examined by the customs house officials. And the city would be more noisy. It is always noisy when *los Americanos de la caravana* are here."

She laughed her low and musical laugh. "My uncle always forbade me from leaving the house except under his escort, while the *Americanos* were here. And it always made me rebellious. He thought them barbarians. I thought them strange and splendid, though perhaps wild in some of their ways."

Con chuckled. "Maybe your uncle knew best. How do you feel about facing him, after skipping out of that convent? Scared?"

Her firm little chin lifted. "I am never scared!"

"I've seen you look considerably worried at odd

times," Con commented dryly, and then could have bitten his tongue for the slip.

Her secret little smile came. "*M'sieur,* one might think that you had known me longer than for merely a few days."

Con coughed. "I—uh—it is because I feel as if I have known you all my life," he countered gallantly.

They passed down the winding road and entered a narrow street of flat-roofed houses and walled patios, leading to the plaza. People gazed at them, astounded by the sight of a lone *Americano* escorting a Spanish girl wearing male garb and riding like a man, both of them dusty and travel-worn. A trim young Mexican officer met them as they entered the plaza. He clicked his polished heels, bowed deeply to Peregrina, obviously recognizing her, and saluted Con.

"*Señor,* it is General Rajimo's wish that you and the *Señorita* Chavez pay him the honor of calling upon him at the Palacio at once," he reported amiably.

"Our compliments to his Excellency, and tell him we will do so later," Con replied formally. "The lady is tired."

The officer bowed again. When he straightened up, his eyes were not so amiable as before. "*Señor,* allow me to escort you both to the Palacio at once," he insisted coolly. "It is his Excellency's urgent wish."

Con glanced up at Peregrina on the horse, and caught her slight nod. A wish, it appeared, became a rigid command when voiced by the great Rajimo. "With pleasure, Colonel," he drawled.

23. HIS EXCELLENCY REQUESTS

CON FELT STRANGE sitting here in Rajimo's executive chamber, sipping a cool drink while Rajimo played host. Rajimo had risen when Peregrina and Con entered, and had remained standing since, his heavy-lidded eyes constantly playing over Peregrina in a way that made Con want to hit him.

"We would have preferred changing our attire before calling on your Excellency," Con remarked, and set down his glass with a bang. "I am sure the lady wishes to don more suitable attire as soon as possible." He had such a deeply rooted hatred for the man, he could barely keep his tone civil. Rajimo had grown stouter, but not softer. His swarthy, heavy-jowled face was as hard and impassive as ever. The bold black eyes were masterful with the forceful stare of a man who knew all the tricks of arrogant domination over others.

"The *Señorita* will be escorted to the house of her uncle in good time, M'sieur Nagennoc," said Rajimo curtly, and took seat behind his massive desk. "First I desire the story of what took place on the trail. A New Mexican caravan was attacked and plundered, at the instigation of American traders who . . ."

"You're wrong," Con interrupted. "It was done by a band of outlaws. I belong to the American caravan. I trailed those outlaws and took the *Señorita* away from them. That should speak for itself."

"It is true, Don Manuel," Peregrina seconded him, and in speaking to Rajimo she spoke as to an equal or to somebody rather less than that. All New Mexico could bow to the upstart tyrant, but she was of the pure Spanish strain, of the House of Chavez which helped conquer some of Rajimo's ancestors on his Indian side. "There can be no such accusations against the Americans," she stated firmly, and dismissed the subject. "Where is my uncle?"

Rajimo played his eyes over her again. "He is under arrest!"

Peregrina rose swiftly, her face growing very pale. "Don José—under arrest? The *Primer* of the Cabildo—under arrest? You have gone mad!"

Rajimo's dark face stayed wooden and unmoved. "I dissolved the Cabildo council two months ago for insolently attempting to oppose me. Don José then very foolishly defied me and called for a meeting of protest. He is now a military prisoner in the Presidio, and he will stand trial for treason!"

Peregrina took a step forward as if to strike him, and Con could well believe that she had never been really afraid of anything or anybody. Her eyes blazed. "Have you lost your senses, Don Manuel?" she flung at him. "You go too far! Some day the Spaniards of the province will call up their old courage—and the *pobres* and Pueblos will follow them gladly—and this country will revolt!"

Rajimo watched her. He even smiled slightly. "Treason appears to be a trait of the Chavez family," he observed tonelessly. "I have suspected it in you before. You may go." He slapped the desk.

Con moved swiftly to Peregrina and offered his arm. She took it, her head high and her eyes still sparking fire, and they both made to pass out through the wide entrance. The same dapper young colonel, with a sergeant and two troopers behind him, barred their way.

"Escort *Señorita* Chavez to the house of Don José," commanded Rajimo, his tone metallic. "The house is to be guarded at all times. M'sieur Nagennoc, you will not be required to escort her."

Con began sliding his right hand under his coat, but Peregrina touched his arm, her eyes signaling warning to him. She smiled up at his set face, and suddenly her air was of intimate coquetry, scornful of surroundings. "M'sieur, I shall always think of my kidnaping as a charming holiday."

Her tone was light and laughing. "I can only pray that when next I fall into ruffianly hands—you will appear once more to save me." The sense of her words was definite enough. "In furtherance of that prayer, I must reward you a little now for gallantry past, so that the future may tempt you."

She stood on tiptoe and kissed him, while the young colonel hastily averted his stare and Rajimo rose behind his desk.

"And in case you should ever incline to forget me, I give you a keepsake—to keep your memory constant." She drew out a rolled handkerchief and pressed it into his hand.

Con pushed the small bundle into his coat pocket.

He bowed, smiling, matching his manners to hers. "Could I ever forget? Believe me, Peregrina—I shall have eyes and ears only for the future."

She laughed softly, turning to go. "You Frenchmen are so understanding!" she breathed, and left with her escort.

CON TURNED BACK to Rajimo, prepared for trouble, but Rajimo had about-faced in his attitude and he gestured for Con to be seated. Con took a mental stance, his gambler's instinct on guard.

Rajimo seated himself and rested his hands on the desk, relaxed and informal. "M'sieur, do not take this little incident too seriously," he advised. "In my position I must often bark, but I seldom bite—and least of all would I be harsh with a charming young lady who is very dear to me."

Now he was the kindly emperor laying aside his majestic luster for the moment and becoming confidential. Con said nothing, recalling some of the corrupt anecdotes he had heard concerning Rajimo's private life. The man was a brutal and conscienceless nabob utterly without honor or scruples.

"I desire your advice, M'sieur," went on Rajimo flatteringly. "It concerns . . ." He paused and asked abruptly, "Have I seen you before? There is something about you that seems familiar to me."

Con had a tense moment. "I hardly think it likely, your Excellency. Since leaving France I have traveled much, but this is my first visit to your country."

Rajimo nodded. "Then I must be mistaken. I was

about to speak of the American caravan. It will arrive soon. It was my belief that the Americans instigated the attack on the Mexican train. You have shown me that my belief was incorrect. However, I have already issued a *bando* which prohibits the Americans from trading anywhere on New Mexican territory."

Con felt that all this was leading up to something he couldn't yet see. "Why not cancel your *bando?*"

Rajimo shook his head. "I never cancel my orders after they become public. The law, M'sieur, must always be immutable, or its power suffers. No, I see only one way. Happily, it is a way in which I may also reward you for restoring the *Señorita* Chavez to me. I am grateful for that—very grateful."

He leaned forward, more confidentially than ever. "You are a Frenchman. You have no foolish ties of loyalty to these Americans, not so? And, as I can see plainly, you are a man of the world. Like myself, you recognize opportunity. Yes? So I shall speak frankly, as one opportunist to another. How many wagon-loads of goods do you own in the caravan?"

"One."

"Only one?" Rajimo shrugged. "There is little profit in one wagon. But there is a way in which I may make it possible for you to earn the entire profits of the whole American caravan! My *bando* forbids any American trader to sell a single article in New Mexico. But you, M'sieur, are not an American! I shall sign a special permit allowing you to sell anything you wish. You understand?"

"I'm beginning to," Con acknowledged.

"I knew you for a man of perspicacity," Rajimo complimented him. "In order to dispose of their goods, the Americans will be forced to sell through your hands. You will be in the position to dictate terms and take all their profits, and I shall support you in every possible respect. Your profits should amount to about two hundred thousand dollars—the usual profits of a large caravan. However, you will be required to pay taxes and customs duties on all that you sell, of course."

He straightened up and became his official self. "The taxes, M'sieur, will amount to one hundred thousand dollars—payable directly to me!"

At last Con found one thing to admire in Rajimo. As a thoroughgoing rascal and schemer, the man topped all comers. "In other words," Con stated bluntly, "we're to corner the market, sting the boys out of their profits, and split the winnings between us. Right? *Hombre,* you must've been born in a bandit camp!"

Rajimo's eyes chilled. "It is my wish that you do as I suggest! You may go!"

Out in the plaza, Con took his bearings and struck off across to the Camino de Chimayo, hoping he would be able to secure lodgings of some sort within sight of the Chavez house. As he walked, he pulled out the kerchief that Peregrina had given him, and unrolled it. Something fell out and he picked it up—a little golden Cupid, broken-winged, scratched, dented, a battered leer on its chubby face.

"Minx!" he muttered softly, and carefully wrapped it up again.

The American caravan, when it came, rolled into Santa Fe with all the shouting and tumult of a wild army. Teamsters popped their long whips, riders emptied guns into the air and rode whooping around the plaza, and even the animals shared in spirit the general abandonment of restraint.

The Santa Fe citizens wholeheartedly joined in the enthusiasm. The coming of a great American caravan always took on the nature of a carnival, and the whole town happily plunged into a gay period of fiesta. To the Americans, made half savage and elemental by their long weeks out of touch with civilization, any town would have looked good, but Santa Fe was the cream of them all. Here was a town, only too ready at all times to declare a holiday, and give itself over to fandango and frolic. And the women—exotic, colorful in thin *camisas,* blue-black hair, fine bleached skins, dark eyes that were bright and soft. . . . Graceful, coy, knowing when to be candidly alluring and when to be distant, but always warmhearted. They liked the big *Americanos.*

People raced through the narrow streets and poured into the plaza. *"Los Americanos! Los extranjeros! La entrada de la caravana!"*

The huge wagons, scarred now by accidents and repairs along the trail, their gay paint cracked and peeled by sun and rain, creaked ponderously into the plaza and drew up. Con made his way onto the plaza with the milling crowds. His rescue of Peregrina had become well known, and it appealed strongly to the Spanish love of drama. Men bowed and women smiled admiringly whenever he appeared on the streets, tall, dark, his brown face made intriguingly sinister by the black eye-patch, thin cheek-scar and upturned eyebrows. With their knack of descriptive nomenclature, they called him *El Corsario de Francia*—The Buccaneer of France. He had heard them whisper it as he passed, and gathered that it was not intended in disrespect.

Within an hour of the caravan's *entrada,* a raging group of traders headed by Dall Burgwin sought out Con. One look at their faces and Con saw explosions in the near offing. Burgwin leveled a finger and his roar could be heard all over the noisy plaza.

"Hey, you! What damn' trick is this you've rigged on us? They won't let us take our stuff through the customs! Won't even let us unload! They're saying you've tied up the whole market and we've got to sell through you. You Judas, you cooked that up with Rajimo!"

"Hold your head!" Con snapped. "But for me, none of you would be selling anything this trip. Rajimo had it all laid out to blame you for that raid. I had nothing to do with . . ."

A hand tugged at his sleeve. He found a shabbily garbed Mexican trying to get his attention. The face of the Mexican was thin and bitter, and Con recognized the man. It was the *teniente* who had ridden in command of the dragoons escorting Rajimo's mule train, and suffered defeat along the bank of the Arkansas. He was no longer in uniform, and on him were the signs of a man who had fallen low. Con had a twinge of conscience. Defeat had brought disgrace to the man, reducing him to beggary. He felt in his pocket for some coins to give him.

The man came close and spoke guardedly. "I bear a message. There is a certain house on the Camino de Chimayo. The patio gate is for the time not watched. A lady asks that you come . . ."

A curse from Burgwin and a warning premonition caused Con to dodge, but Burgwin's fist scraped over his ear and set bells ringing in his head. Con caught his balance, whirled, and lashed out. His eye-patch, the string broken by Burgwin's glancing blow, fell, but he hadn't time to catch it. He struck again, and Burgwin floundered backward into his group. A few of the cooler heads closed around him to stop the fight, but their action wasn't necessary. Burgwin, a hand to his bloodied lips, stood and glared at Con's face.

"He—he's—look at him!" He choked on his own words. "Look at that eye—nothing wrong with it! I knew I'd seen him before—I knew it! He's Connegan, the twisty Texan who shot Rajimo in St. Louis that time and nearly wrecked us!"

Con picked up his eye-patch. "The man's an idiot!" he drawled, and turned away.

The one-time *teniente* was gone. Con saw him slipping off through the crowd. The Mexican looked back at him once, and it seemed to Con that a fierce joy sharpened the bitter face. He hoped he was mistaken and he followed swiftly, but lost the shabby figure before he got to the Camino de Chimayo.

"Looks like we're blowed up, Con, don't it?" The rusty voice of Old Nick sounded behind him.

Con turned. "Maybe so, Nick, maybe so. Burgwin wasn't any too sure, though. Did you see that Mexican who spoke to me? Go and see if you can find him. If he recognized me—phew!"

24. THE LAST OF M'SIEUR NAGENNOC

THE PATIO was entirely shut off from the street, with the house built around three sides of it and a high adobe wall completing the enclosure. The little gate in the wall was not fastened. Con stepped into the patio and closed the gate after himself. Several doors, all closed, led from the house onto the patio, overhung by the upstairs balcony. Nobody came out, so Con began trying the doors.

A plaintive voice called down to him, "Alas, they are all locked!"

Con stepped back, looking up at the balcony, and doffed his hat. "Is this hospitable, after inviting me to call?"

Peregrina gazed down at him over the balcony rail, a chamber door open behind her. Her eyes were very bright, and there was a glow to her face. "I apologize," she returned with mock humbleness. "But do not blame me. It is Rajimo's order. There is a soldier out front, so do not talk too loudly. All the servants have gone to the plaza. Aguirre did not return with you?"

"Aguirre?"

"Our gardener—the man I sent for you," she explained. "But I suppose he is drinking again. He was once an officer, and is not a good worker. I told him to bring you here and stand watch while we talked. He drinks a great deal, poor fellow."

She leaned lightly over the balustrade. "Let me congratulate you, M'sieur, on recovering the use of your eye!" she offered sweetly. "I like you better without the patch."

Con accepted the gentle thrust. "*Touché!* You beautiful little humbug, when did you guess?"

She flushed, laughing. "From the very first. And you knew me—*n'est-ce pas?*"

"Away with your French and Latin man-traps!" Con growled. "Listen, girl, am I expected to stand down here and get a crick in my neck talking up to you?"

She elevated one smoothly rounded shoulder. "It is very proper that I should not entertain a gentleman caller in the house, without a chaperon."

"That's a matter of opinion," ventured Con, and took a high leap. His fingers got a hold of the balcony's edge. He drew himself up, climbed over the balustrade, and stood before her. "Hadn't we better go inside, before somebody comes along and sees us?" he suggested.

Peregrina looked somewhat taken aback. "Why—yes, I suppose so," she conceded dubiously.

Con followed her into the chamber and considerately made a long task of closing the balcony door, while behind his back she flew around hiding away a few scattered garments. She was quite flushed when he turned, and again he was intrigued by her deliriously inconsistent sense of modesty. She, who had flirted with him and tricked him outrageously—who had once almost juggled him into a forced marriage with her—had traveled and camped with him for nine days, dressed as a male—had poured out warm love on dying Rael in the man-crowded prison cell of the Santiago . . . Hiding a few innocent garments from his male eyes, like any flustered maiden! It was one of her charms. In all that she did, she remained so utterly and unfathomably feminine.

"Peregrina, you're marvelous!" he told her with sincerity. "Oh, come, don't look as if I'm getting ready to pounce on you, merely because we happen to be in your—er—dressing room. You're marvelous because you're so downright contradictory. I swear I never know what to expect from you. You've surprised me too many times! Don't change after I take you away with me, will you?"

"No, of course I'll not ch—" She caught herself, and now her color flamed. "What?"

Con chuckled. "Now, just go back to that first impulse and be honest. You know very well I'm going to take you off with me!"

Peregrina was suddenly haughty and aloof. "Your reaction toward a—a certain situation in the past—in Mexico—did not lead me to believe . . ." She paused in her painful speech and bit her lip. "I think I could have killed you that night!"

Con nodded uncomfortably. "I don't doubt it. But there were good reasons for what I did. At that, I nearly turned back. I'm sorry, on my oath I am." He scanned her face quickly. "Is it revenge on me you want?"

"I—don't know," she confessed frankly. "Please sit down. I sent for you to tell you about your brother Lorin. The opportunity may not come again."

"Why shouldn't it?"

"I am a prisoner here." She gestured about her. "Oh, I could slip out of this house easily enough, yes—but where could I go? Nobody leaves or enters Santa Fe without Rajimo's knowledge. The roads are always watched. My uncle and I have many friends, but Rajimo has his army. Sooner or later, Rajimo will . . . But I still have your pistol. Let us talk of your brother."

She settled herself in a chair and gazed down at her small toes. "Your brother Lorin was—impetuous," she said carefully. "Romantic. He carried letters to my uncle, and so we met. He—he thought himself deeply in love with me. I grew fond of him, but I did not love him. I tried to discourage him, for his own safety. You see, my uncle had at that time betrothed me to Rajimo. He—Don José—is my guardian, as you know, and one of his duties was to find a suitable husband for me. Rajimo was very pressing, and Don José then thought it would be an excellent match."

"I reckon he's changed his mind since!" commented Con.

Peregrina inclined her head. "I never intended to marry Rajimo, but I had to pretend to agree. Rajimo was almost as powerful then as now. He set spies over me, and on your brother. It grew very dangerous, but Lorin would not listen to me. I tried to avoid him. Also, Don José became furious when he learned that Lorin was openly paying court to me. Finally I fled to Chihuahua. But Lorin followed as soon as he discovered where I had gone."

"With his gold?" Con asked.

"I don't know. I only know that he was pursued, challenged to a duel—and killed!" Peregrina lifted her eyes to Con's face. "Please do not ask me who killed him. The matter was hushed up and kept secret, because of the man involved—and to save me from scandal. Lorin was buried somewhere along the Chihuahua trail, where the duel took place. He was a very fine gentleman—but very impetuous, very romantic. He would not believe me when I told him . . ."

She rose swiftly with Con as a door slammed open somewhere below. Feet tramped noisily on floors and stairs, coming up to the second floor.

"Servants?" muttered Con.

"No!" Peregrina had paled. "They sound like soldiers! *Querido,* you must hide—quickly!"

"No use." Con drew his pistol, watching the door. "They're coming right up." He stepped to the balcony door and peered out. "Devil an' all—soldiers all over the place! Here—*you* hide, or your fair young reputation is done blowed up this time for sure!"

He tried to push her into a closet, but she eluded him, and from somewhere in her dress she drew out the pistol he had given her. Con drew her to him and kissed her. "Just in case the opportunity may not come again," he muttered, and both faced the door as it flew open.

The same dapper young colonel, who had escorted them into the presence of Rajimo, stood in the doorway. Back of him the hall was jammed with soldiers. The colonel had his pistol out. "*Señor,* on order of his Excellency, General Don Manuel Rajimo, I demand your surrender!" he rapped, and leveled the pistol. "It would be most regrettable, *Señor,* if we caused death or injury to the lady!"

Con slowly lowered his own weapon. "I see your point, Johnny—hell scorch your dirty little soul!"

THIS TIME he was not taken to the executive office in the Palacio. He was marched to Rajimo's military quarters in the gloomy Presidio, north of the town, where the garrison troops had their permanent *quarteles.*

The place smelled unclean: Indian blood predominated among the slovenly soldiers who loafed half dressed in the yard. Only their uniforms and beggarly pay saved them from being paupers and petty criminals of the outlying settlements, from which classes most of them had been recruited. Known detestedly as *los Perros de Rajimo*—Rajimo's Dogs—they and their sullen Indian women kept to themselves, despised by the citizens of the town. The officers, on the other hand, were models of glittering smartness, and their attitude toward the men they commanded was that of masters toward serfs. Most of them lived in town in elegant style, and all swore allegiance to

Rajimo. It was upon his army officers that Rajimo's power rested, and they in their turn owed their well-paid commissions to him.

Rajimo's private military quarters opened Con's eyes to one more side of the man's nature. Heretofore he had seen Rajimo always as the martinet—cruel, cold-blooded, hard as iron—but a gentleman of sorts, splendidly groomed and imperious in his bearing. The executive office in the Palacio had reflected his dourly astringent manner in its bare severity.

But here it was different. The room was littered and dirty, odorous with stale wine and fouler smells—the quarters of a drunken and debauched soldier. From the rafters hung the famous strings of ears that Con had heard about but hardly believed. Other men had their stuffed heads, mounted horns and tusks. Rajimo had his garlands of Indians' ears, trophies of war expeditions against rebellious tribes of the province. Con wondered if there might happen to be any white ones among them.

Rajimo himself lay sprawled on a couch like a gorged and sottish Caesar, dirty dishes and empty bottles on the floor beside him, clad only in trousers and rumpled shirt. Without his uniform and in this attitude and place, the gross coarseness of the man was so apparent as to be offensive, and Con was revolted at the sight. This was not the majestic military governor, a man worthy of vigorous hatred and warily plotted revenge. This was a fleshy and obscene Indian half-breed who had somehow risen to despotic command of a province.

Rajimo lolled his head and stared at Con. He was drunk, but not so drunk he didn't know what he was doing. "Ah!" he breathed, and pushed himself heavily up on his elbow. "Where was he, *Coronel?*"

"In the Chavez house, Excellency, as Aguirre said he would be," answered the colonel. "In the chamber of a certain lady," he added meaningly.

Con took notice then of Dall Burgwin in the room, glowering triumphantly at him, and of Aguirre the ex-*teniente.*

"Ah!" breathed Rajimo again, and fell back tipsily, blinking up at the rafters. "In the chamber of a lady!" A slow and deadly rage was mounting in him, sobering him. It could be seen in the sharpening cast of his face.

"I assure you, Excellency, he is the man!" Aguirre started forward, fiercely eager. "He is the man called Don Desperado—the Texan who . . ."

Rajimo curtly waved him silent. "He is also called Captain Connegan—as *Señor* Burgwin and I know very well! And to think that I did not suspect—!" He rolled over, snatched up a plate, and flung it full at Con's face.

"Texan dog! Aguirre, I give you charge of him! Your commission is restored to you. Take close care of him—take very close care! At my leisure I shall attend to him, and to the certain lady! Yes, at my leisure—!"

I T IS MY PROFOUND CONVICTION," stated Don José Chavez, "that right and truth must always triumph in the end, regardless of whatever we may strive to do about it. Evil brings about its own sure punishment. Wickedness carries the seed of its own eventual doom. Tyranny ultimately guts itself by its own perversions and excesses. Justice is not a negative quality—it is positive, certain. It is a natural law which, like the law of gravity, can never permanently be flouted or restrained."

His thin patriarchal face was pale, haggard, unshaven. He was ragged and filthy, and lack of sunlight had bleached his skin to a bluish transparency. Imprisonment had impaired his health without breaking his courage, but he had fallen back upon a lofty and ascetic philosophy that amounted almost to a religious faith.

"Sometimes," said Con meditatively, "I wonder if I don't cheat myself out of a lot of mental comfort, not being exactly what you'd call an idealist." Such high-flying abstractions were too misty for him to ride on. He suspected them of being substitutes for stoical hopelessness.

At first, yesterday, when Con was thrust here into the Presidio dungeon, Don José, who had been here two months, had been barely civil. He made no reference to the past, but his sunken eyes, so dark and luminous against the pallor of his skin, spoke with eloquence. But a small and smelly dungeon was no place for a feud, as Con pointed out. They were fellow prisoners and had to make the best of each other's company. So by tacit agreement they declared a truce. Last night, with some ceremony, Don José had broken a cigar in two and given Con half. Later, he said, he would receive a few more and perhaps a little decent food.

This morning the cigars had come, furtively smuggled in by the dull and brutish jailer who brought the scanty morning meal. Friends of Don José, by judicious bribery, were keeping in touch with him from the outside. There was a note with the cigars, and Don José shook his head after reading it.

"Bad news?" Con asked, munching his *tortilla.*

Don Jose tore the small note into confetti and calmly disposed of it by eating it along with his own *tortilla.* "They wish to rescue me," he replied. "They want me to lead an armed revolt against Rajimo."

Con sat bolt upright. "Fine! When do we start?"

The Don glanced at him. "Never! It would mean fighting—bloodshed—murder. All New Mexico would break into civil war. We could not hope to win against Rajimo's forces. His soldiers would massacre us, hunt us down, and finally there would be wholesale executions. Rajimo knows his enemies, and it would give him the opportunity he seeks to wipe them out. No, I shall never consent to such a mad holocaust!"

"You mean you'd rot here rather than take a chance?" Con exclaimed incredulously.

It was then that Don José spoke of his profound faith in the ultimate triumph of justice over tyranny. Con gathered that all one had to do was suffer in patience, hold tight to sublime faith, and everything would come out all right in the end—though he might not be alive then to see it. Con wanted to choke him.

"From what my friends write," mentioned Don José, "it appears that your Caravan Captain—Burgwin—has conspired with Rajimo to take control of the trade. Burgwin is the only American given permission to sell goods. The other Americans are furious and everyone is much excited. No customs duties have yet been paid, nothing has been sold, and the plaza is an armed camp. The Americans will have to give in finally, of course, and take whatever terms Burgwin offers them."

Con was not surprised, having figured on something of the kind. "When do your friends expect your answer?" he queried.

The Don delicately took a spoonful of watery soup. "At once," he replied composedly.

"How would you get word to them? How do they know that jailer can be trusted?"

"My reply does not need to be written," explained Don José. "If I agree, then I am to bend the handle of my spoon. We have used that method before on other matters."

"H'm," said Con, and finished his soup. Thoughtfully, he bent the handle of his own tin spoon.

Later, after the jailer had come for the bowls and spoons, Con lay on his back and gazed up at the low ceiling, feeling that he had lighted the fuse to a bomb. It had been simple to bump into the jailer and switch the spoons.

THEY CAME THAT NIGHT. First a patter of feet, faintly heard from the dungeon, and the startled challenge of a sentry. Then a single shot that echoed around the old Presidio. A door crashed in to a shattering blow, and the hurrying feet tramped loudly inside the building.

"Don José—where?"

"Right here!" called Con, and kicked at the iron door. Don José, astounded, was on his feet, stuttering and wagging his head. A pistol roared five shots, blasting the lock, and the door swung open, exposing a mass of figures in the darkness, guns and eyes shining. "Come quickly, please, Excellency!"

They were most polite about it, despite the urgency of the circumstances, and already they gave Don José the highest title in the province. These were not rabble, but *caballeros* and blue-bloods of Don José's own class. Con hustled Don José out with him, almost carrying him.

"His Excellency is not well, gentlemen," he said rapidly. "A little dazed. I wish to join your party. Will someone give me a pistol?"

Someone did. "Haste, please—we must hurry!"

They sped for the yard, Con staying close to Don José, who feebly tried to protest against it all. There was a reckless sort of efficiency about the whole thing. Nobody fired an unnecessary shot, and they were cool while the Presidio erupted noisy alarms. Voices rang out, shouting commands, squads of soldiers poured out of the *quarteles,* and somewhere a frightened sentry was hysterically shooting off his carbine into the night.

The party cut straight across the yard, keeping together and running at a trot. It was not, Con found, a large party. Not more than a dozen men, and most of them white-haired. Members of the ousted Cabildo council, he presumed. Only when a crowd of half-dressed soldiers raced across the yard to bar them did shooting really begin. The soldiers were led by a hatless officer, and Con saw it was Aguirre, now back in uniform. Aguirre screamed a command, and a pistol in his hand spat quick flashes. Con fired, but his aim was spoiled by having Don José stumble heavily against him. He threw an arm around the Don. "You hit?"

"Si," answered Don José. His voice was tired, but composed. "It is as I said, you see—bloodshed—useless bloodshed—and nothing gained!"

Con picked him up and slung him over a shoulder. Gunfire was breaking out in earnest. "He's hit—where'll we take him?" he shouted, and saw Aguirre fall under the wave of his own advancing men.

"Stay with us, *Señor!*" requested a dignified old Spaniard beside him, coolly shooting at the soldiers as he trotted along. "His Excellency must not be caught. *Viva Chavez!*"

It was a rebel battle cry, a new one, and the rest took it up. *"Viva Chavez! Muerte á Rajimo!"*

They got out of the yard, lacking two who fell, and headed directly onto the town. To Con the whole thing had an unreal aspect, a theatrical quality that was quite mad and wholly without any conceivable hope of success. "Where's your army?" he called to the elderly Spaniard beside him.

"Army? Our army, *Señor?*" The old *caballero* airily waved his pistol. "When the people learn of the revolt our army will arise and form itself! All hate Rajimo and his drunken *ladrones* of soldiers!"

"They're almighty scared of him, too!" retorted Con, shifting Don José to an easier position on his shoulder. "Do you mean to say you haven't done anything about organizing an army or—my Lord, Chavez was right!"

The old *caballero* beamed approvingly. *"Viva Chavez!"*

A T T H E H O U S E on the Camino de Chimayo they fired one more shot, which disposed of the soldier guarding the front door. By this time the whole town was thoroughly aroused. Women and men ran helter-skelter through the streets, some to hide, others to find weapons, none of them quite sure as to what was happening except that it was very apt to be explosively dangerous. Con and the Cabildo *caballeros* pushed on into the house, after shouting their *"Viva Chavez!"* through the startled town. Peregrina came running downstairs with a lighted candle and a gun, evidently prepared to stand off invaders, and stood astonished when she saw the nature of the party. When she saw

Con with his burden she darted to him.

"Con—you! But—oh, is he—?"

"He is," Con told her crisply. "I don't know how bad, but he caught a bullet when the rest of us lunatics sashayed out of the Presidio. Let's get him to a bed."

The revolution committee was in earnest counsel when Con came downstairs. Candles had been lighted, some wine found, and the *caballeros* were discussing matters around a table. The house was crowded with male citizens, all brandishing firearms and all talking at once.

Con shouldered through to the counsel table and caught snatches of grandiloquent speeches that were fiery, fluent, but not particularly constructive. The thing was pathetic, all of it. It did not seem to occur to anybody that haste was imperative or that Rajimo might not wait until they were ready before closing in on them. This was a gentlemen's insurrection, and they were going to conduct it along gentlemanly lines. None of the Cabildo *caballeros* knew anything about soldiering. They were statesmen, civic leaders, *muy grandes señores*.

Peregrina followed Con downstairs and touched his arm. "Is there fighting?"

"Not yet, but there will be!" he returned, and brought a hand down on the table with a bang that made the glasses jump. "Gentlemen! We have an army—sort of. We have an enemy. We have a cause. What're we waiting for?"

That brought a semi-silence to the listening mob of citizen *insurrectos*. *"Viva el Corsario!"* piped a voice, and raised a ragged cheer.

A hawk-nosed *caballero* at the table, caught in the midst of a particularly fine flow of seditious sentiment, coughed and frowned. "We are waiting for the fighting to begin!" he stated, and drew himself up.

Con swallowed his first retort. "D'you reckon Rajimo is waiting, too?" he asked. "Damnation, he's got troops—cavalry—cannon! He'll blast us out of this house and pick us off like running buffalo! He'll surround the—Hell, hear that?"

Somewhere a bugle blew a quick ta-ra-ra-ra, and there came the dull rhythm of marching feet. An uneasy hush fell over the packed mob in the house, and the *caballeros* rose to their feet. Con whirled and saw Peregrina fighting her way to the front door. He started after her with a yell.

"Hey, come back here!"

But she was gone, and he paused, amazed. Never had he seen her show real fear or panic. She was gone, fleeing from the house. Well, maybe that was better. She couldn't be any worse off in the streets than here in this doomed place.

"Break up, *hombres!* Upstairs, some of you—take the windows and doors!" Con shouted commands at them. "You too, gentlemen—the fighting is about to begin and you don't have to wait any longer. *Viva Chavez! Viva* all of us!"

"*Viva Chavez!*" echoed a *caballero* gravely, draining his glass and flipping out a horse pistol as ancient as himself.

The mob swarmed through the house to make ready

for the siege. Some of the bemused citizens were not sure whom they were fighting for, but they all knew the enemy.

"Pobrecitos!" muttered Con, and jerked another pistol for himself from an old fellow who was flourishing it around.

26. LOS RENEGADOS

T HEY POSSESSED a wild and fanatical kind of courage, these people, a blind bravado that blazed up in the face of coming defeat. Yet it was not wholly grim nor fatalistic, but had a bright thread of hard gaiety running through it. This thing had come suddenly upon them, catching them utterly unprepared, and volatile emotionalism had played its part in dragging them into it. But they behaved as if they had for years waited eagerly for the day of revolt. They crowded to the windows and yelled insults at the dragoons massing at all points around the house. They shot off their rickety old firearms, hooted, cheered, and shouted their rebel cries.

"Viva Chavez! Viva la Revolución! Muerte á Rajimo!"

Con went and took a look at Don José. The Don, his chest bulkily bandaged under his loose and blood-stained shirt, lay muttering in bed. "Madness—all madness! Ah, the waste of life—the suffering—misery—women's grief!"

His large dark eyes settled on Con, bending over

him. "My answer was 'No'—yet they came. Was that your work?"

"I reckon it was," Con confessed. "I didn't know it would be like this. I thought they were prepared, ready with men—guns—plans."

The somber eyes regarded him steadily. "You are a firebrand, Captain Connegan," Don José pronounced flatly. "A desperado! Yet I have always given you respect for certain qualities—a conscience and a capacity for sacrifice. It is a pity that you will die with the rest of us. It is a pity that you cannot live on—with the memory of this tragic night haunting you!"

A crashing detonation of gunfire exploded around the besieged house, and immediately men were screaming. Don José shuddered. Con raced out of the room and blundered into men carrying others. The first salvo of the dragoons had done deadly work, clearing the windows and doors of the yelling *insurrectos* and preparing the way for attack. Con fought his way downstairs.

"Hold the doors, *hombres*—they're coming at us!"

He got near the front entrance and began emptying his pistols as yellow-and-blue uniformed figures came in a mass. The trapped rebels jumped to meet them, and both parties clashed in the narrow space. Gun butts hammered on the iron grills of the downstairs windows, the dragoons smashing their way into the house, and all sounds mingled into one thunderous clamor.

It subsided as suddenly as it began. A bugle, imperative and insistent, blared its tinny notes down the street. The solid bump and grind of rolling cannon wheels rumbled, coming near. The soldiers broke away from the house, herded by their shouting officers, and grouped again behind walls and near-by houses.

Con no longer had his pistols, but he had a broken musket which he had been swinging as a club. He exchanged it for the sword and pistol of a fallen dragoon officer, taking the cartridge belt as well. Powder burns stung his face, his chest was gashed, and red violence rioted in him. Be damned to Don José's bleating—this was a fight!

"We have beaten them!" whooped a *caballero,* sitting on the floor with a bullet hole in his foot. *"Viva Chavez!"*

Con peeled off his coat and took an experimental cut with the sword. Nice skewer and just the right weight. "The hell we have. Hear that cannon coming up? They'll knock the house down on us and blast us out with scrap iron. Let's get out of here!"

"Retreat? Never!"

Buckling on the pistol, Con looked around at what he could see of their faces in the darkness. They had fighting blood in them, all right, once they got all fired up. Right now was a good time to push the gamble with them, while they were full of glory.

"I didn't say retreat. Let's get out of here and go for that damned cannon! Come on, you *valientes—Viva la Revolución!"*

It was insanity, but they were not sane and they followed him. They swarmed out after him in a mob charge, north up the street where the cannon had halted and most of the troops were gathered.

"Viva Chavez! Viva!"

Behind them, from the direction of the plaza, burst another howling army—howling in another language and in voices more bass than shrill. Con, running, looked back and let out a high Texas squall. "Come on, you wagoneer *renegados*—into 'em!"

Teamsters, packers, traders—they were coming on the run, some riding, some afoot, armed with their Hawkins and Yerger rifles, Colt's repeaters and Pomeroy smooth-bores. In the rear of the whooping *Americanos* surged a horde of citizens brandishing clubs, knives, and here and there a flintlock gun. There were even some women, all shrieking their *vivas*. Santa Fe was rising, snatching up what arms it had, and pitching into the fight.

A scattered volley ripped spatteringly from the Rajimo troops, but the massed ranks were breaking. Officers could be seen dashing about trying to hold their men together, while feverish activity boiled around the huge old brass cannon.

A plunging horse brushed by Con and reared to the tug of reins. Old Nick was in the saddle. "Grab a holt, Con—we'll git thar fust! By glory, what a fight! You done right, Con—you done right, sendin' the boys warnin' to stand by Chavez. Burgwin's the only one wouldn't come, an' a feller broke his jaw for him with a gun bar'l. 'We gotta stand by Chavez,' she says, perky as a . . ."

"Who said?" Con called out, hanging on alongside.

"Look out—they got that cannon set!"

"Your gal—Peregrina! She's back there, ridin' a horse she took from . . ."

There was no time for more. They plowed into the group around the cannon and Con let go, slashing out with the sword. The troops were falling back, breaking into disorder like a rotten fence before a hurricane, leaving their officers to make a stubborn stand alone. When the main rebel body struck, it swept the street clear and left the cannon standing like a mute and useless monument.

Half an hour later they hitched mules to the gun carriage. "They're barricading themselves in the Presidio!" called out a voice.

"Then it's on to the Presidio!" said Con, and looked around for the speaker. " 'Lo, there, minx! Enjoying yourself?"

Peregrina sat on a borrowed horse and grinned at him like a boy. *"Viva la Revolución!"*

They dragged the brass cannon up facing the Presidio, and had just got it nicely aimed when a white flag fluttered urgently from a window of the gloomy old pile.

"Now, that's an almighty shame, boys," complained a trader aggrievedly. "After all our trouble hauling the damn thing up here an' all! I'd set my heart on hearing it pop."

"Mebbe 'tain't loaded, nohow," put in a teamster.

Old Nick, lighting his pipe, settled the matter by dropping the burning stub of his match into the touch-hole. The resulting boom satisfied everybody, scared all the horses into a bolting panic, and brought Rajimo's Dogs tumbling out of the Presidio with their hands up.

A crowd of citizen revolutionaries had ganged under the front columns of the Palacio when Con got there. They were not rioting. Those in the rear yelled and pushed, but a strange lack of action held back those who blocked the way into the governor's executive office. Con forced a passage through for himself and saw the reason when he got to the front.

The door to the executive chamber stood wide open, allowing full view of the lighted interior and the big desk facing the doorway. Every candle had been lighted in the pair of elaborately branched silver candlesticks that graced the desk. Behind the desk Rajimo stood in full uniform—silent, immobile, impressive as an Apache war chief in full paint. The light of the many candles played upon him, so that he stood out in splendid radiance against the dark background of the room's back shadows. His long military cape, dazzlingly blue and of fine texture, he had tossed grandly back over his shoulders, exposing the crimson silk lining, rows of glinting medals, and a hand resting in imperious pose upon the gold hilt of his sheathed sword. The swarthy, heavy-jowled face with its domineering eyes and jutting nose, betrayed nothing but a haughty and menacing anger. By sheer will and majestic bearing he was holding the mob in check.

Con, a gambler himself, appreciated the finished expertness of the man's last desperate gamble. Rajimo was staking everything upon his power to dominate and rouse fear. His imposing appearance had always been his most valuable asset. Tonight he stood alone, his clique of officers killed and scattered, his army defeated, and all Santa Fe ablaze with rebellion. By morning, as the news of the uprising flew through the province, every town and settlement would follow the lead of Santa Fe.

Con gathered together some monumental dignity of his own, and stalked with deliberation into the chamber. "Don't bite him, *hombres*—the poor mongrel's lost his teeth!" he threw over his shoulder, and that broke the spell.

With a muttering growl the mob pushed forward, and Rajimo uttered a dry sound deep in his throat. Con kicked the door shut and bolted it in the face of the livened crowd. He turned back to the desk, hearing the swift *weep!* of the sword drawn from its scabbard.

"It's no use, Rajimo," he said. "You're finished! If you meant real business you'd pull out that pistol you're wearing. You're all through. You can drop the theatrics."

He shook his head as Rajimo clapped a hand to his pistol holster. "I could make my draw and shoot you between the eyes before you got it out. And if you did happen to get me first—what then? That mob out there craves to get its hands on you. I'm the only protection you've got."

He paced around the desk, brushed Rajimo's hand away, and took possession of the pistol. Rajimo let him do it, and slumped heavily into his massive chair, letting the sword clatter to the floor. His majestic hauteur fell from him and he sat like a man beaten and lost, staring dully at Con.

"Protection—from you! Am I to beg for my life? I—Rajimo? No! Kill me!"

He still was acting. Now he was the fallen monarch, fallen but noble, too proud to beg the enemy for his life. Con said nothing, waiting, knowing that soon the true nature of the man must emerge. He had learned that silence was the most shattering weapon to use upon poseurs. Rajimo straightened a little in his chair, malice and hatred burning in his eyes.

"What are your demands?" he growled. "What are your terms? Money? My money is here in the Palacio, down in the *bóveda*. I will give . . ."

Con stopped him. "Nothing is yours any more to give. No, you can't buy me off. You and I are going to ride out of town together. I'll give you back your pistol, and we'll have it out! If you beat me, then you've got the chance to head for Mexico. I'm giving you a better chance than you likely gave my brother Lorin."

Rajimo breathed heavily. "Your brother? I did not kill your brother—I swear I did not!"

Con shot out a hand, grasped the long cloak, and dragged the man to his feet. "Liar! You . . ."

He broke off. Rajimo was telling the truth, and his eyes showed it. His nerve had cracked and he was beyond lying.

"Then who killed him?"

"Don José!"

27. VENGEANCE

ON THE CAMINO REAL they halted, two men alone in the silence of the great plateau, with the lights of Santa Fe visible behind them. Rajimo shifted uneasily in his saddle, his shrinking eyes on Con. It had not been easy for Con to slip him out of Santa Fe unobserved by the inflamed mobs of victorious revolutionaries that roamed the streets.

Con dismounted and drew two pistols. "Get off!"

The bloodshot whites of Rajimo's eyes shone in the moonlight. "It is murder! I—I—am too shaken to shoot well. I swear to you it was not I who killed your brother, but Don José! I was there, but Don José demanded on his right as guardian of . . ."

"I can guess what happened," Con said curtly. "You rigged Don José into it—used him as your cat's-paw. What happened to my brother's gold?"

"I had given your brother permission to store it in the Palacio *bóveda*—the strongroom—for safe-keeping," Rajimo muttered. "After his death, I—I let it remain there."

"You mean you kept it!" Con corrected. "I see. You first played friend to Lorin and got him to trust you. Then you set Don José against him with lies and scandal, and got them both into a duel. Lorin wasn't much of a hand with a gun. But it's not just for that I'll take pleasure in killing you. I'm thinking of that march down to Mexico City, and of the men who died on the trail."

Rajimo's panic was plain in the way he stared at the pistols. "I—I did only my duty!"

"There was one man in particular," Con pursued. "He was my friend. The finest, whitest man I ever knew, God rest him. He died in the Santiago. Damn you, get off and take this pistol!"

He was trying to whip up all his old vengeful fury, but sickening revulsion rose in him instead. To kill this man would be so easy. Too easy. This was not the Rajimo whose vision he had carried in his mind— dominant, cruel, an enemy of resource and power. That Rajimo was gone, crushed, leaving only a fear-ridden Indian half-breed. Con recalled one statement of policy that Rajimo had made in the little *cuartel* room off the San Miguel plaza: "I do not kill those I hate . . ."

Con put away the pistols, and heard Rajimo's shuddering sigh of relief. "I'm going to let you live, *hombre*," he said. "I don't think I'll regret it. You'll be the one who'll regret it—when you're a drink-sodden wreck cadging coppers in Mexico City, without the nerve to kill yourself. Mexico has no use for her ex-generals who come back broke and defeated. You'll sink to obscurity—poverty—beggary. Yes, I'll let you live!"

He waved the man on his way. "It's a long road down to El Paso del Norte. You'll skulk and hide, dodge the towns and settlements, steal food where you can, and be chased by those who used to fear you. And if you reach Mexico alive, you'll find nothing much there for a fugitive commander who lacked the courage to die when his time came. *Vaya!*"

He struck the horse and stood watching until Rajimo was gone, riding south through the night for Mexico and refuge. Then he mounted his own horse and rode back to Santa Fe, thinking of Don José.

PEREGRINA MET CON in the downstairs hall of the house on the Camino de Chimayo. The place resembled something between a hospital and a battered army post. Mobs still roved through the town, singing and shouting, but the violence of the night had burned out. Passing through the plaza, Con had looked in at the Cabildo, seeing lights in there. The *caballeros* of the Cabildo, those not too hurt to talk, were gathered in special executive session. From now on, Santa Fe stood a chance of being ruled by a civil government, not by military decree.

Peregrina curtseyed impudently. "Hail the conqueror!" she breathed with exaggerated reverence. "My uncle—I mean his Excellency, Governor Don José Chavez—has been inquiring for you. Where have you been?"

"Seeing Rajimo off for Mexico," replied Con, unsmiling. "I meant to kill him, but I changed my mind. Sometimes it's a mistake to kill a man. We talked. He filled in one or two gaps that you left open, regarding my brother."

She fell back a step, paling. "He—told you?"

"Yes. And now, if you'll excuse me, I'll go up and see Don José."

"Wait!" She stood in his way. "Please! Give me a

few words before—before you do what you came to do. My uncle is not the kind of man who would beg you for his life, so I am begging for him. He never knew until recently about Lorin's money. When he dueled with your brother, he thought he was guarding me from harm and scandal."

Con said not a word, watching her face, while a devil's impulse took growth in him. Silence could be a devastating weapon at times. He had used it on Rajimo, and now he used it on her.

"From the first minute I saw you and learned your name, I feared you would find out if ever you reached Santa Fe," Peregrina hurried on. "Rajimo feared it, too. I did not know about the money. I thought Rajimo wished to protect my uncle. That was why I plotted with him to keep you from the caravan, and tricked you that night in St. Louis."

She paused painfully, a hope in her eyes that he might say something, but he stood wordless and hard before her. "I—I'm not trying to trick you now. All I can do is ask that you spare Don José. He did what he thought was right. He has sometimes been harsh, but he has been father and mother to me. I can't stand by and . . . Con, I'm begging you!"

"Begging?" Con echoed. He shook his head slowly. "Begging doesn't suit you, Peregrina. Bargaining would be better."

She caught his meaning, and stood very still. Her eyes grew bright and hard. "I—think I understand. Very well. Your terms?"

Her voice was low, and sounded dangerous to Con.

"You!" he said bluntly. "When I leave Santa Fe, you'll leave with me!"

"Like a conquered Indian girl?" she flashed.

Con shrugged. "I told you once that I preferred catching to being caught. You had your try. Now it's mine!"

"*Viva* the Buccaneer!" she whispered mockingly. "Very well, if that is your bargain."

Con bowed, but she whirled and left him, and he went on upstairs, not sure whether he felt like a conquering buccaneer or just a plain damned rascal.

Don José said he was glad Con had come, and Con had no special reason for not believing him, except that the Don appeared a little strained in his manner.

"I am free to confess," said Don José, "that I am astounded at the speedy success of the revolution—or that it succeeded at all. Its success, I believe, was due largely to your excellent generalship and to the help of the Americans."

Con clicked his heels and bent in the middle. "Your Excellency flatters me," he drawled. "I have come to give my report. Rajimo has fled. Most of his soldiers are now cheering for the new governor. The rest will come back out of hiding, soon, and join in. With your permission, sir, it is my intention to take temporary charge of the Palacio—particularly the strongroom. Rajimo owed my brother ninety thousand dollars. I expect to collect it."

Don José eyed him searchingly. "It is very irregular."

"Quite," agreed Con blandly. "So was the revolution."

The Don conceded that with a nod. "Some day there will be another revolution—bloodless, I hope," he made meditative prophecy. "There is a restlessness in the land. Even in the Cabildo, I have heard men regret that better fortune did not favor the Texas Expedition. The rule of Mexico is not popular, but our province is not strong enough to break away and stand alone. More and more, the people look northward, and they make easy friendships with the Americans. It may well be that some future day, Captain, you and I will find ourselves serving under the same flag."

"I'm a Texan," Con reminded him. "But you may be right. Texas will join the States sooner or later. And maybe New Mexico—who knows? Er—by the way, I'd like a free hand in regard to arranging about customs duties. The American traders who pitched in and helped you—they expect lowered tariffs. In fact, they were promised by—uh—the person who enlisted them. Naturally, I know your treasury can't afford to keep that promise, but I think I can adjust the matter. I have your permission?"

His calm assurance left Don José looking somewhat blank. "Well—ah—really, Captain . . ."

"Thank you," said Con briskly. "And now I bid you *buenas noches* and a swift recovery from your wound." He bowed again and swung on his heel.

"Captain Connegan, I have something to tell you," Don José called after him. "It concerns your brother. I have decided that you have a right to know the details of that most distressing and unfortunate affair."

Con turned. "Was it a fair fight?"

The Don met his stare squarely. "Yes. He fired and missed—and died quickly. I . . ."

"That, sir, is all I wish to know."

Con found the Americans celebrating on the plaza, all except Burgwin, who sat apart with his wagons, his jaw bandaged where somebody had clouted him with a gun barrel. Con mounted his own wagon, and shouted his announcement.

"Gather round, you *renegados,* and listen to good news! Would any trader like to hear that tomorrow he can start business without paying a *claco* to the customs house?"

In quick time he was surrounded, every trader yelling questions.

"Well, it's true," Con affirmed. "That is, it's true for those men of foresight and vision who—uh—proved they've got the best interests of New Mexico at heart. For others it's a different story. Gentlemen, the commerce of the Santa Fe Trail has become a reputable and established business. No room in it for rascals and tricksters any more, as I heard a man say once. Burgwin, step over here—*please!*"

Burgwin rose and came sullenly over. He had earned the general animosity of the other traders by his attempt to corner the market with the aid of Rajimo. He had never been popular, and now the crowd was openly hostile toward him.

"My brother borrowed fifteen thousand dollars from you, Burgwin, didn't he?" Con asked. "I'm going to settle that bill in the morning."

Burgwin blinked. "M-mm—thanks," he grunted.

"Quite all right." Con waved it aside. "It'll help compensate you some for not being allowed to sell your goods!"

"Wha-at?"

Con nodded. "You're banned! You sure haven't shown yourself to be an ethical and aboveboard trader, nor a friend to the new governor. But Chavez is a fair-minded man. He thinks you ought to have one last chance. It's up to you to prove you're ready to co-operate with his new civil government and with the rest of the traders."

Burgwin swallowed hard. Perhaps he could guess what was coming. "How?"

"By just footing the customs bill for the whole car-avan!" Con explained cheerfully. "It won't leave you any profit for this year—but it's either that or haul your goods back to Missouri and quit the business. It's a chance to clear yourself, Burgwin. I hope you're grateful!"

28. WAGON WHEELS EAST

THE WAGONS ROLLED AND LURCHED up the long grade of the trail, bound out for the return journey overland to Missouri with their pre-cious packs of fine furs, Mexican silver, and some gold from the Indian-worked mines in the south.

Next year, come spring, they would be returning in

greater numbers. All auspices promised good future trading. The Santa Fe trade was entering upon its golden heyday, freed now of oppressive restrictions and smotheringly heavy taxation.

At the crest of the grade one wagon pulled out of line and halted, letting the rest of the caravan roll by. The dust slowly thinned and settled, and a last look back at Santa Fe showed it as bright and enticing as at the first glimpse.

Roses of Castilla and cottonwood trees. Clear cool water flowing in narrow *acequias* through shaded gardens and *placitas*. Walled houses, aloof on the outside, full of hospitality within, their *portales* opening onto the *zaguán,* the *patio* and the inner *sala.* Tan adobe, cool white *yeso,* soft greenery of trees, multi-colored garden spots, and crimson splashes of red pepper *ristras* drying in the sun. Rambling old houses—men of courtesy—women of charm . . .

"It's a grand place," said Con. "It gets in a man's blood. But I'll never be coming back!"

Beside him on the wagon seat, Old Nick nodded. "Uh-huh. Y'know, Con, I kinda had a notion mebbe you'd have comp'ny on the way back. I mean— hum . . ."

Con shook his head. "No. No, Nick, I failed there. I thought . . ." He shrugged, but not his old jaunty shrug. "I went about it the wrong way. I can see that now. There are birds you can't tame—that you never should try to tame. I should've known. I did know, but I forgot."

He had sought Peregrina that morning all through

Santa Fe, without finding her. He had even gone to the house on the Camino de Chimayo, and asked Chavez.

"Where is she—where's Peregrina?" he had demanded, and his manner had been such that Don José, his bed surrounded by members of the Cabildo, stared at him. "Oh, I'm not drunk! I'm asking you—where is she? I've searched this house. I've searched the town. I can't find her!"

Don José recovered his dignified politeness. "I do not know, Captain. I have not seen her this morning. If you wish to leave her a farewell message . . ."

Con flung out of the house. She had cheated him, as he might have expected. She was hiding somewhere, laughing at his attempts to find her. When he was gone, she would come out and go serenely back to the Chavez house. She was unconquerable. She couldn't be caught and tamed. Con went slowly back to the plaza. He had lost, and he knew why. He wondered if, had he tried a gentler method with her, things might have been different. She was like him. Defeat, to both of them, meant only further challenge, never surrender. With an understanding of himself, he could understand her. And yet, he thought, had she cared enough she would have come.

She just hadn't cared enough.

Old Nick could read his thoughts. He stuck a thumb over his shoulder at the wagon body. "You got what you came for, Con. Cheer up. Nigh a hunnerd thousan' dollars in good Mex gold!"

But Con gazed back down the trail to Santa Fe, vainly hoping even now for the sight of a slim figure on horseback. Maybe she was just punishing him. Maybe she'd come riding out and join him, laughing and impudent as ever.

For a long time he stood up on the wagon seat, peering back, while the caravan drew farther away along the trail. No, she wasn't coming. He had humiliated her once, in just such a fashion, when he broke out of La Caleta and left her preparing to be his bride. This was her revenge. He felt the dull certainty of it, but still he lingered, hating to turn his back on hope, until the mules began stamping.

"She's not coming," he said aloud at last. "I can't blame her. Tried to humble her—break her pride. Lord, what a fool a man can be!"

Curiously, a sharp remembrance of Rael came to him. Rael, with his high ideals and his untarnished code. Unselfish, dreaming, never assertive, a gentleman by instinct. Rael would not—could not—have made this blundering, high-handed error. He would have remained fair and undemanding in victory, even humble, with never a thought of revenge. That was the difference between a gentleman and a rascal. Hard regret cut into Con, the hopeless regret for a lesson unheeded and lost. He knew now the full extent of his respect for Rael, and why he had tried to protect him and stuck by him to the last. His respect had been grudging while Rael lived, and only faultily understood by himself. He realized, too, how much influence Rael and the memory of Rael had had upon him, how it had shaded and curtailed some of his hardest impulses and worst predatory instincts, and prodded alive in him a conscience that he had thought well buried years ago. His mistake had been in forgetting Rael, in the fine heat of his victory, and allowing his own worst side to dictate his actions.

It was damnably hard to be a gentleman—a real gentleman, as Rael had been. It took self-control. It took a self-respect that was not founded upon tangible tricks and transient victories. In that respect, at least, Rael had been the better and stronger man.

Con dragged his gaze from Santa Fe, and sat down. He met Old Nick's wondering eye, and managed a ghost of a grin. "Rascals never prosper, Nick," he muttered, much to Old Nick's bewilderment and disbelief. "Don José will tell you that. All right, let's push on."

Old Nick whipped up the mules and broke into what he believed was song, trying to arouse a note of cheer. The wagon rattled on after the caravan, and Santa Fe sank out of sight behind the rise.

After a while Con requested quietly, "Nick, d'you mind shutting off that racket? Maybe I'll be able to stand it later on, but not right now."

"You sick?" queried Old Nick. "Y'look kinda peaked. Y'know, Con, you sure remind me of ol' Wolf Runner, the way he went all onreason'ble after he seen that Cayuga gal. There was . . ."

"The hell with old Wolf Runner," Con interrupted wearily.

"Most likely that's where he is," the old hunter allowed. "Like I was sayin', there was plenty gals he coulda picked, an' as many as he wanted. But, no, he had to go get crazy set on that'n. Queer. Ain't one 'bout as good as another?"

"No," growled Con, brooding and moody. "Watch the road, will you? That last rock we went over didn't do me any good. What've we got in the wagon besides the gold and our bedding and stuff? Sounded to me like something just fell. Hell, it's the tailgate and it's scared my saddle horse to fits! Pull up!"

"I chained it tight shut last night when I packed up," grumbled Old Nick, hauling on the lines. "Don't see how it could've—Hey! D'you reckin somebody's been meddlin' with the wagin? The gold—!"

"Devil an' all, have I lost that, too?" muttered Con, and jumped to the ground.

The tailgate hung swinging, while the saddle horse shied and danced, fighting its lead rope. The wagon sheet, stretched across the high-sided wagon to form a roof cover, had torn unlaced at the back, jerked loose by the fallen tailgate. Con flung up the dangling flap of tarpaulin, ducked his head under it, and looked into the wagon. The first thing he saw was a trunk that didn't belong to him. It was a large trunk, brass-bound and strapped, and it stood squarely in front of him on the wagon floor. He craned his neck, looked over it for the gold—and froze in that position, speechless.

Old Nick bobbed up beside him. He gulped, made several attempts to speak, and finally mumbled, "Well, by gopher!"

THE GOLD WAS STILL THERE, packed in two iron-strapped boxes. So was the bedding and all the rest of the camping and wagon gear. And on the rolled bedding, trying hard to look cool and poised, sat Peregrina, wearing a full-skirted and tight-bodiced gown that was designed for anything but camping or riding in a wagon. Against the rough gear and coarse woolen blankets, she looked like a girl who had started out for a dance party and somehow got shanghaied aboard a freighter. And she looked a little frightened, though she tried hard to hide it.

Old Nick blurted, "How the—where—how'd you git here?"

Peregrina gazed at Con's face and eyes as if searching for something reassuring. Evidently she found it. A certain subtle air of self-possession settled upon her. She lowered her eyes demurely and smoothed out her dress with a small white hand. It was a delicately flirtatious gesture that took Con back to St. Louis, to the night on the balcony.

"Oh—I just climbed in," she murmured, with a lift of one slim, rounded shoulder, as if the matter were too inconsequential to warrant interest. "Early this morning," she added. "Servants put my trunk in for me. I fear they didn't understand how to fasten the tailgate properly afterwards."

Old Nick was about to say something else, but Con dug him with an elbow. "Go away!"

After Old Nick ducked out, silence fell. It lasted until Con said, a little huskily, "I wouldn't hold you to that bargain if—I mean—just because it was a bargain. Do you—do you—want to go back to Santa Fe?"

She met his gaze. "Do you want me to?"

"No! I'd give anything to keep . . ." Con paused, clamping a check on himself. "Why did you come? Was it because we made that bargain?"

He saw the warm color flood to her face. She bent her head, saying nothing as she went on smoothing her dress.

Con pushed the trunk to one side. "Old Nick has taken my horse and gone on ahead. It—it'll be hot in here later in the day. Wouldn't you rather ride on the seat with me? I'll make it comfortable with blankets."

He was asking, not demanding. He helped her out of the wagon, very carefully, very gently, and she watched him fasten up the tailgate. An unreasonable fear that she might somehow vanish possessed him, and he finished the task hurriedly. He knew why she had chosen this method of leaving Santa Fe with him. This way, she came of her own free will, not because he was the conqueror. Now she could still keep her pride and her independence. Her self-respect remained untouched, unblemished. She had not allowed him to carry her off like a conquered Indian girl.

Con padded the wagon seat with blankets, and lifted her up to it. He climbed up after her and took his place, gathering up the lines, but still he forced himself to hold back from starting the team. Looking at her beside him, so dainty, so beautiful, it was hard to say what he had to say. It was hard to risk letting her change her mind. But fairness and the memory of Rael demanded it.

"If you're not absolutely sure," he said carefully, "it's still not too late to turn back. You know me—you know what kind of man I am. I—I can't change overnight."

She turned her face toward him. "Is that all you have to say, Con?"

Con tied the lines again. "No. I've this to say—Will you marry me? We could be married by a padre in Taos, and catch up with the caravan at Raton Pass."

He was trying desperately to be very calm about it, afraid to startle her with an abrupt act or word, as he would have been afraid to frighten off a bird that he wished to keep without caging. But calmness and Peregrina did not mingle well. He even tried not to look at her, waiting for her answer. A man had to be gentle, discreet, understanding, with a girl like this. She went to his head too easily.

She was smiling when he looked again at her. Her eyes were bright and soft, her lips parted, and the flush still warmed her face.

"I like you as a gentleman, Con," she whispered. "Yes, I do. But—darling—I think I love you best as yourself!"

She pulled down his dark head and kissed him so fiercely that it took his breath and good intentions away.

Minutes later, Old Nick, who had turned back, called out, "D'you two figger on goin' any partic'lar place today?"

"Eh? Oh—sure." Con grabbed up the lines, and Peregrina settled modestly back into her place on the seat beside him.

He grinned down at her. "To Taos!" he whispered.

She smoothed out her dress, her dazzling smile provocative and flirtatious. "To Taos!" she echoed.

"Minx!"

"Ruffian!"

Center Point Publishing
600 Brooks Road • PO Box 1
Thorndike ME 04986-0001 USA

(207) 568-3717

US & Canada:
1 800 929-9108